Our Lives Together

Two Men in Love

Alvin Granowsky

iUniverse LLC
Bloomington

OUR LIVES TOGETHER
TWO MEN IN LOVE

iUniverse books may be ordered through booksellers or by contacting:

iUniverse LLC
1663 Liberty Drive
Bloomington, IN 47403
www.iuniverse.com
1-800-Authors (1-800-288-4677)

Because of the dynamic nature of the Internet, any web addresses or links contained in this book may have changed since publication and may no longer be valid. The views expressed in this work are solely those of the author and do not necessarily reflect the views of the publisher, and the publisher hereby disclaims any responsibility for them.

Any people depicted in stock imagery provided by Thinkstock are models, and such images are being used for illustrative purposes only. Certain stock imagery © Thinkstock.

ISBN: 978-1-4917-2806-2 (sc)
ISBN: 978-1-4917-2808-6 (hc)
ISBN: 978-1-4917-2807-9 (e)

Printed in the United States of America.

iUniverse rev. date: 03/14/2014

Dedication

To Don and John for being there for all these years

Acknowledgments

I need to express my gratitude to the many people who read my manuscript in its many stages of development. Their concerns and suggestions helped shape the novel and their encouragement provided to me the confidence I needed to continue.

They are:

My friends—Bill Blalock, Robert Doyna, Bill Eanes, Sy Lemler, David Krongelb, Gordon Markley, Lon Rogers, Thom Swiger, and Joseph Traigle.

My daughter—Sedra Spano whose helpful suggestions about needed additions made me proud of her sensitivity and intelligence.

My partners—John Glendinning, who was raised in the Southern Baptist Church and focused my attention on the biblical verses that took precedence above all others; and Don LaRue, who patiently read and reread the manuscript in all its many stages and whose enthusiasm for the novel encouraged me to continue.

Finally, I am especially indebted to Joyce Magee for her talents and efforts in editing and formatting my novel—a remarkable act of kindness considering we had never met.

Credits

The quotes from Mary Robinson, a former United Nations High Commissioner for Human Rights, appeared in the Preface to the "Stand Up for Your Rights," a Peace Child International Project, published by World Book Encyclopedia, Chicago, IL., 1998.

The passages from the Platform of the Republican Party of Texas have appeared in Internet postings starting in the year 2004 under the headings: Homosexuality and Texas Sodomy Statutes.

Prologue

The earlier novel, *Teacher Accused, when Homophobia Explodes in a Texas Town*, depicts the coming out of Glen McLean. Idealistic and determined, he arrives in Edgemont, a small Texas town near Dallas, to teach and to build a life authentic to his needs as a gay man—something he could not do living in the bosom of his Catholic family in upstate New York.

He develops a strong bond with Katie Collins, a fellow teacher who falls in love with him and, even knowing that he is gay, proposes marriage. "Glen, I know we care about each other. I see it in your eyes when you look at me. I feel it in your touch when you sit beside me. I hear it in your voice when you say my name. Why couldn't we live together as man and wife? Why couldn't we have children? Why couldn't we both live out our lives as teachers in Edgemont? And if you had someone else you loved, and you wanted to see that person, why couldn't I share you with him?"

Knowing of Glen's relationship with Keith Chamberlain, a deeply closeted lawyer from a prominent Edgemont family, and their breakup over Keith's panic that people might discover he was gay, Katie says softly, "I believe it's an arrangement that Keith Chamberlain might like. He could maintain his image with you as his best friend. You could see each other whenever you wanted. We could even travel together. Just think about it . . ."

As much as Glen cares for Katie and as much as he longs to build a relationship with Keith, Glen will not agree to living a lie. Glen is proud to be a teacher, proud to be on his own and determined to build an authentic life—an open and honest life—true to his inner needs and feelings as a gay man.

His idealism is soon interrupted. The Texas Sodomy Statute has been overturned by "activist" judges, and religious conservatives are paranoid about the "homosexual agenda" and its impact on their children's lives. An effeminate boy, Danny Anderson, is relentlessly bullied after his father forces him to admit his sexual orientation to the church congregation.

Still, Glen's classroom lessons focus on respect and acceptance for all, including homosexuals. Glen's essay assignment ignites an explosion of homophobic hatred. Jeanette Haar, a prominent member of the First Baptist Church and the mother of Mickey Haar, the youth tormenting Danny, leads the drive to have Glen fired. Editorials appear in the local newspaper against the homosexual teacher promoting tolerance of homosexuality in his classroom.

To his horror, Glen is accused of sodomizing Danny, the 15-year-old boy he has tried to protect. A spontaneous outburst of homophobic hatred erupts: Glen is denounced in news reports and editorials as well as from the pulpit of the First Baptist Church. His apartment is trashed and had he been there, he would have been severely beaten—or worse.

But times have changed even in this small Bible-belt community. The intolerance of the few collides with the compassion and respect of the many as large segments of the community stand behind a popular teacher who has been unjustly accused. Glen is exonerated with the help of Keith, who steps forward to protect him from the charges and in so doing, outs himself as a gay man in a gay relationship.

As the novel draws to an end, Glen and Keith are reunited and Katie, reconciled with her former fiancé, plans to move to New York City to build her life with him. However, her love for Glen remains. In a telling moment, she offers to be the surrogate carrying Glen's baby should he and Keith ever try to have a family.

At the novel's ending, Keith says, "Glen, when I thought I'd lost you, I fell apart. I vowed that if you ever came back into my life, I'd never again deny you or our relationship. Edgemont is my home and I've always planned to live my life here. The only difference is that now I'll be living here as a gay man with the man I love instead of as a gay man living alone, pretending to be straight. I think I'm better off this way, don't you?"

They raise their glasses in a toast, "To the rest of our lives together."

This novel—*Our Lives Together*—picks up four years later.

Chapter One

"Gentry, Gentry
He's our Man!
If he can't do it,
Nobody can!"

The Edgemont High cheerleader with the flowing blond hair led the screaming fans to an ever higher pitch of excitement as the player—his face tense with concentration—stood at the foul line, preparing to shoot the game-winning point.

Glen McLean saw the young player's lips moving in prayer. Then, with a quick movement, he sent the basketball arching toward the hoop.

For a moment the ball teetered precariously on the hoop, and the gymnasium grew silent as the watchers held their breath. Then as if in answer to the youth's prayers, the ball dropped through the hoop and a gigantic roar erupted. Edgemont High had won and the elated high school students raced from the wooden bleachers to cheer for their team, and especially for Gentry, the anxious young player whom Glen didn't know.

Typically, Glen avoided athletic events, because his partner wouldn't go. Keith said, "Makes me feel like a monkey at the zoo having all your students staring at me. It's bad enough when they see us together at the mall. I'm not about to spend two or three hours at a game, pretending not to notice students staring and whispering that Mr. McLean is with his gay partner."

Glen was at this basketball game because Mr. Fowler, the principal, had personally asked him to help chaperone the event. It seems like everyone has something going on this Friday evening. Can I count on you to be there? As a favor to me?"

Although he hated giving up an evening with Keith, Glen wouldn't let his principal down. As it turned out, he really enjoyed himself. A number of parents were at the game and several took the opportunity to introduce themselves and make positive comments about his teaching . . . which naturally made Glen feel proud.

Above all, he rarely had the opportunity to be with his students in a social setting outside of the classroom. That was especially enjoyable for him, and even more so for his students. Mr. McLean was a popular teacher and the students couldn't get enough of him. They jostled one another to sit near him on the bleachers and at the end of the game, stayed beside him, trying to engage him in conversation.

"Did you enjoy the game?"

"Will you come to other games?"

"Will you ever bring your partner?"

"That gold band on your left hand . . . is that a wedding band?"

It was almost 10:30 p.m. when Glen finally left the building. He knew Keith would be waiting for him and he wanted to get home as fast as he could to enjoy what was left of their Friday evening. He had almost reached his car, when he saw two people about to enter a silver Toyota. One of them was the player who had made the winning shot. The other was the blond cheerleader.

The youth nodded at him. "Hello, Mr. McLean."

Glen smiled, a little surprised that the attractive youth knew his name. "Sure was a lot of pressure. But you came through. Great shot!"

Gentry smiled back, "Thank you. I appreciate your saying that."

And then their eyes locked. It happened in an instant—unplanned and spontaneous. Glen was startled by the sudden awareness: *this kid is gay.*

****

It was 7:30 a.m. and Keith Chamberlain had just completed his hour-long workout regimen at the gym and was taking a shower. He was deep in thought about the upcoming meeting with his client, a prominent 60-year-old business owner who claimed he had shot and killed his neighbor in an act of self-defense. Keith didn't believe him and suspected a jury wouldn't either as the neighbor was unarmed and the coroner said the bullet had entered his back.

He was mulling over how to convince the client to take a plea, when he became aware he wasn't alone in the shower room.

"Hi, Keith, saw you in here and thought I'd join you."

"Oh, Colby, how you doing?"

"Better, now that the wife and kids are away for the weekend." He turned on the shower next to Keith. "You're looking good, real good." He smiled suggestively. "Six-pack abs and a hot-looking butt . . . any chance you might drop by the house . . . like in the old days."

Keith shrugged. "You know I can't." He lifted his left hand to show the gold band on his ring finger. "I'm in a relationship and . . ."

Colby lifted his left hand as well to display the gold band on his ring finger. "So what does that mean? A ball and chain and no more fun? Not for me." He paused, "It's been a long time since we've enjoyed each other's company . . . too long. No one needs to know."

Keith looked at the tall, lean man standing close beside him: trim body and nice looking face. Just his type. Tempting, but he wouldn't allow it to happen. "If I were single, I'd take you up on that offer, but . . ."

"I get it," Colby shrugged. "Not now, for now. No problem for a salesman like me. Hear it all the time in my business." He smiled, placing his hand familiarly on Keith's shoulder. "I can wait for it to happen, and it will. Your *no* will become *yes*, and we'll have a real good time together."

Keith removed the gold band from his finger before entering the office, placing it in his jacket pocket. It was just something he did, and had done throughout their relationship. Glen knew he didn't wear the commitment ring at the office, and kidded him about the unnecessary subterfuge. "They all know you're gay—so who are you fooling?"

"You're right and I know you're right. No one brings it up, but they know," he admitted. "But I'm just not comfortable wearing a gold band like the married lawyers in our office. Doesn't feel right, and I don't want to start a conversation about the ring and what it means."

3

"I'm not asking you to do something that makes you feel uncomfortable," Glen said, "But I hope one day you'll feel secure enough about being a gay man in a gay relationship that you'll be proud to wear the ring at all times and in all places."

"Hello, Mr. Chamberlain," the office receptionist smiled. "First lawyer here in the morning and last one to leave in the evening. That's the price you pay for having so many clients."

Keith nodded. "Thanks for noticing. By the way, I'm expecting Mr. and Mrs. Clements for a 9:00 a.m. appointment. Please show them to my office as soon as they arrive."

Keith walked down the narrow corridor to his office and shut the door. It was 8:00 a.m. and he knew Glen would be at home waiting for his call, before leaving for school. It was just something they did, an unnecessary something in their relationship that cemented their commitment to each other.

"Hi, just arrived at the office. Everything's fine."

"Fine here too, Keith. You're so reliable: 8 a.m. on the dot. Never even a minute late. I can set my watch by your call. I love that and I love you."

"Love you, too," Keith said. "Looking forward to happy hour tonight at home."

"I'll have your martini ready with two olives as soon as you walk in the door, plus . . ." Glen lowered his voice in a suggestive manner, "a little you-know-what to make you so pleased that you have me in your life."

****

Glen McLean leaned back on his chair, savoring the good feelings. His fourth year teaching at Edgemont High and the ugliness of the past—the false charge that he was a homosexual predator who caused a student, a teenage boy, to commit suicide—was just a blip, a terrible moment now long gone. He was a popular and respected teacher at Edgemont High who happened to be gay and people knew it. For the most part that was not a problem, at least for most people. A movement at the door to his classroom distracted him.

A handsome youth with dark wavy hair, his face suffused with a reddish flush, was standing at the doorway. It had been almost two weeks since the basketball game and at first Glen didn't remember him. It was 4:30 p.m. and students had long since left the building. Most teachers had as well.

The youth hesitated at the doorway, as if undecided about entering. Then, resolving his indecision, he entered the classroom. "Do you remember me?"

Glen smiled. "Gentry, right? You made that foul shot under all that pressure. You were great!"

"Thanks. I didn't know if you'd remember."

"Is there something I can do for you? It's a little late for you to still be in the building."

Gentry cleared his throat, as if he was going to say something . . . and then didn't.

Glen motioned Gentry to be seated at the chair beside his desk. "Is there something I can do for you?" he repeated.

Once again the youth cleared his throat. He looked down and then said, almost in a whisper, "I was told that gay people can tell if other people are gay." His voice tightened, "Is that true?"

"Sometimes. Not always." Glen said, "Why do you ask?"

There was a long hesitation, before Gentry said, "I saw the way you looked at me in the parking lot after the game. I just needed to tell you—I'm not gay."

As Gentry spoke, their eyes locked and the youth's blue eyes took on a darker cast.

"Are you worried that you might be gay?" Glen asked.

"No!" Gentry spoke sharply. "I'm not worried. I have a girlfriend. She's great and . . . I don't know why I'm here. It was a mistake." He turned and walked quickly from the classroom.

****

"Katie called." Glen still had on the khaki Dockers pants and black polo shirt he'd worn to school as he sat close beside his partner on the large, down-cushioned sofa in their formal living room.

Keith sipped on his martini. "Yes?"

"She and David are calling it quits. They're getting divorced."

Keith took deep sip of his drink. "I'm not surprised."

"Why do you say that?" Glen asked. He turned to face his partner.

"She loves you," he said. "You're the one she really wanted to marry." Keith reached into his martini for an olive.

"Oh, I don't know about that," Glen responded. "It's true we care about each other, but only as friends."

"Really? Only as friends?" Keith placed his martini on the red lacquered cocktail table in front of the yellow damask sofa. Turning toward Glen, he said, "Do you recall that evening at dinner when she said she'd love to have your baby? You think that's how friends talk to one another?"

Glen waved his hand in dismissal. "That was just talk. Remember, I had said I'd love to have a child. Maybe Keith and I could find a surrogate mother. Anyway she was just being supportive . . . a friend."

"Whatever you say," Keith said, obviously not accepting Glen's explanation. "So what are her plans? Will she remain in New York?"

"No, she's planning to return here. "I'm picking her up at DFW on Saturday. She's moving back to Edgemont."

Keith reached for his martini. *She's moving back to be with Glen.* He tried to keep his voice even as he asked, "After living in New York City, I'm surprised she'd want to return to a small town like Edgemont? Won't that be rather limiting for her?"

"Katie was raised here," Glen said. "Her friends and relatives are here. She still has her home here. Where else would she go?"

Keith took a deep breath. "She's moving back to be near you." He paused to remove the remaining olive from his martini. "She loves you . . . *like in love.* It was obvious to me the first time I saw you together."

Glen said nothing. He lifted his wine glass for a sip of cabernet and waited.

"You know what I wish?" Keith said "I wish sometimes you weren't so handsome. I see the way people look at you . . . the way that they come on to you, men and women. Now Katie is moving back. She's returning to be with you. You admitted you slept with her once and now . . ."

Glen raised his hand, palm out to stop him. "Keith, I'm committed to you. That's what matters, the only thing that matters. Besides, you're forgetting how appealing you are. Remember that sexy young guy at the gay party in Dallas last Saturday . . . the one in the tight Levi's with the bubble butt? He came on to you, big time." Glen reached for Keith's hand. "Not just that guy either, and that's before they know you're a successful lawyer."

Glen caressed Keith's hand. "I have no interest in anyone but you, and I know you're committed to me. It gives me a good feeling to know that I have a lover that other men want. That I have a lover who still excites me."

Upon arriving home from the office, Keith had removed his suit jacket and tie and opened the top buttons of his long-sleeved white shirt. Without another word, Glen undid the remaining buttons. "You're so buff!" He placed his hand on Keith's bare chest and caressed his hardening nipples. "I love you—*like in love* with you. You're the one who makes my heart go pitter-patter." He leaned forward to kiss Keith. Their lips parted as they pressed against one another. "You're the one I want, the only one."

Glen stood up and reached for Keith's hand. "Come, let's go upstairs to the bedroom for some before dinner delight."

****

"Katie!" Glen saw her as soon as she entered the airport's baggage claim area. He ran to embrace her, then stepped back, admiringly.

"Wow! You are so pretty! Chic! A New York City girl, for sure. A new hair style for your gorgeous auburn hair . . . and, hey, what happened to your freckles? I love those freckles!"

Katie laughed. "Don't worry! They're still there, just hidden." Her hazel eyes sparkled as she reached for his hand, "I can still remember the first time I saw you. It was the start of the new school year and the superintendent was introducing the new teachers. He called your name 'Glen McLean.' You stood, and my heart went flip-flop. So handsome!"

"And now?" Glen laughed. "I was 28 years old back then, young, innocent and so virile . . . and now I'm 33, long in the tooth, past my prime and . . ."

"The best looking man I've ever seen!"

Later, together in Katie's home, seated on the small brown sofa in her narrow living room, Glen held his glass of cabernet and looked inquiringly at Katie. She had said there was something she needed to tell him. Glen assumed she wanted to talk about her separation from David, her husband.

"So, what is it you want to tell me? But wait. Where's your glass of wine? Don't tell me you've given up on wine."

"That's what I want to talk to you about," Katie said. "She turned to face him directly. "I won't be drinking for a while."

"Why?"

"I'm pregnant," she said softly.

For a moment, Glen was too taken back to speak. "How does David feel about that?"

"David doesn't know," Katie said.

"But he needs to know," Glen's brow furrowed. *What is she saying? Of course he needs to know.*

"No, he doesn't," Katie said. "David has two daughters to support from his first marriage. The last thing he wants is to be responsible for another child. He had told me that from the start, but I hoped he'd change his mind and I thought he had. One evening after several glasses of wine, David agreed that we could try, and we did very briefly."

Katie shook her head, "Less than a week later, he came home from work and I could sense something was wrong, very wrong. He was quiet over dinner, like something was eating at him. Finally, I said, 'What's the problem? Something's obviously bothering you?'

"And he went ballistic. He accused me of manipulating him— wearing him down—so that he had agreed to something he didn't want. 'I don't want another child! I told you that from the start! If you want a baby so badly, you need to find someone else!'"

She paused as her eyes grew moist. "I told him, 'we've had unprotected sex for a week. For all we know, I might be pregnant. What will we do then?'"

"'Have an abortion!' That's what he said, and he meant it. He wanted me to have an abortion!" Katie shook her head. "I was so angry! It was like, I don't know who this man is."

Katie placed her hand on Glen's thigh. "I'm sorry. I just get so upset when I think about what he said."

For a long moment, Katie said nothing. She removed a thread from a fraying sofa pillow and twisted it in her fingers. "You told me you wanted a child. That you wanted to be a father. Do you still feel that way?"

"Yes, I do," Glen spoke without hesitation. "I've talked to Keith about it, and he's agreed. One way or another, we are going to have a child, maybe two."

Katie was looking at him intently. She started to say something, but stopped."

Glen paused, waiting for Katie to speak, but she didn't. He took Katie's hand in his, "Katie, you're pregnant with David's child and he needs to know."

Katie shook her head to stop him, "It's been a long day and I'm real tired. Let's talk about that another time."

****

Earlier that day, Glen had passed Gentry in the school's front corridor by the principal's office and nodded in greeting, but the youth looked away.

Gentry was with that very pretty cheerleader with flowing blond hair and a slender figure. Upon seeing Glen, he placed his arm around the girl's waist so that anyone watching might see that they were a pair.

Now the school day ended and the school buses long departed, Glen heard a footstep. He looked toward the doorway and saw Gentry standing outside his classroom, just as on the other occasion. He waited to see what the youth would do.

Glen watched as Gentry, with a quick, nervous motion, brushed his dark wavy hair back from his forehead. Adjusting the collar of his blue polo shirt, he entered the classroom. "Are you busy?" he asked.

"I was getting ready to leave," Glen said, rising from his chair. "Is there something I can do for you?"

"Oh, I'm sorry," the youth said, "I don't want to keep you." He was obviously disappointed.

Glen smiled, "I'm in no rush. We can talk if you'd like." He sat back down and motioned Gentry to be seated on the chair beside his desk.

"Thanks," Gentry said as he sat down. "I'd kinda like to ask you something, but I don't know how to say it."

"It will be all right. If it's important to you, I want to hear it."

Gentry cleared his throat. "Well, I kinda guess you know what folks say . . ." he stumbled for the right words, "that you're gay."

Glen nodded. "Yes, I am gay. It's not a secret."

"I was kinda wondering . . . I don't mean to pry," Gentry took a deep breath, "but I sure want to know. I mean need to know, how did you know you were gay?"

"That's a rather personal question, but I assume you're asking because it's important to you. Am I right?"

Gentry nodded. He cleared his throat. "Yes."

"I'm going to tell you and I'll be totally honest with you, but first I want you to be totally honest with me. Can you do that?"

"Maybe . . . I'll try," The youth spoke softly. He lowered his eyes.

"Tell me why you're asking that question?" Glen said.

Gentry looked down. "I don't know. I'm not sure."

"You need to be honest with me," Glen said. "You're wrestling with something and you probably need to talk to someone—a friend you can trust. I can be that friend, but only if we're honest with one another. Can you be honest with me?" Glen looked directly at the handsome youth who was fumbling with the collar of his shirt.

Gentry swallowed and cleared his throat once again. "I don't want to be gay. It would be awful to be like that, but I . . . I'm so scared." His eyes grew moist and his voice became hushed. He turned his head as if to reassure himself that no one could hear.

Impulsively, Glen took the boy's hand in his. "It's all right. You don't have to be scared. Now let me tell you how I knew I was gay."

For a moment, Glen looked about his empty classroom, with its cement block walls painted a pale green as he gathered his memories of a very confused and upsetting time. Then looking into the eyes of the anxious youth seated beside him, he said, "I didn't want to be gay either. It wasn't a good thing to be, even more difficult than now. Looking back, I can see that I was gay from an early age. It was always other boys that I was attracted to . . . that I wanted to be with. And that was okay, wasn't it? I mean boys like to be with boys. That's normal, isn't it? At least that's what I told myself.

"In high school I really began to worry that something was wrong with me. My friends were obsessing about girls. They wanted to be with girls, date them, and have sex with them. I acted as if I wanted that too, but I really didn't. I just wanted to be with my best friend. And when he started to date one particular girl, I was so upset. I felt abandoned. I didn't understand what was going on inside of me. Or maybe I suspected, but couldn't accept that I might be . . . you know." He sighed, "I just couldn't deal with it."

Gentry cleared his throat. "What about girls? Did you ever want to be with girls? Like sort of do things with them." His face reddened. "You know."

"I liked girls, but only as friends. Not someone to date. But then I did date girls, even went steady, because I thought I needed to. I thought people might think something was wrong with me, if I didn't have a girlfriend.

"That all changed my first year in college. I was at the library at Cornell and I saw an upperclassman who I found so attractive and appealing. Our eyes met and he smiled and my heart did a flip. We dated . . . became lovers and that was it. I knew that I was gay.

"Is that what you wanted to know?" Glen started to smile, but stopped. Gentry was crying.

The youth wiped at his tears. "I don't know what's wrong with me. I need to go." He stood up and walked rapidly from the classroom without turning back.

Chapter Two

Glen turned toward Keith as they lay beside each other on their king-size bed. "I love you, even more now than four years ago when we first became a couple."

"Really?" Keith said. "I hope that's true."

There was something in his tone that bothered Glen. "Keith, honey, is something wrong? Have I done something to upset you?"

"No, everything's fine. You haven't done anything."

"Does it have to do with Katie?" Glen asked. "Are you upset that I spend time with her?"

"Maybe . . . maybe a little," Keith admitted.

"She's having a difficult time," Glen said, "She needs me. I have to be there for her."

"She's in her third month of the pregnancy and she hasn't told her husband." Keith said, trying to make it sound like a casual comment when it wasn't. He had been obsessing with a very upsetting thought. *Why hadn't Katie told her husband? If he was the father, didn't he need to know? There were legal issues.*

But what if he wasn't the father? Katie had been in Edgemont that past November for the Thanksgiving Holiday to be with family, she said. And Glen had cut his visit to his parents in Albany short so that he could be with Katie on the Saturday following Thanksgiving. That Saturday evening was a sticking point in Keith's memory. Glen came home very late. It was almost midnight and Keith had waited up.

Glen seemed ill at ease, as if something had happened that shouldn't have. The look on his face was etched in Keith's memory. *Glen's feeling guilty*, Keith had thought, assuming that it was about being out so late.

But now another possibility had wormed its way into Keith's thinking, threatening and unnerving him: Glen and Katie were having sex. He willed himself not to go there. Yet, in spite of himself, he began to visualize the scenario. *It was Katie's last night before returning to New York. They had been sitting on her sofa, close beside one another. They were so close and then* . . . Keith tried to block it from his thoughts—*Stop! Don't go there!*

But what if in the temptation of the moment, they did have sex, unprotected sex? If Katie was pregnant with Glen's child, wouldn't that explain why she hadn't told her husband? That would make sense because the child wasn't his.

"I love Katie, but only as a friend, a best friend," Glen said. "Our relationship is spiritual, not physical. You're the one I sleep with, no one else." That's what Glen said, but Keith had experienced Glen's passion—his strong sex drive—and was unnerved by what it might mean if Glen also enjoyed sexual pleasure with Katie.

They had made a pact early in their relationship that being open and forthright with one another was critical for a long-term relationship— the lifetime together they both claimed to want. If ever an issue or concern arose, they would talk about it—resolve it—rather than allow it to fester as a wedge pushing them apart.

Now that an actual situation was at hand, Keith just couldn't talk about it, at least not yet. His feelings were too raw, unsettled—he wasn't secure enough to start the conversation.

****

During his planning period, Glen noticed that the door to the counselor's office was open. On impulse, he stepped inside to see if Ms. Hancock was available. She was. The stocky woman with the short cropped hair was seated behind her large walnut desk and motioned for him to join her.

"If you have a moment," he said, "I'd like to ask you about a student."

"Yes," the counselor said, "Which student?" She leaned back in her swivel chair.

"I don't know much about him except that he's on the basketball team."

"What does he look like?" she asked.

"He's about 6 feet tall, trim, with dark, wavy hair. A good looking boy, soft-spoken and very polite. His first name is Gentry."

"That has to be Gentry Phillips!" Ms. Hancock smiled. "He's a senior and a fine young man. An excellent student . . . very popular. I've been guiding him on his application to Bob Jones University in South Carolina. His father went there and . . ." She lowered her voice, as if revealing a secret. "Reverend Phillips never said it to me, but I'm confident he'd love his son to become a minister, just like him. Gentry is such a credit to his family!"

Glen was silent for a moment. "I didn't know his father was a minister."

"Yes, he's our pastor at the First Baptist Church, a very prominent and respected man. Reverend Phillips is so proud of that boy, his only child. He's referred to him in several of his sermons. But why do you ask?" the counselor said.

"No reason," Glen said. "Just curious. I'd seen him in the halls with a very pretty girl and . . ."

"Oh, that has to be Betty Jean Farris," Ms. Hancock interrupted. A lovely girl from a fine Christian family. Such a good looking couple! She's sent in her application to Bob Jones University as well. To be with Gentry, I'm sure." The counselor smiled. "Wouldn't surprise me one bit to hear that they marry one day. Warms the heart of this old spinster lady to see young folks in love like that."

As he left the counselor's office, Glen rubbed his hand across his mouth. He was filled with compassion for Gentry Phillips. *That poor gay kid! No wonder he's an emotional wreck!*

****

Katie sat at her kitchen table across from Glen, watching him as he ate the sausage and peppers dinner she had prepared.

"So sorry that Keith couldn't join us," she said, not meaning it at all.

"Another late night at the office," Glen said. "It's that criminal case he's trying about that elderly man who shot his neighbor. It was front page in the *Gazette*."

Katie believed it was just an excuse. Nothing had ever been said, but it didn't have to be. Katie understood. She was a rival for Glen's time and affection.

She reached across the table to take Glen's hand in hers. She loved being together with him like this in her home—a cottage actually, with two tiny bedrooms, one bathroom, and white walls that needed repainting. But it took on a glow when Glen was there. Just like in the old days before her marriage to David.

If her estranged husband was actually the father of her baby, she would have to tell him. She dreaded having to do that and resolved to assure David she expected nothing from him. If her mother was able to raise her on a secretary's salary after her dad's death, she could certainly raise her child on a teacher's salary.

But there was another consideration. One that excited Katie greatly. What if the baby wasn't David's? There was the possibility—that wonderful possibility—that Glen was the father. The very thought caused her spirits to soar. She felt certain Glen would be thrilled and she anticipated with great pleasure telling him what she had done. Just not now.

Ending the marriage was so upsetting, but it had to be done. Having a child—becoming a mother—was too important. Once Katie accepted that it wasn't going to happen with David the marriage had to end. And it had! Thank goodness!

Now almost everything else was falling into place. She would be hired as a substitute teacher in the Edgemont Schools for the remainder of the spring term and was assured a full time position for the fall semester. The school district was growing, and just as she had hoped, there was an opening for a math teacher.

Mr. Fowler, the high school principal, told her the job was hers. If need be, he would even use a substitute teacher for a few weeks if she needed that time after she had the baby. "Katie, you were one of our best teachers. We were so sorry to lose you and so happy to have you back."

Not only did she have the job, she had her home and close relatives in town. Her loyal Aunt Molly was so supportive. "You don't need to tell nobody about your breakup and the pregnancy, I'll handle that for you. No decent man would want his wife to have an abortion! He should be horse-whipped!"

That Sunday at The First Baptist Church service, Katie knew by the sympathetic looks and especially warm greetings that her Aunt Molly had indeed spread the word: "So happy to have you back! Edgemont is your home! You never belonged in New York! Why would anyone with any sense raise a baby in New York?"

The only thing missing to make her life complete—her perfect world—was a man to love and share her life.

"You're so quiet," Glen said. "What are you thinking? Good thoughts?"

"The best," Katie smiled.

"Care to share them?" Glen asked.

Katie shook her head. "No, I'll keep these thoughts all to myself. It's like making a wish at your birthday party. Share the wish and it won't happen. Keep it to yourself and well . . ."

Katie closed her eyes, "I wish . . ." She then completed her fantasy of the ideal life, *Glen and I living here in our home with our baby. Working together as teachers at Edgemont High . . . having two children . . . spending the rest of our lives together deeply in love.*

"That's a long wish," Glen said. "Must be something special."

"Very special," Katie said.

Glen finished the last bite of his dinner. "That was delicious! I'd almost forgotten how much I love your cooking. Too bad Keith couldn't join us. He loves Italian cooking! Then as if tuning in to her thoughts and needing to assert the boundaries of their friendship, he said, "I find it hard to believe that Keith and I have been together for four years. Seems like just yesterday that we met and I fell in love with him."

Katie's fantasy evaporated, crushed by the unyielding reality: Glen was in a relationship with another man. *Katie Collins, you're a fool for holding onto a dream that can never be. Why do you do this to yourself?*

Chapter Three

"Thomas Jefferson was a founding father of our nation, the third president of our newly created country, the author of our Declaration of Independence, and a person whose ideas influenced our nation's Constitution and Bill of Rights."

Glen was excited by the new unit, the final big one of the year. "That's why Thomas Jefferson's thinking is so important to us as we consider changes past and present in the development of our nation. As an elder statesman, Jefferson made this analogy: *If a young boy wears a coat that is a perfect fit, will that same coat still fit when he is a grown man?* The answer, of course, is no.

"Jefferson believed that this comparison must be applied to the laws and customs that governed our young nation as it matures. As new knowledge and truths are revealed, our society and the laws that govern it must also change to properly reflect the growth in knowledge. Our nation's Constitution, written in 1787, was designed to allow for the changes that Jefferson knew would be needed as our young nation grew and matured.

"Twenty-seven amendments have been added, and each one represents a change that people felt was necessary. We will be going to the library today, and each day this week, so that you will have the opportunity to do research on one of three amendments that had an especially profound impact on our society and the lives we lead today."

Glen wrote on the chalkboard:

The 13th Amendment abolishing slavery, enacted 1865

The 15th Amendment ensuring the right to vote for men of all races, enacted in 1870

The 19th Amendment establishing women's right to vote, enacted in 1920

"Mrs. Harris, the librarian, will guide you in using research skills to find the information you need to write an essay depicting the way things had been, the new thinking that gave rise to a questioning of what had been, as well as the inevitable debates and conflicts among those that wanted the change and those who did not. And finally the changes made, and the impact those changes have made in your lives and the society we have today."

He sat down on the edge of is desk. "I expect you are going to find a whole lot about our nation that you never knew, and may shock you. You will also find that change never comes easy and things we take for granted today came about only because some courageous people stood up to fight for what they believed was fair and right.

"We will also have panel discussions in which each of you will be assigned a position, either for or against the proposed changes, arguing for the benefits or harm those changes might create for the peoples of our nation."

Glen smiled at his 10th grade students. "We are living through a time of change today, and I hope this unit reflecting our nation's past will provide insight into our current times—its conflicts and challenges— and the ongoing struggle for equality for all people."

****

Over the past several weeks, Gentry had stopped by Glen's classroom a number of times, always after school when other students were gone. His conversation predictably returned to one theme: how did anyone know if they were gay? Perhaps it was just a phase—something that would pass with time? If a person could choose to be gay, couldn't that same person choose not to be gay? Why not?

Glen sensed that one time soon, Gentry might be secure enough— trust Glen enough—to raise the possibility that he might be gay, which up to this point he had never done, and in fact had strongly denied.

"Do you have a moment?" Gentry asked, as he always did, when entering the classroom.

Glen smiled at the very attractive youth, and his thoughtful politeness that Glen found very appealing. "Yes, of course." He motioned him to the chair beside his desk. "I enjoy our talks."

Gentry returned the smile. "I guess you're kinda wondering why I ask you so many questions about being gay . . . folks who are gay. It's just . . ." the youth hesitated as if he might be making a mistake, perhaps revealing something that he shouldn't.

"Gentry, I know why you're asking those questions, and it's all right. You need a friend and I can be that friend for you."

"What do you know?" Gentry said quickly, his hands clenching in a nervous gesture.

"How long have you been worried about being gay?" Glen sensed this was the time for directness.

Gentry looked down, unable at first to meet Glen's eyes. When he looked up, he was crying.

"A long time," Gentry said softly. "I pray every night that those feelings—those dreams—go away. That I'll awaken in the morning and I'll be normal, like other folks."

"Have you ever talked about this to anyone?" Glen felt his pain— understood it fully—and wanted to hold him and reassure him. *It's all right. You're all right. Just give it time.*

"Just as most people are born straight, some people are born gay." Glen said, "It's not a choice and it's not a moral failing. It's just the way things are."

"My dad says God made all people straight, but that some succumb to satanic influences and become gay."

"I don't believe that" Glen said. "In the past, it was believed that homosexuality was a perversion, a disease . . . perhaps, a satanic temptation. But science has revealed new truths—knowledge—that have changed the way people think."

Gentry shook his head. "My dad says that the Bible is God's book and the Bible says that homosexuality is an abomination. Dad's a minister and has spoken out against homosexuality in his sermons. He's angry that gay people want to change our society."

"Do you agree with your father?" Glen asked.

"I don't know," Gentry said. "I just pray that one day I'll wake up and those feelings will be gone." His lower lip quivered, "If Dad found out that I was gay, he would be devastated." Gentry began to cry. "I would be such a disappointment to Dad."

Glen reached for Gentry's hand and held it tightly. "You're a fine young man who's going through a really difficult time. You're being very hard on yourself—too hard. You can trust me—count on me—to be there for you."

Gentry's eyes were downcast and Glen said, "Gentry, look at me. I have some understanding of what you're going through and I want to be there for you. Let me be there for you. Can you do that?"

"Yes—and thank you." He wiped the tears from his eyes and tried to smile. "Thank you so much. You're a very kind man." Then rising from the chair he turned and left the classroom.

Chapter Four

Keith closed the hotel door behind them and then turned toward Glen. "Did you notice the room number?"

"Not really," Glen said. "Something special about it?"

"To me there is," Keith moved to stand before Glen. "You remember the last time we stayed at the Melrose Hotel?"

Glen smiled. "How could I forget? It was our first time together, and it was wonderful."

"This is the same room. I wanted everything to be the same . . . even the sex we're going to have." His voice became husky. "Do you remember what we did and how many times we did it?"

Keith's jealousy over Glen's relationship with Katie was destroying his peace of mind. He obsessed about it during the day, and tossed and turned thinking about it during the night. Something had to be done, and Keith determined that going back to where they had been—reviving the initial passion—would be the best answer.

"I just remember how excited I was to be with you, and suddenly I had all these romantic thoughts about you and me being together," Glen said.

"Well, we've been together almost four years now and I love you more than I've ever loved anyone before. It's been wonderful." Keith placed his hand on Glen's shoulder. "But I also remember the sex we had that night and I want to repeat it."

Glen felt a tingling in his groin as Keith began to fumble with his belt. He leaned forward to kiss Keith, gently and then passionately as he felt the touch of Keith's hand inside his pants.

Later, lying in bed naked, Keith asked, "Was it as good as you remembered?"

"Better," Glen laughed, "Obviously, I've taught you some things—improved your technique—in the years we've been together."

"Really?" Keith smiled, "I was thinking the same about you. You were a novice back then and now you' re a WOW! The credit belongs to me."

"But you know what I really remember," Glen said, "The next morning at breakfast when I told you that I felt we had a connection. That perhaps we could turn our being together into something that could last. And you said you weren't interested in a relationship. I was so upset."

"And I remember that you just got up and left," Keith said. "One moment everything was wonderful—great night! great sex! I was thinking about a repeat the next weekend. And then you left. Just got up and left! I couldn't believe it."

"So, fast forward four years and now," Glen said," if I say I can see our relationship lasting for a long, long time. Hopefully, the rest of our lives together. What will you say?"

"That's what I want . . . more than anything," Keith said. "I had no idea how wonderful a relationship could be until I found you. I don't know what I would do if you would ever leave me." He leaned forward to kiss Glen. "You are my sweetheart, my life."

****

Later, as they ate breakfast at the hotel's upscale Landmark Restaurant, with its elegant marble floors and tables covered in white linen cloths, Glen said, "Katie has asked me to be the godfather of her baby."

"And what did you say?" Keith took a bite of his Eggs Benedict.

"I told her I'd be honored."

"Are you aware," Keith said, "There's an assumption that the godparent of a child will assume responsibility for the child, if something happened to the parents."

Glen nodded. "I would want to do that. It wouldn't be a problem for you, would it?"

"Don't think so," Keith said, "But what about the baby's father? Shouldn't Katie's husband have a say in the matter?"

"He should," Glen said and I asked Katie about that. She said, "What if David isn't the father?"

After the passion of the past evening, and the good talk about the lasting relationship they were building, Keith had relaxed, felt secure once again in their relationship and was able to dismiss those obsessive thoughts that Glen and Katie were more than devoted friends as just nonsensical thinking. He was blindsided by Glen's comment.

"So who could be the father, if not her husband?" Keith tried to sound unconcerned, casual, as he reached for his Bloody Mary.

"I have no idea," Glen said. "I was shocked at the possibility that it might not be David. I waited for Katie to explain, but she didn't. I asked, and she said she was foolish to say anything because she had no way of knowing at this time." He took a sip of his Bloody Mary and shrugged, "I'm totally puzzled."

Keith looked at his partner's face: the wavy blond hair, the high coloring and deep blue eyes, the perfectly-shaped lips and cleft in his chin. So handsome! He felt his stomach churn. This was the first shoe to drop and he suspected others would follow. He took a big swallow of his drink, as he raised his hand to get the waiter's attention. "I'll have another Bloody Mary." Keith smiled at Glen, determined not to allow his inner turmoil to show.

****

The warm April sun was nearing the horizon when Katie suggested they go for a walk. "I need the exercise and there's something exciting I want to tell you."

"So tell me," Glen said, as they left the front porch of Katie's home. "Good news. Right?"

"Very good," Katie smiled and little pinpoints of light danced in her hazel eyes.

"I had an ultrasound today and . . ." she paused, allowing the tension to build.

"And?" Glen prompted.

"My baby boy is healthy."

Glen heard the emotion in her voice and saw the tears forming in her eyes. "Wow!" He reached his arm around her waist. "A baby boy! The only thing better would be a baby girl, just like you." Then, laughing, "That was a politically correct comment. I'm thrilled it's a boy!"

For a moment neither spoke as they walked together down the tree-shaded street of modest, neatly maintained homes, similar to hers. Then Glen said, "Katie, I would love to be the baby's godfather and I want to be there to help raise the baby. There's nothing I want more."

"So, is there a problem?" Katie asked.

"There is because your baby has a father and that father should have a right to . . ."

Katie stopped him. "Are you certain that you want to be there for the baby and me?"

"Yes, of course, but that's not the point." There was a tension in her voice that surprised Glen. He turned to look at her.

"Then there's something else I need to tell you. I hope you won't be angry or resent me for what I've done."

"Angry at you? Why?" Glen had no idea where this conversation was headed. "I don't understand."

"Before I tell you, I want you to know you're not responsible. It was my choice and . . ."

"Just tell me. I promise whatever it is, it won't be a problem." Glen reached for her hand.

"I was so upset with David saying I should have an abortion that I determined, come what may, I'd have a baby. That it would be my baby and he would have nothing to do with my baby. I was distraught and . . ."

Katie fumbled to find the words. "Remember when you came to visit shortly after David and I had married. Do you remember what we did?" she asked. Katie stopped walking as she turned to face him.

"The fertility clinic?" he said. "We went to that fertility clinic."

"You had said that you wanted children and would consider a surrogate mother. And I told you, we should harvest my eggs so that your child would be mine as well."

Glen nodded, his excitement growing as he began to anticipate where this might be heading.

"Remember, I asked you to donate your sperm as well, so that if David would not agree to having children, I could become pregnant with your sperm."

"But that was almost four years ago. Can sperm be viable that long?" Glen asked.

"It's frozen—time doesn't matter—at least I hope it doesn't. The day after the blow-up with David, I went to the clinic and—I'm pregnant."

Glen said nothing.

"Are you angry? I didn't have the right to do what I did." Katie spoke rapidly. "Not without asking you. But you're not responsible and . . ."

Glen took her in his arms and kissed her. "Angry? I'm elated. Nothing could make me happier than my wonderful Margaret Katherine Collins having my baby! Wow! This is the best day of my life!" He pinched himself. "I'm not dreaming, am I?"

All those anxious years worrying about being gay, hiding that he was gay. Fearing that his life would be spent as an outsider, his face pressed against the window watching the heterosexual people—the normal people—finding acceptance and love, a partner to cherish and children to nurture and love. Never to be his. And now this . . . all because of Katie, his wonderful Katie!

"Glen, honey, I hope it's your baby. I pray it is, but I can't know for sure. It could be David's."

Noticing that a neighbor watering her front lawn was watching in the dimming light of the lovely April evening, Katie laughed and waved at her. "Just wait 'til she gets to the phone. 'Can you believe it! I saw Katie Collins kissing this good looking man right in the middle of the street. Can you imagine what she's doing in private, if she's doing that in public? It's living in New York City that's done it. No doubt about it, Katie Collins has become a tramp!'"

Then, laughing, Katie said, "Since you've ruined whatever little reputation I had, go ahead, kiss me again. That will give my neighbor something extra to gossip about."

Chapter Five

Gentry's visits with Glen had taken on a warmth based on trust and liking and the sharing of a secret. Glen found himself growing increasingly protective toward the tormented youth and looked forward to his visits at the end of the school day.

"So what are we going to talk about today?" Glen asked, feigning innocence.

Gentry gave a short, embarrassed laugh. "I kinda need your advice about a decision I have to make 'cause it's driving me crazy."

"Yes?" Glen asked.

"Dad wants me to go to his alma mater, Bob Jones University in South Carolina. He has close friends there. Professors and clergymen who'd watch out for me 'cause they know him. But I don't think that would be right for me. You see, it's a Christian school with strict rules about . . ." Gentry fumbled for the right word.

"About homosexuality," Glen said it for him. "I'm familiar with Bob Jones University."

"If I went there, I'd have to live in fear of being found out."

"Then your decision should be clear. Don't go there."

"But if I did go there," Gentry said, "It could keep me from being gay and that would be good."

"Why would it be good?" Glen asked. "If accepting that you're gay means being true to yourself, why would that be bad?"

"Dad says that being gay goes against biblical teaching. It's an immoral choice that condemns a person to a life of perversion and the torment of hell."

"Do you believe that?" Glen asked.

"I don't know what I believe," Gentry looked imploringly at Glen. "I just know I'm falling apart inside. My girlfriend is planning to go to Bob Jones. We'll be together and we're talking about becoming engaged. She thinks that's so cool."

"Is that what you want?" Glen asked.

Gentry didn't answer.

"Where would you really like to go to college?" Glen asked. "It's your life, not your father's."

"I'd like to go to the University of Texas at Austin, but there's a problem. There's someone there who I kinda can't be near 'cause . . ." he stopped. "I just can't be with him. It would be a mistake, a very bad mistake."

Glen waited for the youth to continue. When he didn't, Glen said, "Gentry, I can't be helpful to you if you withhold information from me. Tell me what's really upsetting you."

Gentry swallowed hard. "You asked me once if I'd ever had sex with a male and I said no. But that wasn't true. I have . . . had a best friend. We kinda did everything together and you might say we loved each other. He's a year older than me and during the Christmas Holidays when he was home from school I was over at his house and . . . we had sex." Gentry cleared his throat. "It was just one time. We never did it again," he added quickly. "He wanted to, but I wouldn't."

"I take it that he's at U.T. Austin," Glen said.

Gentry ran his hand through his hair in a nervous movement. "I keep thinking about him. About what we did and I'm afraid it might happen again. I have dreams about him. He wants me to be his roommate if I go to U.T. Austin. It's driving me crazy."

"Would you like to be his roommate?" Glen spoke softly.

Gentry looked down. "That would be so cool, but I know what it would lead to . . . what it would mean."

"Yes?" Glen asked. "What would it mean?"

"That I'm gay, and that would ruin my life."

Glen reached for Gentry's hand. "I'm gay and I have a partner. We have a good life, a very good life. Maybe sometime you could meet him. He's a fine person and we have a very good life."

****

Happy hour was a ritual at their home. Martinis with two olives for Keith. Red wine—typically cabernet—for Glen. It was their time to relax and share the happenings of the day.

Keith had just taken his first sip of his drink when Glen said, "I have some very exciting news."

"Yes?"

"I can't believe this is real, but Katie says it is and, well, I'm so happy!" Glen spread his arms in a show of amazement. "Katie said that I might be the father of her baby!"

"Really?" Keith felt a heavy weight in the pit of his stomach. *They were having sex!* Just as he had suspected. "Isn't that what happens when a man and woman have sex?" Keith spoke in a matter of fact manner, not allowing the upset to register on his face, his voice.

"But we didn't have sex," Glen said. "Katie and I are friends, wonderful friends. There's nothing sexual in our relationship. We're friends, not lovers."

Keith tried to sound nonchalant. "Then this is one of those virgin birth tales, like the second coming of Jesus."

"No," Glen laughed. "Nothing like that. Katie went to the fertility clinic where her eggs and my sperm were frozen and stored."

"Your sperm was at a fertility clinic?" Keith stared at his partner. *Does he actually expect me to believe that bullshit?* "And where exactly is this fertility clinic?"

"In New York City. It was Katie's idea. When I visited Katie shortly after she had married David, she suggested that we go to a fertility clinic and register as a couple in a committed relationship. Her eggs and my sperm were to be frozen and . . ."

Keith interrupted, "Are you telling me that Katie could obtain your sperm without your knowing? Seems to me the clinic would require a release signed by you for that to happen."

"If I remember correctly, we did sign a release allowing each of us the right to use the other's sperm or eggs. Yes, that's what we did."

"And what's the name of that fertility clinic?" Keith asked.

"I have no idea. It was almost four years ago."

Keith thought to himself, *I don't believe this! It's a bunch of bullshit! They're having sex.* Keith took a gulp of his drink, loath to continue the conversation. What if he pushed too hard and Glen would say that he really did love Katie, like *in* love? That he wanted to leave him and live with Katie now that she was pregnant with his child?

Keith needed time to get his emotions under control—time to absorb this new information and what it might mean for his relationship with Glen. "So let's have another drink," he said, hoping to sound nonchalant, as angry thoughts of ending the relationship consumed him—*I'm not going to put up with this goddamn crap!*

"Okay, but first, tell me," Glen said. "Aren't you excited at the possibility of the baby being our baby? Isn't that something!"

Keith smiled. "Yes, it's really something."

****

Assuming that Keith would go to the law office Saturday morning, as he always had, Glen made plans to be with Katie. But Keith surprised him with a suggestion that they drive to Dallas, visit the Nasher Museum to see the new modern art exhibit, and then have lunch at the Mansion. It was to be a special treat.

Unfortunately, Glen had already made plans to be with Katie.

"How about going tomorrow? Wouldn't that work, just as well." Glen said.

"If that's what you want, we'll do it tomorrow," Keith agreed, but he seemed disappointed and that disturbed Glen.

Keith had yet to complain about the time he was spending with Katie. But Glen anticipated a moment when Keith would confront him, and he dreaded that moment. He cared for Katie, always had. She was the girl he would have married had he been straight. He knew that and she did too. It was a bond that joined them together. And now with the possibility that her baby was his, Glen was drawn to Katie more than ever.

He loved Keith with all the intensity that a heterosexual man might love a woman—there was passion, excitement—a feeling of completion when he was with Keith. His love for Katie was different: calm and secure—a quiet peacefulness that came from being with a warm and trusted friend. He wanted—needed—both of them in his life.

There was the feel of rain in the air and a blustery May wind shook the branches of the live oak trees, as Katie and Glen walked hand in hand. "I have something exciting to tell you," she said.

"Yes?"

"Last night, I felt a fluttering—the baby. I'm beginning to feel the baby. And this morning, I felt him again. Several times."

Later, as they sat beside one another on the small sofa in Katie's living room, Glen placed his hand on Katie's abdomen. They waited silently and then Glen exclaimed, "I felt a movement! I really did! It's either the baby . . . or gas."

Katie leaned forward to kiss Glen lightly on his lips. "It's our baby," she said. "A lady never has gas."

Glen laughed. "Katie, you're the best! I'm so happy you went to that fertility clinic."

"So am I" Katie said softly. "She leaned back on the sofa and closed her eyes."

"Are you making another one of your wishes?" Glen asked.

Katie nodded. "A wonderful wish that I hope will come true."

"Oh, by the way," Glen said, "When you're through making wishes, I want to ask you about the minister at your church."

"Reverend Phillips?" she asked.

"Yes. What's he like?"

"He's all right, I guess. Too conservative for me, but highly respected, especially by the older members of our church. Before you came to Edgemont, we had a young, very appealing minister at the First Baptist Church. He got in the cross-hairs of several influential members, because he wouldn't say that women should be obedient to their husbands as the Bible taught."

Katie shook her head. "There was a huge brouhaha and the young minister whom I adored was removed. I seriously thought about going to another church, but I had been raised at the First Baptist. My relatives and friends belong. So I stayed even though Reverend Phillips who replaced him is one of those ultra-traditionalists who believes women are less than men and," she paused, "I don't have to tell you his views about gays. It begins with the Bible says and ends with the everlasting fires of hell."

Then, taking Glen's hand in hers, she asked, "Why did you ask?"

"Just that I know his son and was wondering about his father." Glen said.

"You know Gentry? His father is so proud of him. Gentry is such an appealing young man. And so handsome! When Reverend Phillips and his family arrived, the young girls at our church went gaga over Gentry. They just loved that boy with his dark wavy hair and those deep blue eyes. But then he saw Betty Jean Farris and that was it," Katie said. "Do you know his girlfriend as well?"

"Not really," Glen said. "I've seen them in the halls together. She's a very pretty girl."

"Betty Jean is an angel. I know her mother real well. They're so happy that Betty Jean and Gentry are so much in love. Just last week after church, her mother told me that they'll be going to Bob Jones University in South Carolina." Katie smiled, "It's supposed to be a secret, but everyone knows, Gentry and Betty Jean are planning to get engaged at the end of their freshman year."

****

"Hi, Gentry," Glen said as the youth entered his classroom door. "Haven't seen you in a while. I was beginning to wonder if you were all right."

"I'm fine! Actually, better than fine," Gentry appeared buoyant and confident. His blue eyes sparkled and there was a liveliness in his step that hadn't been there before.

"I guess I've got some catching up to do," Glen said. The last time we were together you were a very unhappy young man."

"Well, for one thing, I've received my letter of acceptance at Bob Jones University and Mom and Dad are thrilled. Dad has been telling everyone that I'm fixing to go to his alma mater and that I'm probably going to be a minister, just like him."

He paused, before adding, "Betty Jean, she's my girlfriend, has been accepted as well. We're going to be together! We're going to get engaged at the end of our first year of college. Isn't that cool?"

Gentry continued in an excited, almost manic manner, "The big thing—the biggest thing of all—is that I've allowed Jesus to enter my heart. *He* has taken away my sins and brought peace to my soul."

Glen was silent, dumbfounded at what he was hearing. After a moment, he said, "What about U.T. Austin? I thought that's where you wanted to go. That you had a friend there . . . ."

Gentry stopped Glen with a shake of his head. "That would have been a terrible choice! I emailed my friend telling him that I didn't want to have anything to do with him ever again. That what we did— what he wanted me to do—was a perversion. Homosexuality is a perversion!" Gentry repeated forcefully. It's a choice to allow Satan to control your life.

"I was tempted, but I turned to Jesus and found the strength to say no." Gentry sounded triumphant. His face was flushed and his eyes gleamed.

"Did your father help you make that decision?" Glen asked, already knowing the answer.

"Yes, he showed me the way," Gentry said. "Two days ago after Sunday church, Dad asked me why I seemed so upset. I started to cry and told him about my fear of being gay. Dad was wonderful! He took my hands in his and said, 'Let the spirit of Jesus enter your heart. Trust in Jesus.' Dad said Jesus would help me stand up against Satan. And Jesus did, just like Dad said he would. I've felt wonderful these past two days!"

Gentry hesitated. There was something more he wanted to say. He started to speak, then stopped.

"Yes?" Glen asked.

"You're a kind person, Mr. McLean. I know you want to lead a good life. I can see that. So I just need to tell you that it's not too late."

"Too late for what?" Glen asked.

"To allow Jesus to enter your heart. To trust in Jesus to save you from the sin of homosexuality. My Dad told me that people who make the choice to be homosexual will never be allowed into God's Kingdom. They will surely spend eternity burning in the fires of hell. Dad placed his hand on my shoulder as he prayed for Jesus to enter my heart and free me of Satan's temptation. If I asked, I know Dad would do that for you."

Glen considered saying nothing. What good would it do? Gentry appeared too high on religious euphoria over his imagined release from homosexuality to consider another reality, a different perspective.

Still, Glen felt the need to say, "Gentry, I want you to know that I don't agree with your father. Being gay is not a choice and it's not a sin. I'm a gay man living with a gay partner and we are living a good life, a moral life. I don't feel less than others because I'm gay, and you don't have to either."

For several moments after Gentry had left, Glen sat quietly at his desk, fighting back the insecurities of his youthful years, when talk of sin and judgment triggered panicky feelings of hell and damnation and a life without love.

Glen shook his head to break the spell. The teachings of his Catholic Church were wrong! He was living the good life—the best life! He had Keith and now the baby. That was his family. If he could have that, he wouldn't need anything more.

****

Katie was exhausted. She had worked all week as a substitute teacher and loved being with the students and her former colleagues. But teaching five classes, plus a study hall, each day had left her drained. At home, she collapsed on her bed and closed her eyes, hoping for a short nap before dinner.

That didn't happen. That tiny lump in her right breast had not gone away. She had discovered it when examining herself midway through the second month of her pregnancy, and froze. It was nothing, a lymph gland, nothing more she had reassured herself.

But her mother had died from breast cancer when barely 40, and Katie was paranoid that would be her fate as well. If she hadn't been pregnant, she would have rushed to her doctor. The pregnancy changed everything. If it was breast cancer, she would be told to have surgery immediately, followed by chemotherapy, possibly radiation. The baby wouldn't survive, or if it did, it would have birth defects.

So she waited and prayed obsessively. "Dear Lord, please, let me be well. Let my baby be healthy. Please, dear Lord Jesus, Please."

Everything was going so well in her life. She was back in Edgemont in her own home, secure in knowing she would have a job. Surrounded once again by her relatives and friends, and she was back with Glen. She loved him—always had—and despite his being gay, she felt certain he loved her, too. Didn't she see it in his eyes when he looked her way?

In his voice when he spoke her name? In his touch when he held her hand or lightly kissed her on the lips?

"Oh, dear Lord Jesus, please let the baby be Glen's. That would be so wonderful! My life would be perfect—Glen and me and our little boy!

She felt her breast once again, hoping this time that lump would be gone, or at least smaller and no longer hard. It wasn't. The lump was still there and bigger. It was growing. Katie closed her eyes.

Four more months to go in the pregnancy. Once her baby was born and she knew he was safe, she would have the surgery and all the treatments that had to follow. Just not now when her life was brightly colored with wonderful images of Glen and their baby.

Chapter Six

Keith's suspicion that Glen and Katie were in a sexual relationship had become an obsession. He could not put it to rest. He was jealous and intensely possessive. Glen was his! Each time, Glen would leave to be with Katie the anxiety that they might be having sex would torment him—driving him to distraction.

They were out for dinner at Outback Steak House and the waitress had just brought their order. As Keith raised his knife and fork to cut into the thick pork chop, he said in a casual manner, "Ask Katie the name of the clinic where she went to get pregnant."

"Why does that matter?" Glen asked.

"Just curious," Keith said. "One of my clients told me that he and his wife were having a problem conceiving and I thought maybe that clinic Katie went to might help him." He paused to take a bite of his pork chop. "I know so little about those places. I mean when you and Katie first went there, did you give your real names. Tell me how it works?"

Glen laughed. "Why wouldn't we give our real names? We weren't doing anything illegal or something to be ashamed of. We told them that we were in a committed relationship and wanted to ensure that her eggs and my sperm would always be available. It was like an insurance policy in case something bad happened to either one of us."

A few days later, Glen handed him a slip of paper with the name and address of the clinic. "Here, you can give this to your client. Katie said the place was great."

35

Saturday morning at his law firm, Keith closed the door to his office. He looked up the phone number of the fertility clinic, and called.

"Hello, this is Glen McLean and I'm calling to thank you and ask a question.

"What's the question?" the woman who had answered said.

"My girlfriend, Katie Collins, went to your clinic several months back for a procedure to become pregnant with my sperm, and I wanted to know if there's a record . . ."

The woman stopped him. "I'm the receptionist. Let me switch you to someone who can help you."

A moment later, a man responded. "Yes, can I help you?"

Keith repeated, "This is Glen McLean, my fiancé Katie Collins went to your clinic in November to obtain my frozen sperm for a procedure to become pregnant."

"Did it take?"

"Yes, it did." Keith said.

"That's great!"

"I just wanted to know," Keith said quickly, fearing the man was about to hang up. "Was all my frozen sperm used? Do I need to come back again?"

"Tell me your name again. And the name of your fiancee. I'll need to check our records. Can you hold a moment?"

Several minutes passed. "Hello, Mr. McLean, I'm not finding those names in our computer. There is a Margaret K. Collins who was in here in November. But not a Katie Collins. I don't see any record of your name. Are you sure you're calling the right clinic. You know there are several with similar names."

About to hang up, Keith grasped at a possibility, "How are you spelling McLean?"

"M-a-c-L-a-n-e."

"It's M-c-L-e-a-n. See if that helps," he said, not believing that it would. It was all bullshit and he knew it. He clenched his hand into a fist and hit his desk. The next time Colby came on to him at the gym, he would say *yes*. Why not? If Glen was carrying on with Katie, why shouldn't he carry on as well? Their relationship—their talk of love and commitment for life—was bullshit. Nothing more than fucking bullshit!

A moment passed and then another. "Yes, Mr. McLean, I did find it and yes, Ms. Collins was the recipient. You will have to come back as the file shows there is none of your sperm remaining."

"Thank you," Keith said. "Thank you so very much!"

He placed the phone back on the receiver and felt relief wash over him. First the good feelings: *Glen is wonderful—honest and loving, kind and thoughtful, committed to me and always there for me. I'm so lucky to have Glen in my life!*

Then the guilt and self-recrimination. *You should have trusted Glen. You should have known he wouldn't lie. You have to make it up to him . . . and Katie too.* She'd been back in Edgemont for over two months and he had yet to see her, in spite of Glen's requests that he invite her to their home for dinner. Keith felt he had some serious making up to do.

****

Saturday afternoon, shortly after returning from the office, Keith said to Glen, "Why don't we invite Katie here for dinner?"

"That would be great!" Glen said. "I was hoping you'd be open to doing that."

Keith was the chef in their home. Whenever asked about his role in preparing a dinner, Glen would laugh, "Keith prepares the menu because he thinks I wouldn't know how to develop a menu. He does the shopping because he believes I wouldn't know what to buy. Keith prepares the dinner because he says—and he's right—I wouldn't qualify to cook a hamburger at McDonald's. And after the guests have departed, Keith arranges the dishes in the dishwasher, because he says if I load the dishwasher, he has to remove everything and do it the right way—extra work for him.

"What do I do? I peel, chop and dice, because according to Keith I am good at following his directions, so long as I am not in one of my negative moods. Recently, he has granted me permission to clear the table and rinse the dishes and flatware so that he can then place them in the dishwasher, the correct way. At the end of the evening, I am *always* allowed to take out the garbage because, according to Keith, I have a talent for that.

"There's a few other things I do at the end of every dinner party. I kiss Keith and pat his sexy butt and tell him what a fabulous dinner we just had. Why? Because I have no interest in cooking and am so grateful that my control-freak partner is a wonderful gourmet cook. What a lucky break for me!

"So when should I ask Katie to come?" Glen asked.

"Tomorrow evening would work, if she's free. I could do the shopping today and have Sunday afternoon to prepare the dinner."

Keith had worked all day Sunday to prepare a special dinner for Katie and Glen: Caesar Salad, Chilean Sea Bass with potatoes au gratin and asparagus, and a strawberry tart for dessert.

"Wow! You've gone all out!" Glen was pleased. "I'm so happy you're doing this." He leaned forward to kiss Keith. "You are such a sweetheart and probably the world's best cook!"

"Once I learned that Katie might be pregnant with your baby—our baby—I thought we must have a celebration. I was so happy when you told me."

"Were you happy? I thought you seemed a little upset." Glen said.

"Why would I be upset?" Keith asked, and then wanting to change the subject, pointed to the red and yellow roses on the dining room table. "Do you like the roses?"

"They're beautiful, and I know Katie will love them. Keith, sweetheart, I can't tell you how proud I am of you and the life we're leading and this beautiful home we live in. I can't wait for Katie to see it."

****

A soft North Texas breeze rustled the leaves of the giant live oak trees on this balmy April evening as Katie stood on the sidewalk admiring the stately Victorian home set off with a flowing lawn and a large wrap-around front porch. This was one of the town's wealthy neighborhoods, a street of large homes built in the early decades of the 20th century by the prominent families.

People who grew up in Edgemont knew of the Chamberlains. Keith's grandfather had been the mayor and a street was named after him. Keith, who had inherited the family home, was several years ahead of Katie at Edgemont High. Before they ever met, she had heard about him from gushing older girls: "What a dream! So smart and good looking! The star quarterback on the football team! Can you believe a fabulous guy like that is still available?"

At the dinner table, Glen did most of the talking. He was obviously excited to have his partner and Katie together. And so proud of the home he was sharing with Keith. "How do you like that staircase? It seems to be suspended in air, doesn't it? And look at these tall ceilings! They're 14 feet high! Did you know that Keith's great-grandfather built this house and a Chamberlain has always lived in it?

"And Keith is such a great cook! I'd put him up against any chef in any five-star restaurant. I really would! I can't believe my good fortune in winding up with this man."

Glen reached over to take Katie's hand in his. "Keith and I have talked so many times about having a child—raising a child in this house—and now you're making our dream come true. You're my angel and I love you and hope you know how happy Keith and I are to have this baby to share with you."

It was painful for Katie to be with Glen and Keith in their home. When she and Glen were alone, just the two of them, she could make believe that they were in love, like a man and woman should be, and one day they would share a life, a bed and a family. Now, witnessing the reality before her—two gay men in a loving, committed relationship—she felt the folly of her delusion. *It's just pretense—you and Glen and the baby. It will never happen! Why do you do this to yourself?* Katie felt the wetness on her cheeks.

"Katie, honey, why are you crying?" Glen said. "Is something wrong?"

"Oh, no, everything is wonderful! I just felt the baby move and I was thinking how fortunate my baby will be to have the two of you in his life."

Chapter Seven

The 19th amendment establishing voting rights for women elicited strong reaction. Many students, especially the girls, found it inconceivable that when our country was founded women did not have the right to vote, because—according to biblical teaching and custom—women were not the equal of men and should not be involved with challenging issues involving the governing of a nation: a woman's mind was not made for intellectual thoughts such as those.

"That is so stupid!"

"It's wrong!"

"Who decided that women had to be obedient to men?"

"It's what the Bible teaches. That's what our minister says."

Another very emotional topic involved slavery. A number of the students hadn't fully realized that the Bible and our founding fathers condoned slavery, and that laws were passed in a number of the states to protect the rights of the slave owners.

"Black folks had less rights than anyone! They were treated like dirt!" a black student said. "They couldn't vote until 1870 and . . ."

"Well, that was a long time before women had the right to vote!" Jennifer Arrendale called out.

And that started a heated discussion over who was more abused.

"Blacks still face discrimination in their jobs!"

"So do women!"

On several occasions, Glen had to intervene as the feelings ran so high about the past treatment of women and black people.

"But we're not just talking about the past. Growth in knowledge providing new perspectives and understandings is ongoing. That means our societies must constantly re-evaluate and adjust current laws and attitudes that are based on discredited thinking and bigotry. The wonderful thing about our Constitution is that it recognized that changes would need to be made, and it included a procedure for this to happen, so that our nation's Bill of Rights guaranteeing life, liberty and the pursuit of happiness may one day hold true for all people."

A number of parents sent notes, emailed Glen, or stopped him when they met in public to thank him for the positive influence he was having on their children.

"I've never seen my son so excited by a teacher. You're teaching civics as well as English. Thank you!"

"My daughter loves your class. She says you're the best teacher ever!"

Not all parents were impressed. Inevitably, there would be an irate note, such as this one:

The Bible is God's Book. His truths are eternal and unchanging. My wife and I do not appreciate you teaching our daughter to think otherwise.

****

On the first Wednesday in June, the long summer recess began. Whoops and hollers from students echoed through the halls, and the buses departed shortly afterwards. Glen was cleaning out his desk and thinking about his plans for the summer break, when he heard someone entering his classroom.

Looking up, he saw Gentry. "Hi," he smiled. "Haven't seen you a while."

Gentry looked hesitant. "I thought you might not want to see me anymore."

"Why?" Glen asked.

"Because of what I said about gay people . . . about your being gay."

Glen shook his head. "No, I didn't hold that against you, because I've been there. Liking yourself isn't easy, not when you've been taught—as you and I were—that what you are is unacceptable."

"I'm glad that you understand. That you're not mad at me. I . . . I need you to be my friend."

"Sit down," Glen pointed to the chair beside his desk. "When I was your age, and coming to realize that I might be gay, I desperately needed a friend. Someone I could talk to about my fears and feel safe." Glen reached for Gentry's hand. "I'd like to be that someone for you."

"Thank you so much. I do need to talk to someone . . . to you." Gentry's voice broke as his eyes filled with tears.

Glen waited for Gentry to continue.

I don't know what to do. I'm being torn apart. My friend will be back from college next week. He wants to see me—be with me—and I'm afraid." Gentry ran his hand through his hair, a habit of his when nervous or upset.

"What are you afraid of?" Glen asked.

"I can't stop thinking about him and wanting to be with him."

"Are you afraid that you love him?" Glen asked.

Gentry looked down. He sighed. "I've been fighting with myself, trying so hard to block the thought. But then it comes in my dreams: we're together holding each other, saying words like, 'I love you, and I love you too.'"

"You can't deny love. It's too powerful. You're fighting a battle you won't win." Glen smiled gently. "Trust me, I've been there." He patted Gentry's hand. "You need to accept that you love your friend, so that you can move on to the next step: what you are going to do about it."

"I don't know. My father says it's a perversion. It's Satan tempting us to sin." He ran his hand through his hair once again.

"Do you really believe that?" Glen said. "My church—the Catholic Church—taught me that. But I don't believe that now. Not only scientists, but even religious scholars have rejected that way of thinking. Your father may not be willing or able to change his way of thinking, but you can change yours. I did and I'll be there to help you, if you want me to."

"Would it be all right if I called you during the summer? Would that be all right?"

Glen smiled. "Yes, that would be fine." He reached for his pen. "Let me write down my cell phone number. You can call me whenever you need to talk."

****

Katie sat down beside Glen on her sofa. "David called."

"Yes?" Glen said, "Any reason?"

Katie nodded. "He had heard from a mutual friend that I was pregnant. He was worried that the baby might be his. I could hear the tension in his voice."

"What did you tell him?"

"I told him what he wanted to hear. The baby wasn't his. That I had gone to a clinic and had become pregnant by a procedure using your sperm."

"But what if it turns out the baby is his? Shouldn't he be told there is that possibility?" Glen reached for Katie's hand.

"No. David didn't want another child. He couldn't have expressed it more strongly than telling me to have an abortion, if I were pregnant." She shook her head. "I don't want my baby to have a father who doesn't want him."

She turned to look directly at Glen. "I want my baby to have a father who loves him and thanks God every day for having this baby in his life. I want you to be my baby's father."

Glen squeezed Katie hand. "I understand."

"I've been thinking about the birth certificate," she said. "Would it be all right if I name you as the father."

Glen was deeply touched. For a moment he didn't speak. Then hugging Katie to him, he said. "From this moment forward, I will be the father of your baby, and I will love him and care for him all the days of my life."

Katie moved his hand to her belly. "Our baby is moving. Can you feel him? I hope he knows that he will have the best daddy in the whole wide world." She leaned forward to kiss Glen lightly on his lips.

Later, after Glen had left, Katie stood naked before the full-length mirror in her bedroom. She was entering the seventh month of the pregnancy and it showed. That was so fulfilling and exciting. Her baby was growing and she could feel his movements throughout the day. There were times, when lying in bed, she could see the ripple on her belly and she wondered, *Is that his hand or his foot?*

She was seeing her obstetrician on a regular schedule now to make sure that everything was progressing as it should. And it was. Her baby was healthy and that was what was most important to her, especially as the lump in her breast was growing. She checked several times each day, hoping that it might be smaller and less tender. It wasn't and she realized something had to be done, just not yet. It was not something she would discuss with anyone, even her obstetrician, because she knew what she'd be told, and she wasn't going to do it.

If I have surgery now, Katie reasoned, *they will need to follow up with chemotherapy and possibly radiation. What would that do to my baby? The baby is due in just two months. I'm going to wait.*

****

Upon his return to Edgemont for the summer break from college, Jason contacted Gentry about his decision to end their friendship. "We've been friends for so many years . . . more than friends. We need to talk—face to face—not end it with a text message."

"I don't know if that's a good idea," Gentry said. "Our friendship needs to end . . . our meeting will only prolong it."

"It's important to me that we meet. I don't want it to end like this. Not after all we've shared . . . all that we've meant to one another," Jason's voice broke.

"All right," Gentry agreed, "Let's meet, face to face and end it that way." *Just one meeting, one time.* That's what he told himself. *We'll talk, shake hands for old time's sake, and it will be over.*

Gentry had suggested they meet at the park where they could talk in private as they walked along the dirt pathway bordering the lake. He figured a half-hour would be time enough for an amicable ending of their friendship.

Gentry sat on a stone bench hearing the squawking of the mallard ducks as he watched a pair of white swans dunking their heads into the water for whatever it was they ate. He rehearsed his words to Jason. "We were best friends for so many years, and I'll always think of you that way: a friend—a very good friend."

He intended for them to reminisce about the many good times they'd shared—positive memories of a friendship that was wonderful in its time, but needed to end now before it led to something bad—a sinful perversion, an abomination. He was confident he could make Jason understand that there was no other choice: their friendship had to end before it would lead them into sin and make them regret they ever knew one another. He and Jason would shake hands and it would be over. The issue resolved, he would then depart for his date with Betty Jean, his conscience clear and his mind at peace.

Looking up, Gentry saw Jason heading his way, and his heart did a flip. He ran his hand through his wavy hair and tried to calm his emotions as he responded to Jason's trim body and athletic walk, his short-cropped sandy hair and the large brown eyes that suggested intelligence, sensitivity and fun. The sight of Jason made his heart beat faster.

"Hi," Jason smiled and the lights in his dark eyes shone bright.

"Hi, yourself," Gentry said, a greeting they had shared for years. He rose to shake Jason's hands, but the handshake unexpectedly changed into an embrace—and the spontaneous pressing together of their bodies excited Gentry: he felt a sexual surge that he hadn't anticipated. Gentry's resolve to end the relationship evaporated and the words he had so carefully rehearsed weren't spoken.

They walked along the meandering pathway—their shoulders touching, and occasionally one or the other would put his arm around the other's waist. Jason did most of the speaking as a love-smitten Gentry, listened enthralled to Jason's tales of college life in Austin. Before they parted, Gentry had agreed, "Yes, we can get together tomorrow evening at your house. I'll be there at 7 p.m."

Why had he agreed to meet Jason this evening? And why was he meeting him again tomorrow evening? He knew where this was heading. It was a mistake! Jason would want to have sex . . . expect that they would. Could he stand firm? Just friends, nothing more! *Yes, I'll be firm. I'll . . .*

He stood motionless watching Jason walk down the pathway toward his car. Then his mind in turmoil, he headed quickly to his car and his date with Betty Jean.

****

Even as Gentry told himself that this coming evening with Jason would be nothing special—just time together with his friend—he knew it wasn't so. He changed his outfit several times, before he was satisfied with his look: navy-blue Calvin Klein jeans and a yellow polo. He ran his hand through his dark hair over and over again to ensure that no unruly lock was out of place.

Gentry hadn't known that Jason's parents would be out: they had driven to Dallas for dinner at the French Room and the theater. They wouldn't return until late, and that left the two of them alone in his home.

"Would you like a glass of wine?" Jason pointed to the bar, as he led Gentry into the dimly lit den.

"I don't know," Gentry said. "Do you think that's all right?"

"I drink at home with my parents and . . . let's do it. Okay?"

"I guess that'll be cool," Gentry smiled. "My dad wouldn't like it, but then he's not here."

For several moments they sat beside each other on the large leather sectional, quietly sipping the red wine. Gentry, who had little experience with wine or any alcoholic drink for that matter, began to feel its calming effect. "I like this," he murmured as he touched Jason's hand.

"I do too," Jason said. "very much." He cleared the huskiness from his voice. "Do you remember the first time we met? You had just moved to Edgemont and Betty Jean invited you to her party."

Gentry nodded. "I didn't know anyone there except Betty Jean."

"I didn't know who you were, but I thought you were so good looking," Jason said. "Dark hair and blue eyes and the whitest teeth I'd ever seen. "I wanted to get to know you but I thought you didn't like me."

"No," Gentry said. "I thought you were so attractive. I saw you as soon as I came. You were wearing blue jeans and a red shirt . . . and had a wonderful smile. "I asked Betty Jean who you were and she said, "Oh, that's Jason Glendinning. Isn't he great! He's one of the most popular boys in the eighth grade. I'm so glad he came to my party!""

"But you didn't seem friendly when I came over to talk to you," Jason said.

"I was this shy kid in seventh grade and I just froze when you came over. I couldn't think of anything to say. But I couldn't keep my eyes off you that evening . . . and then later when we'd pass in the corridor at school. I wanted to say something to you, but you were in the 8th grade and had so many friends. I thought you wouldn't be interested in knowing me."

Jason took Gentry's hand in his. "But I was interested." He paused. "Remember we started to walk home from school together, and then we started to play tennis and go bike riding. We became friends."

"We did everything together, didn't we?" Gentry said, "Even double dated in high school." He paused, as he felt Jason's grasp on his hand tighten. "Did you know that Betty Jean was jealous? She told me that I cared for you more than her."

"So what happened?" Jason said simply. "Why did you send me that text that we couldn't be friends—our friendship was over?"

Gentry sighed deeply. "We crossed a line. What we did was wrong and . . ." He saw the tears welling in Jason's eyes. "I'm so sorry. I don't want to hurt you. But what we did was a sin, an abomination."

"I never planned to love you in that way," Jason said. "We were friends, very good friends. Two guys who just wanted to be together until . . . last year. Something changed—I don't know when it happened exactly, but you started to come to me in my dreams, and we held one another and made love. I couldn't believe that I was having those dreams.

"When we were together last Christmas, I couldn't help myself. You were so close. Your hand was touching mine. It was like a dream. I leaned forward and kissed you, and you kissed me back. Before then, I was afraid to say something—do anything—because I didn't know how you felt. I thought you might be repelled . . . but you kissed me back. And I knew that you loved me in the way that I loved you."

Jason leaned forward and kissed Gentry lightly on his lips. "I can't stop thinking about that evening and what we did. It was so exciting—just like a dream, but it was real." He looked into Gentry's eyes. "You do love me, don't you?"

"I don't know if we should do this," Gentry said. "This isn't right. It's . . ." He felt Jason's hand caressing his thigh, and a growing sexual excitement ended his protest.

Jason kissed him again and then again. Their lips parted. "I love you," Jason said, "and I know you love me."

Gentry took a deep breath. "I do love you . . . very much. It's just that . . ."

"Don't fight it. We love each other and that's what matters." Their kissing became passionate. "Tell me you love me . . . tell me it again." His voice was husky.

"I love you . . . very much," Gentry said. He pulled Jason tightly against him. "This is what I want—you're what I want."

****

As Glen handed Keith his martini, he leaned forward to kiss him. "Thank you for having Katie for dinner last Sunday. I know it was a lot of work for you, but it meant so much to me. It made me very happy."

"I'm pleased that everything went so well," Keith smiled. "And above all, I'm happy that you're happy. As the saying goes, 'If Mama ain't happy then ain't nobody happy'."

"In our case, I believe the saying should be, 'If Papa ain't happy then ain't nobody happy.' You're the Mama. I'm the Papa," Glen laughed. Then he grew serious. "Earlier today when I visited Katie, she told me that David had called her. He had heard about her pregnancy and, according to Katie, he was worried that he might be the father."

"So what did she tell him?" Keith took a sip of his martini, then reached into the glass for an olive.

"She told him she became pregnant through a procedure using my sperm. That he wasn't the father."

"Did he believe her?" Keith removed the olive pit from his mouth and placed it in a saucer on the red lacquer cocktail table.

"According to Katie, he was relieved. He's in his 40s and is already responsible for two children from his first marriage. He doesn't want another one."

"Well, that's now. But people have been known to change their minds, especially if the baby is his. In the almost 13 years I've been a lawyer, I've seen a lot of unexpected happenings. You can never predict what people might do."

Glen shrugged. "Katie is going to put my name on the birth certificate as the father. Won't that take care of any future issue about who's the father?" He took a final sip of wine and placed the empty glass on the cocktail table.

"Not necessarily," Keith said. "What if it can be proved that the baby isn't biologically yours? Maybe David doesn't want more children and won't care, but someone else might."

"Who? I don't understand what you're saying?" Glen raised his hands, palms upward. "Why would anyone care?"

"Glen, sweetie, I may be a little paranoid, but this is Texas, and you're known to be a gay man. We are a gay couple and there are people here—fundamentalist Christians—who go ballistic at the thought of a gay person raising a child."

Chapter Eight

On summer recess for almost two weeks, Glen had immersed himself planting and tending to the flowers and shrubs in the large back garden of their home. He loved the celosias with the red feathery heads, but was especially taken with the white caladiums with their pale green veining. He had stepped back to admire them when his cell phone rang, startling him.

"Yes?"

"Mr. McLean, is that you?"

"Gentry?"

"You said it would be all right for me to call you. I hope it is."

"Of course, it's all right. Tell me how you're doing?"

"I need to talk to you. Something's happened and I don't know what to do."

"Are you comfortable telling me about it on the phone?" Glen asked.

"It would be better if we could be together. Can I come to your home? I know where you live."

"That will be fine," Glen said. "What time works for you?"

"Now? Can you see me now? I really need to see you now."

Glen guided Gentry to the formal living room.

"Your home is so cool," Gentry said. "I had no idea a teacher might live in a home like this."

"It's the family home of my partner, Keith Chamberlain." Glen motioned Gentry to be seated on the Chippendale armchair facing the sofa. "But tell me what's upsetting you. It's been two weeks since I last saw you. So what's happened?"

"A lot. It's hard to know where to begin. My friend—his name is Jason—returned from college for the summer and called me. He had received my email saying that our friendship was over, but he wouldn't accept it. He said we needed to talk face to face. I agreed. One time, and that would be it.

"Only it wasn't. Once we were together, I couldn't break it off. We met again. And it happened, just as I was afraid it would. We had sex and I told him I loved him and he told me he loved me too."

Gentry took a deep breath. "During this past year in Austin, Jason said he had come to accept himself as a gay man, and he knew that I was gay too. That we needed to be honest and admit that we were gay and that we were in love."

"Can't be more direct than that," Glen said. "So what did you say? Did you admit that you were gay?"

Gentry nodded. "I told him he was right and yes, I did love him. Then he said my going steady with Betty Jean was a farce. It wasn't fair to her and I needed to end it. 'You need to come to U.T. Austin and be with me.'"

Gentry looked down, pausing before saying. "I am gay. I've known that for a long time, but couldn't accept it. I just couldn't." His voice was choked. "And I do love Jason . . . very much, and I don't know what to do."

"I didn't come out to my parents until I was 28, just five years ago," Glen said. "I couldn't do it until I was able to deal with the shame about being gay that I carried inside. So I understand what you're going through. But I do know from my own experience, if you're ever to find happiness and the fulfillment that comes from a meaningful relationship, you'll need to stop hiding from the authentic life that would be right for you to live."

Gentry shook his head. "I can't do that. It would break Dad's heart. He's so proud that I'll be going to Bob Jones University. And Betty Jean loves me. Her parents think we're going to get engaged."

"It won't be easy. I know that," Glen said, "But you'll never find peace of mind and happiness, unless you're true to yourself and honest with the important people in your life. Gentry, you have some very big decisions to make, important decisions that will affect your life and the lives of others."

Gentry began to cry. He hunched over, placing his hands before his eyes. Glen walked over to him and placed his hand on the youth's shoulder. "I'll be here whenever you need to talk."

****

"I had lunch with my Aunt Molly," Katie said. It was late afternoon, as she and Glen sat beside one another on the white wicker bench on her front porch. "She's so excited about the baby! And typical of Aunt Molly, has opinions on just about everything. When I told her the baby would be in daycare while I was teaching, she had a fit. To quote her 'Ain't gonna happen! Ain't none of my flesh and blood gonna be with all those black and Mexican babies.'"

Katie laughed. "She's really something else. Anyway, Aunt Molly has retired from her bookkeeping job, and insists that she will take care of the baby while I'm at work."

"Sounds like your Aunt Molly is a first-class bigot. But her bigotry could be a break for you," Glen said. "Do you think she'll follow through?"

"Absolutely! What she says is what she does. She was Dad's older sister and sees herself as the matriarch of the Collins clan. She was always there for Mom and me, especially after Dad died. She's not exactly a refined southern lady," Katie laughed. "Actually, she's the opposite: rough around the edges and a little hard to take, but always there to do for family."

"I know the type," Glen said. "She sounds like a bona fide redneck sweetheart. I'll look forward to meeting her."

Katie smiled, "You might want to take that back. Aunt Molly is a pious Christian lady. Five minutes after she meets you, she'll ask if you're a Christian, and no matter what you say, she'll witness for Jesus."

Glen laughed, "In that case, I won't be in a rush to meet her."

"She asked if I was going to put David on the birth certificate as the father. I told her no, I wasn't going to do that. 'You're letting him off too easy,' she said. 'He's the daddy and has to pay for the baby.'

"I reminded Aunt Molly that we broke up over his not wanting a child, and I was not going to impose that responsibility on him. To end the discussion, I told her that you would be named as the father on the birth certificate."

"So? Did she have a problem with that?" Glen said.

"That might be an understatement," Katie said. "But I've grown up with Aunt Molly and I've had a lot of experience ignoring her opinions, just as I'm going to ignore this one."

"Did you tell her that I might really be the father of the baby?"

Katie shook her head. "I didn't want to get into that."

Nor did Katie intend to relate to Glen the extent of Aunt Molly's conniption.

"Katie, what are you thinking? I know you're real close to him, which I'll never understand! But that don't change the fact that the man is a homosexual. You'd have to be dumb as dirt to put a pervert on your baby's birth certificate! What if something happened to you and that homosexual tried to lay claim to your baby?"

Aunt Molly shook her finger in Katie's face. "I ain't gonna stand for you naming that man on the birth certificate as the baby's father! You hear me? I ain't gonna let you do that!"

Lunch with Aunt Molly had been very upsetting, and Katie had no intention of relating to Glen all that had transpired. To change the topic, Katie pointed to a robin that had just appeared on her lawn. "When I was a little girl, I used to see robins all the time and now it's rare to see one. Just like the fireflies that used to light the skies at dusk."

Chapter Nine

Glen was relieved by the change in Keith's attitude toward his friendship with Katie. Instead of a grudging nod whenever he said he planned to be with her, Keith seemed comfortable with them being together.

"How's Katie doing?" Keith asked.

"I guess she's doing fine. At least that's what she tells me, but I just don't know."

"You think there's a problem with the pregnancy?"

"No. I think that's fine. The baby's moving a lot and Katie tells me her doctor thinks it will be a fine, healthy baby."

"So what's bothering you?" Keith was in the kitchen working on the raspberry vinegar and olive oil dressing for the spinach salad he was preparing for their dinner. Glen was standing by the doorway, sipping from a glass of cabernet.

"It's just Katie. She seems pale and has no energy. She's listless and that's not like her."

"Glen, she's in her eighth month and Texas in July is hot as Hades. The heat would cause anyone to be listless, even if they weren't pregnant. You worry too much. I'm sure everything is fine." Keith opened the oven and removed the pan of bubbling King Ranch Chicken.

"I hope so," Glen said, but he wasn't convinced. The previous day, she had felt too tired to take a walk. "Is something wrong? Is there a problem you're keeping from me?" he had asked.

"No, everything's fine. I'm just tired. The baby is moving so much I don't get enough sleep."

But then she added, "Once the baby is delivered and I know he's safe, I'm going to have a complete checkup. And if I need surgery . . ."

"If you need surgery? For what?"

"Glen stop worrying," Katie put him off. "Everything is fine. The baby is healthy and that's what matters."

****

Wearing only white gym shorts and sandals, Glen was in the back garden watering the caladiums in the late morning when his cell phone rang.

"Hello?"

A muffled voice, that he could barely recognize said, "Mr. McLean this is Gentry. I'm so sorry. So very sorry."

"For what?" Glen asked, alarmed by the emotion in the boy's voice.

"Dad's going to call you and—I'm so sorry that I got you involved. I never meant this to happen."

"Why would your father call me? Tell me what happened."

Gentry was clearly overwrought and apparently crying. "I told Mom everything—about Jason and me—and that I loved him. That I was gay and I didn't know what to do. I told her I had come to you for advice and you helped me. You said I needed to be true to myself and not live a lie."

"Yes? How did she respond?" Glen asked.

"Mom told me that she loved me. She cried and I cried. She told me that she had known something was wrong for a long time, but couldn't figure out what it was. That I shouldn't worry. She loved me and that she would be there for me no matter what."

"So what's the problem?" Glen asked.

"Mom told Dad everything and that was a mistake. He confronted Jason and told him that he knew he was a homosexual and was tempting me to join him in his perversion. Dad warned Jason never to see me again. That he needed to fall to his knees and pray to Jesus, lest he live a life of sin and spend eternity in hell.

"I sent a text to Jason asking if he was all right. He texted back, 'No, I'm not.' He was very upset. He said he could never have anything to do with me again." Gentry's voice grew husky.

Glen was quiet as Gentry continued, "Dad is going to call you. I don't know when, but I know he will. I'm so sorry. I begged him not to. I never meant to get you involved. I'm so sorry. Please—please forgive me."

****

"So how was your day?" Keith asked when he came home from the office, the jacket of his black pin-striped suit draped over his shoulder, and his long sleeve white shirt soaked with sweat.

"Just another hot summer day making the garden pretty and waiting for you to come home." Glen gave him a quick hug. "I'll fix your martini with two olives while you shower and change into something comfortable."

Glen shook his head, "I can't understand why lawyers in Texas wear a suit and tie in July when it's going to be 100 degrees in the shade. Violates common sense! I'd be out there in my all-together instead of these skimpy shorts, if I didn't know I'd be locked up for indecent exposure. Anyway, there's something I need to talk to you about."

Later dressed in black gym shorts and a white T-shirt, Keith sat down beside Glen on the large down-filled sofa. He placed his hand on Glen's bare thigh. "So what do we need to talk about?"

Glen sighed, "Remember I told you about that high school senior who was gay and having a rough time accepting it."

"I do." Keith took a sip of his martini, then reached in for one of the olives. "Great drink! For someone who can't cook, you sure make a perfect martini!"

"Appreciate your noticing." Glen said. Then returning to the conversation, "What I didn't tell you was that his father is a minister."

Keith ran his hand through his short-cropped hair, then patted Glen's thigh. "Seems like a rather significant detail. Did you tell the boy something that might upset his father?"

"I told him what I believe," Glen said. "That being gay wasn't a choice or a sin. That he could have a good life—an ethical and moral life—as a gay man. The important thing was for him to be true to himself and to others."

Keith took a deep breath. "I sure hope his Dad's not the minister at the First Baptist Church on Main Street."

"Why did you say that?" Glen asked. He took a deep sip of cabernet.

"Reverend Phillips is the minister there, and when the Texas Sodomy Statute was overturned in 2003, the year before you moved to Edgemont, he gave a series of sermons on the topic: *Homosexuals Versus the Bible*. The *Edgemont Gazette* was so impressed with his rants, that it ran a special issue containing the full text of those doomsday sermons. The town's religious fundamentalists were delighted that such a fine Christian man was here to save us from the onslaught of the homosexuals. You should have seen the letters to the editor. You'd have thought Jesus himself had arisen here in Edgemont."

Glen took another sip of his cabernet. "The boy told his mother everything, including that he was in love with his best friend and that I had counseled him to be true to himself and his feelings. His mother told his father, and a distraught Gentry Phillips called this morning to tell me his father would be calling me."

"Gentry Phillips?" Keith closed his eyes, and once again ran his hand through his hair. "So tell me what you're going to say when Reverend Phillips calls?"

"I thought you might have a suggestion to offer." Glen said.

"Keith tried to smile, but failed. "If you mean, what would I do? I can tell you that I'd listen—just listen and not argue or disagree. I'd let him finish saying whatever he wanted to say. And then when he orders you, which he undoubtedly will, not to see or speak to his son ever again, I wouldn't argue. In a contrite and penitent tone, I'd assure him: I will never see or speak to your son again!"

****

The next day, Glen received the phone call he was dreading.

"Hello, is this Mr. McLean . . . Glen McLean?"

"Yes."

"This is Reverend Phillips. I'm the senior pastor at the First Baptist Church. I believe you know my son, Gentry."

"Yes, I do. He's a fine young man. You must be very proud of him." Glen spoke in a neutral tone, not allowing his feelings to show—or that he might know what this call was about.

"Yes, he is a fine young man. His mother and I are very proud of him. We trust that he will lead a good Christian life and have a bright future ahead of him. But I am very concerned about a temptation he has and a direction you are guiding him to choose."

Glen didn't respond and Reverend Phillips continued. "God made a man to love a woman and a woman to love a man so that they marry and have children. That is God's plan for men and women." The minister spoke in a calm, precise manner, much like a teacher talking to a slow learner.

Then his voice hardened and anger showed. "He did not make man to lie with another man. The Bible is very clear. That is an abomination. It is Satan's temptation, a perversion that will lead to an unchristian life, death and eternity in hell.—Leviticus: 20:13."

Just as Keith had advised, Glen kept silent, allowing the minister to have his say.

"I have spoken to parishioners who know of your work at the high school. They speak highly of you and the contribution you are making to their children. I was pleasantly surprised to hear that. Apparently, you are a good person who has made a very bad choice. That is your choice and I will not attempt to judge you. That will be for God to do on Judgment Day."

"I'm sorry. I don't understand what choice you're talking about?" Glen could be silent no longer.

"Mr. McLean, I believe you know exactly what choice I'm referring to. Your decision to be a homosexual."

"I didn't decide to be a homosexual. I was a homosexual from birth and my life's journey has been to lead a moral, ethical and honest life as the person I was born to be. That is what I believe God wants of me."

There was a moment of silence as the minister was apparently taken aback by Glen's response. Then he said, "Mr. McLean, I believe I know what God wants far better than you. The study of the Bible has been my life's work. The teachings of the Bible have been my guide in all I say and do. It is the inerrant word of God."

"Really? The inerrant word of God? I am confident that as a moral Christian you do not believe or follow all that is in the Bible such as approving of slavery,—Leviticus 25:44, or killing a man who works on the Sabbath,—Exodus 35:2." Glen was not typically argumentative or confrontational, but he did have a stubborn, idealistic streak and would not back down when he felt truth and fairness were on his side.

"Mr. McLean, I did not call to debate you on the merits of the Bible."

"I'm sure you didn't," Glen said, "But since we're talking I'd like to ask, why do you obsess about the few passages against homosexuality and ignore so many other Bible prohibitions, especially when you as a minister must know that Jesus never said one word against homosexuality. If it was such a vile perversion, why didn't Jesus warn against it?"

"That's enough!" Reverent Phillips spoke firmly. "I'm calling to advise you not to have anything more to do with my son. I have forbidden him to have any contact with you. And I am warning you not to have any contact with him. Do you understand?"

"Yes, I understand," Glen said. "I feel very sorry for your son. He is a fine young man who is suffering because of you."

"Did I hear you say that you will not contact my son?"

"Yes, I will not contact your son."

"Thank you, Mr. McLean. I trust this is the last time you and I will be in contact with one another." There was a loud click, and the phone line went dead.

Glen sighed deeply, thinking, *I probably should have listened to Keith.*

Chapter Ten

Katie was excited. "Come, you've got to see Aunt Molly's gift. It arrived just a short time ago." She took Glen's hand and led him into the smaller bedroom that would be the baby's room.

"Look!" she pointed to the crib. "Aunt Molly is such a sweetheart!"

Glen nodded as if in agreement because he didn't want to squelch Katie's excitement. Actually, he felt he should have been the one to purchase the big items his baby needed. It annoyed him that Aunt Molly had beaten him to it, staking her claim to a significant role in his son's life.

To change the topic, he said, "I can't believe that in just a matter of weeks we'll be holding our son. By the way, are you planning to nurse the baby? I've read that nursing is the way to go."

The excitement that had lit Katie's hazel eyes faded, and she looked tired and pale. "Let's sit down on the sofa. There's something I need to tell you."

"Yes?" Glen asked once they were seated beside one another. "You seem so serious. Is something wrong?" He placed his hand on her swollen belly. "Is everything all right with the baby?"

"The baby is fine. My obstetrician wants to induce labor in two weeks at the beginning of my ninth month. He says the baby will be close to full term and will be fine. I told him I'd prefer to wait to have the baby naturally. It would be safer for the baby, but he insists I don't wait any longer. He doesn't think that's wise."

"I don't understand," Glen said. "Is there something I don't know?"

Katie nodded as her eyes welled with tears. "Just when everything was going so well, this has to happen."

"What?" Glen felt the tension in the pit of his stomach.

"I'm going to have surgery on August 10 at Medical City in Dallas. I've met with the surgeon and he wants to perform the operation as soon as possible so that they can start the chemo without any more delay."

Katie seemed reluctant to say specifically why she needed surgery, but if chemo was involved, Glen knew it was cancer. He held her hand. "Katie, is it what your mother had?"

"Yes, I had a biopsy last week and just received the results. It's a very aggressive form of breast cancer. It's probably spread."

Glen embraced her. "Katie, I love you, and I'll be there with you through it all."

"I know that. But there is something I want to ask of you. I've thought a lot about it and I want you to promise that no matter who turns out to be the father of my baby, you or David, you'll love my baby and care for him and protect him as if he were your own."

"Yes, of course, I will. It doesn't matter to me who the father is. The baby is yours and I'll love him for that reason alone."

"If it doesn't matter," Katie said, "let's not check the baby's DNA. It would serve no purpose and could affect your feelings. I just don't want anything to get in the way of your loving and protecting our son. Does that make sense?"

Katie was looking at him intently, and he realized how important this was to her. "If that's your wish, then it's my wish too. We won't do any testing."

For several moments they sat beside each other in silence. Then squeezing her hand, Glen said, "There's a wish that I have, and I hope you'll make it come true for me."

"Yes?" Katie asked.

"I'd like my son to carry my name. I would be so proud to have my boy named after me: Glen Thomas McLean II."

"Done!" Katie said, and for that moment the pinpoints of light returned to her hazel eyes. She leaned forward to kiss Glen. "I love you with all my heart and soul, and that's how I want you to love our baby."

****

Mary Phillips stared at the largely untouched meatloaf on her son's plate. This was Gentry's favorite and she had prepared it especially for him, hoping it might make him feel a little better. But he took just a little bite and asked to be excused from the table.

"Your mother made this dinner especially for you," Reverend Phillips said, but Gentry shook his head, "I need to be excused."

When Gentry left the room, Reverend Phillips rose from the table, his dinner only half finished. "I'll be in my study. I need to . . ." his voice broke and he stopped.

Mary began to clear the dishes from the table. She hesitated, not knowing whether to save the food for another meal or just throw it out. "I don't know what to do. I just don't know what to do." She spoke the words aloud. Then she began to pray, "Please, dear Lord Jesus, help me. I don't know what to do. I just don't know what to do."

Mary Phillips was a small woman, just an inch over five feet tall. She had always been slender, but recently as she approached her 50th birthday had gained several pounds, most prominently about her waist. She was not a vain person, dressing simply and wearing no make-up other than lipstick, and the weight did not particularly bother her. What concerned her greatly was the sadness that had been enveloping her son. Something was wrong.

Finally, Gentry had confided his problem, trusting her to understand. "I love you. Dad loves you. Please don't worry. As long as you have Jesus in your heart, you'll be safe. Everything will be all right. You'll see."

It never occurred to her to keep secret from her husband what Gentry had told her. In 24 years of marriage, she had always deferred to him and depended upon him. He would know what to do. He was her rock—her strength.

She was comfortable allowing him to make the important decisions. That took the responsibility from her, and even when his decision was not one she would have made, it was not difficult for her to accept. She had been raised in a devoutly Christian home and had been taught to accept the biblical teaching that a wife be submissive to her husband.

But in this case, her husband had made a decision that was affecting her son. For the past two weeks, she had watched as her boy fell deeper into depression. Mary Phillips was beside herself with anxiety and guilt for her role in the pain and sadness her son was now experiencing.

As was her habit, she prayed for needed guidance, and when that didn't ease her worries, in desperation she sought out information on the internet about homosexuality. There she found so much that she had not known, or in truth had not been open to know. New understandings, based on science and research, that confronted the biblical condemnations of homosexuality that her husband held.

She had never been comfortable with her husband's condemnation of homosexuals. Several years earlier, he had delivered a series of sermons on the homosexual agenda and its violation of God's plan for a good Christian life. He began and ended each sermon, "*If a man lies with a man as with a woman, both of them have committed an abomination . . . their blood is upon them*"—Leviticus 20:13.

She had felt concerned enough to question him. "Aren't homosexuals also God's children? Doesn't God love all his children?"

Reverend Phillips shook his head, "No, homosexuals have turned from God and biblical teaching. They have chosen to follow in the path of perversion, permitting satanic temptation to corrupt their lives. They must be condemned and contained, lest they entice children to their perverted lifestyle."

Disturbing thoughts now kept her awake at night. *If Jesus taught love and non-judgment of others and her husband taught hate and condemnation, would it not stand to reason that God might be angry?*

As a young girl she had committed to memory the passage from Mathew that her Sunday school teacher had said was the most important teaching in the Bible:

Teacher, which commandment is the greatest? He said to him, "You shall love the Lord your God with all your heart and with all your soul, and with all your mind. This is the greatest and first commandment. And a second is like it: You shall love your neighbor as yourself. On these two commandments hang all the law and all the prophets.

Yet her husband, as a pastor, the leader of his flock, had taught condemnation and hatred of homosexual people. He had counseled his parishioners to shun them as perverted and under the influence of Satan.

Did God make our only child gay to teach us that all people must be loved? As each sleepless night lightened into day, Mary Phillips came to believe that the all-knowing and compassionate God of the New Testament was testing them: It was God's will that she and her husband love their son just as he was. God had made him gay to teach them a lesson: *all God's children must be loved.*

God the creator rules the universe and all that happens within it. Nothing happens by chance. This is what she believed. But that meant she would have to stand firm against her husband and his teaching. She had never done that before and didn't know if she could do it now. *Does God really want me to confront my husband?* She felt herself crumbling.

Now seated alone in the living room, she hunched forward, her hands before her eyes and sobbed. Then moments later, visualizing the suffering in her son's eyes, she came to a decision. Mary rose from her chair and walked slowly to her husband's study.

"Yes?" Reverend Philips looked up from his desk.

"We need to talk," she said.

****

Aunt Molly could hardly contain her excitement. "Don't you just love that crib! And this bumper guard with the Little Boy Blue drawings. Ain't it adorable! I just couldn't stop myself from buying it."

"I love it too!" Katie laughed. "Thank you so much. You're an angel for doing that."

"An angel, am I? More like a fat old Baptist woman," Aunt Molly dismissed the compliment with a wave of her plump hand. "You're the daughter I never had, and your baby boy will be my grandson. Do I plan to spoil him? Does a bear poop in the woods?" She laughed and her blue eyes crinkled in her round face.

Then in a more serious tone, she asked, "Tell me why the doctor's gonna induce the baby? Ain't it better to wait?"

"Come, let's sit down in the kitchen." Katie said. "I've made a fresh pot of coffee. There's something I need to tell you."

Later, reaching across the small kitchen table to hold Katie's hand, her aunt asked, "How long have you known about the problem?" She couldn't bring herself to say *breast cancer.*

"I didn't know for sure until the biopsy results last week. But I did feel a small lump several months back and I suspected there might be a problem."

"Katie, darling, why'd you wait? You know what happened to your mama" Aunt Molly repeated, "Why'd you wait?"

"What choice did I have? If it was cancerous, I'd need to have chemo or radiation following the surgery. Do you realize what that could do to my baby? In those early months some doctors even recommend an abortion."

Aunt Molly touched the gold cross on her necklace. She nodded. "You done right."

"The surgery is set for August 10ᵗʰ at Medical City in Dallas," Katie said, "Can I count on you to be there for my baby and me?"

The heavy woman nodded somberly. "Of course I'll be there. Ain't I always been there for family?"

Aunt Molly, the eldest of three children, the only daughter with two brothers, had never married. "Just never found a man good enough for me." Her life was centered on Jesus, her family and the First Baptist Church of Edgemont, where she played the piano on occasion and sang in the choir.

Wanting to end the seriousness that was settling upon them, Aunt Molly asked, "Have you picked a name for the baby?"

"Yes, as a matter of fact I have. "His name will be Glen Thomas."

Aunt Molly mulled that over. "Has a nice sound, but I'd of thought you'd name the baby after your daddy, David John."

"I thought about that, but I'm going to name the baby Glen Thomas."

"What about his last name? Guess he'll have your husband's name, won't he?"

"No," Katie said. "I don't want the baby to have any connection to David."

"Then his last name will be Collins?"

"No, I've decided not to do that."

Aunt Molly was confused. "I don't understand. If you ain't using your husband's name and you ain't using our family's name, what name will you be using?"

Katie hesitated.

"Katie, the baby will be here next week, and you'll have to put his name on the birth certificate. So what'll you do?" She looked perplexed, her brow furrowed in confusion.

"I'm planning to name the baby Glen Thomas McLean," she said softly.

"McLean? Where in God's name did you come up with McLean?" Aunt Molly said, and then, "I hope that ain't the name of that homosexual friend of yours. Katie, don't tell me you're thinking of giving your baby boy that man's name!"

Katie lifted the coffee cup to her lips and took a sip.

Aunt Molly referred back to an earlier conversation. "I thought you was just joking—trying to get an old woman all riled up—saying you was gonna name that man as the daddy on the birth certificate. You ain't gonna do a dumb thing like that, are you?"

Katie took a deep breath. "I believe you know the answer to that."

The heavy-set woman rose from the chair, her abrupt movement shaking the table. "Katie Collins, I forbid it! Ain't no way that man is the father of your child. He's a homosexual and has no connection to that baby, and you know it."

"I conceived the baby using his sperm. I went to a fertility clinic in New York and . . ."

The table shook as Aunt Molly sat back down with a thud. She stared at her niece. "That's a bald-faced lie and ain't nobody with a lick of sense would believe it."

"It's the truth and my baby will be named after his biological father, Glen Thomas McLean II." Katie did not waver. "Aunt Molly, I love you and I need you, but I'm not going to allow you to run my life."

"If anything ever happened to you, God forbid, that homosexual man could claim custody to your child. I shudder to think what that might mean for the boy!" Aunt Molly placed her two hands on the table's edge. "Katie Collins, your daddy would turn over in his grave if he knew what you was doing!"

****

The hostess at Applebee's Restaurant guiding Katie, Glen and Keith to a table, paused at a booth. "Would you like to sit there?"

Noting the size of Katie's belly, she laughed. "Sorry, I doubt that you'd fit. How about that table nearer the window? That should work."

She handed them the dinner menu and said to Katie, "Looks like you're fixing to have that baby real soon. Do you know if it's a boy or a girl?"

"It's a boy and . . ." Katie smiled. "I expect I'll be holding my baby in my arms within 48 hours."

"How exciting!" the hostess beamed. Then, "Which one of these two handsome men is the daddy?"

Katie pointed at Glen. "He's the guilty one, and I'm hoping my baby looks so much like him that he, and everybody else, never suspects that some other man might be my baby's real daddy."

"Good point!" the hostess laughed. Then looking at Glen she asked, "What's your name. I read the birth announcements in the *Gazette* every morning, and I'll watch to see when your baby's born."

"The name is Glen Thomas McLean and our son will be named Glen Thomas McLean II," he said proudly. "And I'd be very happy if he gets his looks from this lovely lady," he pointed at Katie, "so that nobody ever wonders who his real mommy might be."

Later, after the waitress had taken their order, Katie said to Keith, "I know how excited Glen is about our baby, but how do you feel?" Keith was typically reserved, especially with her, just the opposite of Glen, who was effusive and brimming with warmth. Katie was concerned that Keith might have reservations about the baby—about what it might mean for his relationship with Glen.

"Truthfully, I'm not as excited as Glen. But then who could be? His feet haven't touched the ground since he found out that you might be pregnant with his child. That's all he talks about. How he's going to do this and that with his son. They're going to ride their bikes together and play tennis and . . ."

"Okay, that's enough. You've succeeded in embarrassing me," Glen laughed. "No need to say anything more." Then more seriously, "Tell Katie what you told me yesterday about how you feel."

"I told Glen that just as I love him, I will love and cherish this boy of his."

Glen placed his hand on Keith's. "Katie, can he say anything better than that?"

"What if it turns out the baby isn't his?" Katie asked. "Would that be a problem for you?"

"I don't think so," Keith said. Well, it might make some difference. I mean . . . you know . . ."

Katie took a deep breath. "I need to know my baby will be loved completely, without reservation. That' why I've asked Glen to promise that he won't have the baby's DNA tested. I hope with all my heart that the baby is his, but what if a test showed he wasn't the father? I fear it might make a difference in his feelings."

Katie continued, "I want both of you to believe in your heart that Glen is the daddy of my baby and that you both love him as Glen's baby without reservation. Glen has promised he would never have the baby tested. Keith, will you promise that as well?"

Keith remained silent for a moment. He looked at Glen to see his reaction, then back at Katie. "I understand . . . I can see where it might make a difference." He nodded, "Yes, I promise to honor your request."

Chapter Eleven

Reverend Everett Phillips had moments earlier called a well-connected colleague in the Southern Baptist Convention to ask his opinion on Exodus International, the Christian organization known for successfully changing homosexual orientations. Loath to admit it was for his son, he pretended it was for a parent in his congregation whose gay son needed the love of Jesus to free himself from his sinful attraction to other men.

The Reverend had been given a contact number which he had called, and spoke to a wonderful man who assured him of the benefits of the program and that indeed gay people could be cured—were cured—by the program.

Later that evening, he planned to talk to his son about enrolling him in the program. He felt relieved and hopeful, now that he had a viable plan, a direction, to help Gentry. Reverend Phillips sat down at his desk and clasped his hands in prayer. "Thank you, Lord Jesus. Thank you for showing me the way. My son is a fine young man, a wonderful boy, who loves you and needs you to help him withstand a satanic temptation. Please offer him your hand. Please, I beg of you. In your name I pray."

He looked up to see his wife standing in the doorway to his study. "Yes?" He adjusted his bifocals.

Mary looked distraught. She spoke rapidly, running her words together, "God made our son gay because he has a lesson for us to learn. It's so clear to me. This is all God's doing!"

"What are you talking about? What lesson does God want us to learn? Mary, you're not making sense."

"It's so clear to me, Everett. Don't you understand?" She quoted from memory:

Teacher, which commandment is the greatest? You shall love the Lord thy God with all your heart, and with all your soul, and with all your mind. This is the greatest and first commandment. And a second is like it. You shall love your neighbor as yourself. On these two commandments hang all the law and all the prophets.

"Mathew: 22," Reverend Phillips said. "I know it very well and have quoted it many times in my sermons. What's your point?"

"But you don't live it. You don't love your neighbors as God requires above all else. You preach against gay people and that's why God made our son gay. To teach us—to teach you—that you must love all God's people, not just some." Her voice was pitched high with anxiety.

"But I do love all God's people, just as it is commanded." Reverend Phillips was perplexed by his wife's accusations. *Why is she doubting me? Isn't my position obvious?* "What I don't love is sinful acts . . . perversions that the Bible speaks out against.—Leviticus: 20:13 is very clear: 'If a man lies with a man as with a woman, it is an abomination.' The teachings of the Bible are the teachings of God. They must be obeyed."

"Leviticus?" Mary stared at her husband in disbelief. Why do you obsess with this hate-filled passage from Leviticus and ignore the New Testament teachings of Jesus about loving your neighbors and non-judgment?"

"Mary, I believe you've gone far enough. This conversation needs to end." He was frankly shocked that his wife, typically so gentle and submissive, was challenging him. This was not like her and he did not appreciate it. He fully expected her to back down under his disapproving look. Instead she looked back at him defiantly.

"Everett, you do not love gay people and that is why God made our son gay. You have preached hatred against gay people, God's children, and God is angry. God is judging us—you!"

"Stop it! It is wrong for you to talk to me like that and I won't stand for it." Reverend Phillips was a tall, slender man, who typically projected a gentle, compassionate exterior that people found reassuring.

But when angered or challenged, as he was now, he would lean slightly forward, his expression stern and intimidating.

Still his wife did not back down. "For all the years of our marriage, I deferred to you," she said. "I did as I was taught—that a Christian woman must support and be obedient to her husband. That is what I've always strived to do, even when I've disagreed with your decision. But this is different. This is about my son. You are hurting my son!" Her voice rose with fear and anger.

"Hurting him? I would never hurt Gentry! He is in my thoughts each waking moment. He is my son and I'm doing all that I can to save him from a life of perversion. Can't you see that? Why just before you came in, I had called a colleague about Exodus International, a wonderful Christian organization that helps homosexuals become straight through love of Jesus. He gave me a contact to call, someone high up in the organization. I'll be talking to Gentry later this evening about entering him in their program."

Reverend Phillips took a deep breath. He believed his wife was overwrought and didn't realize what she was saying. He walked over to her and took her in his arms. "Mary, I know you're worried about our boy and you're upset. That's understandable. Please just trust in me. Have faith that with Jesus' love and guidance, I will lead our son in the path of righteousness. Everything will be fine. We're just experiencing a bad moment—everyone has them—and it will soon be over."

****

"Keith! I cut the umbilical cord! Can you believe it? I cut my baby's umbilical cord!" Glen was talking on his cell phone and his raised voice echoed down the corridor where the two nurses at their station could hear him.

The older nurse looked at her colleague and burst out laughing. "That guy is so adorable! You should have seen him in the delivery room. He was shaking so badly that I was afraid he might pass out. When I placed the baby in his arms, he started to cry. I said to him, "Relax, it's over and you have a honey of a baby. Best looking baby I've ever seen." She smiled. "I tell that to all the new dads and . . ."

The other nurse motioned for her to be quiet. "I want to hear what he's saying."

"The baby is wonderful! Yes, he's healthy—five fingers on each hand and five toes on each foot. He's perfect. Do you know what the nurse in the delivery room said? She said my son is the best looking baby she's ever seen.

"Yes, that's what she said and that nurse is an old-timer. She's probably been a nurse a hundred years, and she said she's never seen a better looking baby than mine! Isn't that something!

"And Katie's fine! What a trooper! She's the best. When the nurse put the baby beside her, she cried and I did too. Keith, I can't believe this is happening. It's the most wonderful thing that has ever happened to me." He caught himself, "Except for you, of course.

"Yes, honey, I do love you and can't wait for you to see the baby. Can you come to the hospital after work? Visiting hours extend to 8 p.m."

The nurses looked puzzled. "Who's Keith?" the younger one asked. "Could it be his father?"

"Doesn't sound like a father to me. Have you ever heard a son call his dad honey?"

****

A nurse brought the baby to Katie. "When you leave the hospital tomorrow, you'll be given six bottles of formula and complete instructions for feeding the baby."

Katie had wanted to breast feed the baby but, because of the upcoming operation, couldn't. Nervous and not sure if she were holding the bottle correctly, she placed the nipple tentatively to the baby's lips, hoping that he would begin to suck. And he did! Katie gave a big sigh of relief.

She smiled at Glen who was standing beside the bed. "Now isn't that a smart baby? He knew how to suck without anyone having to teach him."

"Takes after his dad," Glen laughed. "Smart as they come and so good looking!"

"I do think he looks like you," Katie said.

"Really?" Glen doubted that. "He has your coloring: auburn hair and hazel eyes and—freckles. I think he's going to have freckles, just like you."

"It's too soon to know if he'll have freckles!" Katie laughed. "Besides I hate my freckles and would not wish them on anyone!"

"Well I love them and would be so pleased if my son had them." Glen's voice resonated with excitement and happiness.

Aunt Molly, who had been sitting in rigid silence in a chair near the window, came over to the bed for a closer look. "Actually, that baby is the spitting image of your daddy, Katie. Yes, he has your daddy's ears and nose. It's a shame he ain't being named after your daddy."

"That would have been nice," Katie said, "but he has a father that he's being named after—Glen Thomas McLean II. I just love the sound of that name." Then, taking a closer look at the baby, she exclaimed, "Look! He has a cleft in his chin! Just like Glen."

"Your daddy had a cleft in his chin," Aunt Molly said.

"My father did not have a cleft in his chin!" Katie snapped.

"And I say he did," Aunt Molly placed her hands on her broad hips. "I distinctly remember your daddy had a cleft in his chin. Makes me sick that he ain't being named after your daddy!"

"Well, there are a lot of clefts in this world, aren't there," Glen said, hoping to ease the tension. I have a cleft, my son has a cleft, Kirk Douglas has a deep cleft in his chin and it wouldn't be at all surprising if Katie's dad had a cleft as well"

"My you Yankees do talk fast," Aunt Molly said. "I can't hardly follow what you're saying."

Glen laughed, trying to make light of her words. "Seems to my northern ears that you southerners talk slow."

"That's because we don't have nothing to hide, like some folks around here." Aunt Molly said.

Katie cleared her throat. "It's been a long day and I'm feeling very tired. I'd just like to be alone with my baby for a while and then go to sleep."

Glen leaned over and kissed Katie. Then looking at the baby, he said, "Katie, you've given me the greatest gift anyone can ever give another person. I thank you with all my heart."

He gave a perfunctory nod to Aunt Molly, as he left pondering, *Does she think I'm hiding something? What? That I'm not a normal man? That I couldn't have sex with a woman? That I couldn't father a baby? Is that what she thinks?*

To hell with her! Why should I care what she thinks? She's a nasty old bigot! Her opinion means nothing! But he did care. Her disdain pried open his insecurities, releasing that confidence-shredding mantra locked within his being: *you're defective—less than others—you're gay.*

****

It was almost midnight when Reverend Phillips came to bed to find his wife still awake.

"You were with Gentry for a very long time. What did you tell him?" she asked.

He smiled. "It was a very productive talk. I told Gentry that I had been in contact with an important person in Exodus International. The man was confident they could help rid him of his impure thoughts as they had helped so many others. He's setting up a meeting for us in Dallas tomorrow with a man who once was a practicing homosexual and now is cured."

Reverend Phillips was clearly pleased with his handling of the issue, believing that the problem was well on its way to being resolved. He nodded reassuringly at this wife.

"Then I led Gentry to my study and together we went through the passages in the Bible against homosexuality. I read to him the warnings in Leviticus and the passages in Jude about Sodom and Gomorrah. I pointed to the passages and had him read them back to me.

"These are God's words and you must be guided by them." I told him. "You understand that now, don't you? Homosexuality is a perversion. You must never give in to it; for if you do, God's judgment will surely come down upon you.

"My contact at Exodus stressed that for him to succeed in ending his homosexual attractions, he must have no further homosexual contacts or thoughts . . . and I agree fully." Reverend Phillips nodded in affirmation. "I told Gentry how important that was and made him repeat his promise never to see his friend Jason again—or even think of him."

Reverend Phillips took his wife's hand in his. "Mary, I told you I would handle it and I have. Now you stop your worrying and try to have a good night's sleep."

Instead she lay awake for most of the night, not at all comfortable with her husband's reassurances. After he had mentioned Exodus International earlier that evening, she researched the organization on the internet and was upset by the critical reviews. Rather than helping gay men and women, critics claimed, it filled them with anxiety and guilt because gay people cannot change their orientation.

This is how God made Gentry, she thought. *And God wants all his children to be* loved as he had made them.

She also was especially upset with her husband for having their son focus on that unforgiving Leviticus passage with its harsh ending: ' . . . *they shall surely be put to death; their blood is upon them.*' No! That was not something Gentry should be told when he was so depressed and vulnerable.

Mary Phillips tossed and turned until the first rays of the morning sun lightened the sky. She quietly left their bed so as not to disturb her husband, who was sleeping soundly. Slipping on her light summer robe, she left their bedroom, thinking she would put up coffee and then prepare a special breakfast for Gentry: fresh squeezed orange juice, ham and scrambled eggs and the homemade sausage biscuits he loved.

Passing her son's room, she saw a light illuminating the space between the floor and the bottom of the closed door. Assuming that he must be up, she knocked softly on the door.

"Gentry, you're up early this morning. I was thinking you might enjoy my homemade sausage biscuits with your breakfast."

There was no answer so she knocked a little harder. "Gentry, honey, are you up?"

As there was no response, she opened the door. Surely if the light was on, he must be up. She didn't see him in the bedroom. Then she looked toward his bathroom and saw his body on the floor.

"Oh my God! Oh my God! No!" The large bottle of aspirin, now almost empty, was on the floor beside him. She reached for his hand and felt a pulse . . . faint but there. Numb with anxiety and fear, Mary Phillips ran to the phone and called 911.

"An ambulance . . . send an ambulance!" she screamed, "My son needs help! Hurry! For God's sake, hurry!" Then she fell to her knees and prayed. "Oh, Jesus, my beloved Jesus, I beg of you let my boy live!"

Awakened by his wife's scream, Reverend Phillips came running to his son's bedroom. He saw his wife on her knees, and then he saw his son. He reached down to lift him from the bathroom floor. Holding the unconscious youth in his arms, he began to sob.

****

Glen called his mother in Albany, N.Y. to tell her the exciting news. "I'm a Dad! Yes, everything's fine. My son weighed 6 pounds, two ounces. Great looking little guy. The nurse said in all years she'd never seen a better looking baby. Now isn't that something!"

"And how is Katie?" Mrs. McLean asked. "I hope it wasn't a hard delivery!"

"Katie is fine. She's great! So happy. She says the baby looks just like me, but that's not true. It has her coloring—and, oh, yes, he has a cleft chin, just like me."

"Was it a hard delivery?" His mother asked again.

"Maybe . . . I don't know. I don't think so—anyway, everything is fine!"

"I've never met Katie, but from what you've told me she sounds like a wonderful person and now that you have the baby, I hope you're planning to get married."

Married?" What was she thinking? "Mom, did you forget that I'm gay? If I were to marry anyone it would be Keith."

He heard his mother sigh. "Glen, you can't marry Keith because you're both men, so that's foolish talk. I'm thinking about the baby— what's right for the baby. A baby needs a mother and a father and for his parents to be married." She paused, apparently disturbed by a new thought. "Oh, dear, what will it say on his birth certificate?"

"It will say that the mother is Margaret Katherine Collins and the father is Glen Thomas McLean. That the baby's name is Glen Thomas McLean II and he was born on August 1, 2008, at Edgemont Community Hospital, Edgemont, Texas."

"You didn't tell me the baby would have your name. That's so nice! I've always loved your name: Glen Thomas, and now your boy will have that same name. That's so wonderful!"

Glen was relieved at his mother's delight with the baby's name. Hopefully, that would distract her from further talk of marriage to Katie . . . at least for now.

"Tell me, when will the baby be baptized? He needs to be baptized as soon as possible. And by a priest—a Catholic priest."

"Mom, Katie isn't Catholic. She's Baptist. I'm sure she'd want the baby baptized in her church."

"Oh, please don't do that!" his mother said. "According to the teaching of our church, the baby must be baptized by a priest to be assured a place in heaven if anything were to happen to him."

"Mom, you really don't believe that, do you?" Glen took a deep breath. This was not a discussion he wanted to have.

"What you or I believe doesn't matter. Our church teaches that unless a baby is baptized by a priest, he could spend his life in purgatory if anything, heaven forbid, happened to him. That would be so awful! Please make Katie understand how important it is that the baby be baptized in the Catholic Church."

"Yes, Mom, I will talk to Katie and help her to understand that her Baptist Church does not have the same standing with God as our Catholic Church."

"Glen, please don't make fun of me. I might sound like a foolish old woman to you, but this is how I was raised to think and I had hoped that you had been raised to think the same way too."

"All right, Mom. I just want you to be happy about my baby and proud of me for being a daddy."

"I am very proud of you! It's just that I want everything to be perfect and I worry that . . ."

Glen stopped her. "Mom, I know you love me and I love you too. Please try to focus on enjoying and not worrying. That would make both of us so much happier."

"Yes, I know what you're saying and I'll try. But I love you so much and I just worry . . ."

"I understand," Glen said, hoping to end the conversation on a light note, if that was possible. "You're a mother and can't help yourself. I bet Katie is going to be just like you. She's already worrying that this or that might not be exactly the way she wants it for our son. Anyway, tell, Dad, I love him and that everything is wonderful here."

"Yes, I'll tell your Dad. "But before you hang up, I want to plan a visit. I've never been to Edgemont and now it's time. I want to meet my new grandson and of course, I want to meet Katie. You know, being a new mother is so stressful. Please tell Katie I'd be happy to come and help her care for the baby."

His mother hadn't met Keith either. She knew they'd been partners for almost four years. Still, she didn't include meeting Keith as a reason to visit Edgemont. He clenched his hands and started to say something. Then wanting to end the conversation without further conflict, he let it pass. "That's very thoughtful, Mom. But right now Katie has an aunt who lives in Edgemont and is staying with her. It will be better to wait for things to settle down."

****

Late that afternoon, as they drove home from the hospital, Reverend Phillips tried to engage his wife in conversation. "The doctor said he'll be all right—no lasting damage."

She continued looking straight ahead, as if she hadn't heard him.

He tried again. "Mary, our son will come home tomorrow. Everything will be all right. God is watching over him."

His wife maintained her silence and he gave up.

Reverend Phillips had been shaken to the core of his being. He had almost lost his son, the only child that God had given them. They had tried so hard to have children, but couldn't. They had endured the heartbreak of one miscarriage after another, and then at last after years of prayers, when they had almost given up hope, God gave them Gentry. And he was wonderful! Bright, handsome, kind, respectful—you couldn't hope for a better son.

"Mary, I need you to forgive me," he said later that evening as he came to the living room where his wife was seated, her Bible in her lap. "Please say something . . . anything. I need to hear you say that you forgive me."

His wife looked up at him, her face pale and wet with tears. "We almost lost him and if we had, I don't know what I'd have done. I can't imagine life without Gentry."

She paused and read from the open Bible, "Judge not, that you be not judged. For with the judgment you pronounce, you will be judged . . ."

"Mathew 7: 1-5," the Reverend said.

"Yes, you know the passage well but you didn't honor its meaning." She looked directly at her husband. "God sent his beloved son Jesus to us to teach us to love one another," she said. "To be kind to one another. You are a minister who claims to speak for God, but you've taught judgment and condemnation, not love, for all God's children. That's why God made Gentry gay. Yes," she nodded, "God had a lesson for you to learn. He gave you a wonderful son to love and he made that son gay."

Reverend Everett moved to his wife. He was a tall man, well over six feet, and he knelt at her feet. "Mary, please forgive me for the pain I've brought to our family. I will pray for God's forgiveness. I never meant to hurt anyone . . . never."

"Everett, when we bring our son home tomorrow, I want to hear you tell him that you love him completely, just as he is. That's what Gentry needs to hear. Can you do that?"

The Reverend sighed deeply. "I will pray over it tonight. I will talk to God and ask for his guidance."

"And Everett, there is one other thing you need to tell Gentry."

"Yes?"

"Tell him he can be with Jason again."

"I don't want to do that," he said. "I'm not comfortable with that." Reverend Phillips lowered his eyes to avoid looking at his wife.

"You need to become comfortable with that," she said, and quoted from memory, "'The soul of Jonathan was knit to the soul of David, and Jonathan loved him as his own soul.'"

"Samuel 18:1," Reverend Phillips said.

"There are other passages as well telling of the intense love that David and Jonathan shared. Their love was so powerful . . . '*surpassing the love of a woman*' another passage says. Tell me, Everett, what exactly do you believe the nature of their relationship to have been?"

Chapter Twelve

Glen had been tense, his body rigid, when holding the baby, and the judgmental look on Aunt Molly's scowling face didn't help. He said to Katie when they had a moment alone, "I can't relax holding the baby when your Aunt Molly is watching with that constipated frown on her face. Can I count on you to do something about that? Like arrange it so that she's not here when I am?"

Now, after one week of practice, he was holding and feeding his son like a pro. "I love this," he said to Katie as they sat beside each other on the small sofa in her living room, "especially when your Aunt Molly isn't here. Thank you for that."

Katie sighed. "I'm sorry. I've tried to talk to her, but Aunt Molly is . . . well, Aunt Molly." She shook her head. "I know she's been just awful to you and I'm so sorry about that."

"Is it just about my being gay? Or is there something else about me that offends her?"

Katie placed her hand on his. "Aunt Molly never misses a church service and has often heard Reverend Phillips preach against homosexuals and their agenda, especially that part about preying on children."

Katie wiped the dribble of formula from the baby's mouth. "I'm sorry, Glen, but that's the way it is with her." Then to lessen the sting, she said, "Just so you don't feel alone, Aunt Molly has a problem with a whole bunch of people—blacks, Hispanics, atheists, Catholics, Mormons, and most recently, Muslims, although I don't expect she's ever met one. She told me just the other day that those Muslims better not try to build one of their mosques in Edgemont. Other than that, she's a dedicated Christian filled with love and good will for all God's people, just as Jesus taught."

"So what does she think about my being the baby's father?"

Katie took a deep breath. "We've had several intense conversations on that topic, and the bottom line remains that you're not the baby's father."

"She's sure about that?" Glen asked.

"Yes, because you're a gay man and gay men can't have sexual intercourse with a woman. Plus I am her niece and her niece is a fine Christian woman who is not, and never will be, an adulteress."

"What about the fertility clinic? Did you tell her about that?"

"More than once, but to quote Aunt Molly, 'That's a bald-face lie and nobody with a lick of sense would believe it.' She's confident that David is the baby's father, because he was my husband when I became pregnant. While his being Jewish is not a plus, in her ranking system, it's better than your being gay. Aunt Molly has let me know she's very disappointed in my choice of men."

"Why do you put up with her?" He shook his head and grimaced. "I'd never have anything to do with someone as narrow-minded and bigoted as that."

"I was raised with her. Aunt Molly was always there to love us, offer her help if it was needed, and, unfortunately, her opinions about every little thing we might be doing, which would drive my mother up the wall. Mother once said, 'Aunt Molly is like a good old milk cow. First she gives you a full pail of milk, and then before you can thank her, she kicks the pail over.'"

The baby had finished his bottle and Katie reached over to take him in her arms and burp him. "By the way," she said. "I went through a bunch of photos in my family album and Aunt Molly was wrong. Dad did not have a cleft in his chin. I knew he didn't but there's no arguing with her when she gets something in her head, or in this case wants to make a point."

Glen hesitated before asking, "What about David? Does he have a cleft?"

She squeezed his hand, "No, honey, the only one with a cleft is you—and our baby."

"Good! That's what I was hoping to hear." He looked at the baby and whispered. "Hi, little Glen, your daddy loves you!"

"Glen, I can't blame you for not liking Aunt Molly, and not wanting to have anything to do with her, but I hope you understand that I need her. I depend on her help and I know she'll be there for the baby and me. Just put up with her, for my sake, please."

"For your sake, okay. I can understand where you're coming from as I just had one of my classic conversations with my adoring mother. She loves me unconditionally and I love her as well. But oh, can she get to me," Glen said.

"Mom is thrilled about the baby. Couldn't be happier, except that we're not married. That is a big problem for her. Katie, my mother wants me to marry you."

"Well, that's not such a bad idea. Actually, it might be a good idea." Katie smiled. "Mrs. Glen Thomas McLean—sounds good to me."

"Except for a couple of not so minor details," Glen said. "Like I'm gay and in a committed relationship with a wonderful partner who loves me and I love him, which apparently is not a relationship that counts with my mother."

"Well, there's another detail," Katie said. "David and I are legally separated, but not legally divorced at this time."

"Oh, I wish I had thought of that!" Glen exclaimed, "I could have said to Mom, "Unfortunately, Katie is still legally married. I can't marry her as much as I might want to!"

"By the way," he said, "marriage is only one of Mom's concerns. She's also worried about the baby's baptism. Mom feels the baby must be baptized by a priest—a Catholic priest. And as soon as possible so that if anything happens to him, he will not have to spend eternity in purgatory."

"Wouldn't a Baptist minister do?" Katie asked.

"This may come as a surprise to you, being a lifelong Baptist from Texas, but according to Catholic teaching only baptism by a Catholic priest qualifies for a place in heaven. Sorry."

Then more seriously, "If it's not a problem for you, it would make Mom very happy. She's a good Catholic woman who'd know little peace of mind if she had a grandson who could not be admitted to heaven. Katie, honey, would it be a big problem for you if I had our son baptized by a priest. What do you say?"

"Well, I might say yes to that, if you will accept that Aunt Molly will be a part of my life and the life of our baby. And that you won't make faces at her whenever she turns her back. Is that a deal?"

"It's a deal." A broad smile lit his face. "Mom will be so relieved!"

****

Keith and Glen stood beside the baby's crib absorbed by the wonder of little Glen Thomas McLean II, who was sound asleep.

Earlier that day, Glen had driven Katie to Medical City in Dallas where she was to have surgery early the following morning.

"I don't want you worrying," Katie said. "The operation is routine. It's a common procedure. The doctor says I should be able to go home in about two days."

"Okay, I promise I won't worry, at least not a lot."

"Now remember, he baby gets a bottle every four hours and he has to be burped. Don't forget that! He must be burped. Make sure you have plenty of Pampers at your home and be sure to check if he needs changing. I've typed out all the directions. You have them so just refer to them if anything comes up." Katie was tense, her brow furrowed. "I've included Aunt Molly's phone number if you need her help. She'll be there as fast as can be."

"I'm sure she will be," Glen said, "but you can rest assured, I won't be calling her."

Then, laughing he said, "Katie, sweetheart, I know you're a devoted mother and you love your little guy. But relax. I've been with him every day since he was born. I've watched you and your Aunt Molly care for the baby. I've even read a book, cover to cover, that the *New York Times* highly recommends for taking care of baby.

"And since I made the mistake of telling Mom that Keith and I would have the baby home with us for two days, she's been calling at least twice each day to share her latest worry about something we must do—or must not do—for the baby."

For several moments, they drove in silence. Glen glanced her way and saw Katie chewing on her lower lip. She was still worried. After parking his car at the hospital's garage, Glen leaned over to give Katie a quick kiss as he reached for her hand.

"Katie, please don't worry about the baby. I know you were raised to think that women instinctively know how to care for babies while men know only about killing lions and other men. But that does not hold for me as I'm a gay man which means I have a super sensitive nature that makes me ideal for loving and caring for our baby. So *please,* stop worrying*!*"

As the daylight faded in the baby's bedroom, Glen and Keith stood side by side watching him. "Do you think he looks like me?" Glen asked.

"Do you want me to say he does?" Keith placed his arm around Glen's shoulder.

"That might be nice," Glen smiled. "And then if you'd like, I'll say he looks like you."

"He does have a cleft in his chin." Keith placed his index finger on Glen's chin. "Just like you."

"That's because he's my boy," Glen said. "Come, he'll probably sleep for the next four hours. Let's go downstairs. I'll turn the monitor on so that we'll hear him if he wakes up before his next feeding.

"My mom feels that I should marry Katie. Do you think I should?"

Keith was wearing white gym shorts and a gray T-shirt as they sat close beside each other on the sofa.

"Tell me what you told her," Keith said. "Then I'll tell you what I think."

"I told her I'm a gay man and that if I were to marry anyone it would be my wonderful partner of four years."

"Really? Did you say that?" Keith cuddled closer.

"I did," Glen said. "Does that upset you?" He placed his hand on the edge of Keith's shorts.

Keith leaned forward to kiss him. "Right this minute, if you'd ask me to marry you, guess what I'd tell you?"

"That men don't marry men—'tis against God's law. Isn't that what good Christian folks in Texas say."

"A whole bunch of Texans might, but I'm not one of them. "I'd say, I love you, Glen McLean, and nothing would make me happier than to marry you and be your husband until death do us part."

"If we lived in Massachusetts we could get married." He ran his hand under the edge of Keith's shorts.

"What about living in Texas and pretending we're married?" Keith said. He held up his left hand with the gold commitment ring. "By the way, I'm going to keep the ring on my finger, even when I'm at the law office."

"Really? No more hiding it in your jacket pocket? That would be wonderful! Remember how paranoid you used to be about anyone finding out you were gay?"

"If you hadn't come into my life, I'd still be paranoid." Keith said. "You gave me the incentive and strength to leave the closet, and now you've given me a son to enrich our lives. I'm so grateful that you came into my life."

"Thank you for saying that," Glen said. "I've worried that I've taken you to a place—an openly gay life—you hadn't wanted to be in. As for me, I'm thrilled to be living a life I never imagined possible: a terrific partner, a wonderful son, a beautiful home. It's everything I wanted and didn't think possible for a gay man." He moved his hand higher up the inside of Keith's shorts.

"Neither did I." Keith sighed as Glen's hand reached its target. "But it is possible and . . . it feels wonderful." He placed his arm around Glen's shoulder and kissed him lightly once, twice and then they made love.

****

Gentry was with his parents in their comfortable living room. His father was seated in the yellow Queen Anne style chair across from the traditional red and yellow striped sofa where Gentry sat beside his mother.

Seeing his mother wipe the tears from her cheeks, he said, "Mom, I'm so sorry. I never meant to hurt you this way. I wasn't thinking. I just was overwhelmed with guilt . . . of doing wrong . . . of bringing shame to you and Dad."

Mrs. Phillips reached for her son's hand. "Don't ever say that or even think it. You are the finest son a mother could have, just the way you are—the way God made you."

She looked at her husband, waiting for him to speak.

Reverend Phillips adjusted his wire-rimmed glasses and cleared his throat. "Son, you are the pride of my life. No father could want a better son than you. When I feared we might lose you . . ." his voice broke and he stopped.

Gentry saw the tears welling in his dad's eyes and that upset him greatly. "I'm so sorry."

"Please, don't ever do anything like that again. Your mother and I—we—could never live with ourselves . . . forgive ourselves," he fumbled for the words.

"Everett, please tell Gentry what you told me."

"I prayed to God for understanding. 'Why did you make my son gay?' I asked. 'Because he is my child as well as yours,' God said, 'I love him as he is and so must you.'"

Gentry could see that his father was struggling. "Dad, you don't have to . . ."

"I do," his father stopped him. "I have judged and guided others to judge, when that is not my right. That is for God to do. And so God gave me a wonderful son whom I cherish, and created him gay. It was God's way for me to learn."

Reverend Phillips nodded. "God is the greatest teacher. Gentry, I love you, just as you are."

Gentry rubbed his eyes and sobbed.

Reverend Phillips walked to the sofa and placed his hand on his son's shoulder. "Forgive me. I have caused you such pain. I never meant to do that, but I did."

"Dad, please, you did what you thought was right. I know that, and if I could have changed—rid myself of those feelings—I would have. I just couldn't and was overwhelmed with guilt about everything: my feelings for Jason, going to Bob Jones University, misleading Betty Jean. I didn't know what to do, and I felt so bad."

"Don't say anything more," his mother said. "You need to be who you are. Your father and I have talked about Bob Jones University and we agree that's not where you should go. You do need to have a conversation with Betty Jean so that she understands who you really are. You must do that."

She looked up at her husband. "I believe there's something else your dad wants to say."

Reverend Phillips cleared his throat and in a soft voice said, "Son, your mom and I would like you to ask Jason to join us here for dinner."

****

Glen placed Katie's overnight bag in the trunk of his new Toyota. Then he moved quickly to open the door on the passenger's side for her.

She had remained at the hospital longer than originally planned, and now she seemed strangely quiet, and that disturbed him. He tried to reassure himself that all was as it was supposed to be. After all, she had just had a mastectomy. That had to be traumatic.

But Katie was always upbeat no matter what. Typically, she'd find a way to find something positive in whatever was happening. As he helped her into the car, he was shocked to see her pallor and the dark lines under her eyes.

"Katie, honey, is there something I don't know. Something you need to tell me."

She didn't respond until a few moments later as they were on the highway driving back to Edgemont. "I won't be able to start my teaching position next week when the new school year begins."

"I don't think anyone expected that you would. When did the doctors say you would be ready? Two weeks from now? Maybe at the beginning of September?"

Katie took a deep breath. "Glen, the cancer has metastasized."

Glen turned to give Katie a quick look. "Metastasized? What does that mean exactly?"

"It means that it has spread to my lymph nodes and other parts of my body."

Glen could think of nothing to say. Then, "So what do you need to do? How do they treat it?"

"I'm to meet with my oncologist at the end of the week to consider a combination of treatments: possibly chemotherapy and radiation and maybe surgery. I'm not sure, but I don't think I'll be returning to teaching this fall."

"Have you told your Aunt Molly?"

"Yes, I called her as soon as I was told. She was wonderful as I knew she would be. She said I could count on her to care for me and the baby. She's been through this all before with mother and . . ." Katie's voice broke.

"I'll be there too," he said. "Doctors have come a long way in treating cancer. They know things they didn't know ten years ago. Katie, honey, we're going to beat this. You'll see."

"No matter what happens," Katie said, "I need to know my baby will be loved and cared for. I can accept whatever God has planned for me. I'll handle it. But my baby needs to be safe, and cared for and loved.

"Glen, I wanted to have a baby to make my life complete. It was so important to me and I'm so grateful that God allowed that to happen.

"But I also wanted to have the baby for you. It was my dream to have a baby that we could share together." She placed her hand on his thigh. "In my perfect world, it would have been you and me and our baby.

"Glen, no matter what happens to me, I want to know that you will be there for our son."

"Katie, I promise that I will love and cherish our baby all the days of my life. But, Katie sweetheart, don't talk as if you won't be there. Don't give up. I won't let you give up!" His voice was choked and Katie saw that he was crying.

****

"My goodness, Chrissie, you've brought enough food here to last me a week." Katie said as she opened the basket on the kitchen table.

"And I hope it will." Her cousin said. "What with the baby and everything else in your life, you don't need to be fussing with cooking. There's a big pot of stew and corn bread, plus a homemade apple pie.

"And look at this? Isn't it adorable?" She held up a pair of blue pajamas with a big red Superman across its front. "I just couldn't resist getting it for the baby."

Chrissie and Katie, only a year apart, had always been close, more like sisters than cousins. They even looked alike: they were the same height and until Chrissie put on several pounds with the birth of her two daughters, had the same trim figure. Their coloring was different: Chrissie had brown hair, brown eyes, and much to Katie's dismay, not a freckle anywhere.

"Come, let me show you the baby." Katie took her cousin's hand. "I know Aunt Molly must have told you what a beautiful baby I have. She's told everyone else judging by the phone calls I've been getting. Come, you'll see for yourself. It's about time for his bottle and I heard him stirring."

Later, seated beside each other on the sofa in the living room, Katie held the baby in her arms. "I've heard mothers gush about how much they love their babies, but I never fully understood the depth of feeling until I had my own baby. I'm just bursting with love for him."

"You and Aunt Molly," Chrissie laughed. "She's crazy about your baby. Claims he looks just like your dad. She says it was as if she was looking at her own baby brother: same nose, same ears, same coloring, same cleft in his chin."

"Dad didn't have a cleft in his chin," Katie said.

"Aunt Molly thinks he did," Chrissie laughed, "She's said more than once that the cleft in your baby's chin is identical to the one your dad had. According to Aunt Molly you need only take one look at Katie's baby and you know it's a member of our family. No question about it."

Katie smiled, "Well I'm happy that Aunt Molly is so pleased with my son".

"He's a boy," Chrissie said, and that in itself scores points. It appears I let everyone down by having two girls. My husband is so envious. When he heard you were having a boy, he said flat out, 'Why couldn't you have had one of those.'" She laughed. "It's not that he doesn't love his girls. He's crazy about them. But you don't go hunting and fishing with girls, and that's a problem for Jerry.

"Do you mind if I hold the baby?" Chrissie said. "I'd really love to hold him."

"Yes, of course," Katie placed the baby in her arms.

"Oh, he is darling. I'd forgotten how good it feels to hold an infant."

The cousins sat silently looking at the baby. "He is so adorable!" Chrissie said. Then looking at Katie, she said, "Have you told his father anything about him?"

"His father?" Katie looked confused, "His father sees him every day."

"No, I mean his real father . . . David, your husband."

Katie took the baby back. "You've been hearing a lot of things from Aunt Molly."

Chrissie shrugged. "A few things."

"Now you'll hear this from me." Katie was annoyed and it showed in her voice. "Glen McLean is the father of my baby. His name is on the birth certificate and he is the one who will be there with me to raise my son."

Chrissie was quiet. Then changing the topic she said, "Aunt Molly told me that—well, your cancer has spread."

Katie sighed. "It has. The oncologist said a combination of treatments will be needed to control it."

"Everything will be fine." Chrissie said. "Doctors have learned so much since your mother . . ." she stopped. "We will be there for you . . . Aunt Molly and me. You can count on us. The Collins family takes care of its own."

Chapter Thirteen

Now at the onset of his fifth year of teaching at Edgemont High School, Glen felt excited, energized by the positive vibes and compliments he had just moments before received from the office staff.

"Mr. McLean, our office phone has been ringing off the hook all summer long with calls from parents insisting that their child be placed in your English class. You would have such a swelled head if you could have heard what parents think about you." Mrs. Mumford, the principal's secretary, laughed, "Now the down side of all this is that your English classes are filled to capacity."

"Thanks for telling me about the good comments," Glen said. "Now tell me about the others. Last year there were five. Am I doing better this year?"

In his first year of teaching at Edgemont High, the accusation that he had sodomized Danny Anderson, a ninth grade student who committed suicide, outraged the community: there was an explosion of homophobic hate. In a rush to judgment, the *Edgemont Gazette* as well as ministers from their pulpits denounced Glen McLean, an English teacher who had come from New York State.

Just as an outraged community had turned against him, it rose in support for him, once his innocence and his efforts to protect the tormented youth from unrelenting bullying became known. The *Gazette* published an editorial praising him and the PTA held an assembly to honor him and the positive impact he was making on their children. The school board trustees met in special session to declare their public support for him and express hope that he would continue to teach at

Edgemont High. One moment he was a homosexual predator, the next a respected and honored teacher—an asset to the community.

That was the past: a bad moment in Edgemont, except each year there were several parents who would not allow their child to be taught by a homosexual teacher.

Mrs. Mumford nodded. "You're right. Not everyone loves Mr. McLean. There were two, well actually, three calls from parents, and we made sure their children will not be in your class. For your sake, not theirs," she quickly added.

****

Standing before the new chalkboards mounted on his classroom's cement block wall, Glen copied the words of Mary Robinson, written years earlier when she was the United Nation's High Commissioner for Human Rights.

The objective of all human rights action is simply this: to ensure a life of dignity for each person on this earth. The question is, How?

He turned to face his students, the majority of whom were Anglo, as in past years. But the balance was changing and the gap between the numbers of Anglo and minority students was closing. The demographics of Edgemont, as in all of Texas, were changing.

In his first year of teaching he had introduced this unit in the second 6-week period. In subsequent years, realizing the positive impact this unit made on student interactions with one another, he introduced it as the opening unit of the year.

"We will begin this school term with a unit that is very close to my heart, and I hope you will agree is very important. Imagine the world as it was in 1900, the beginning of the 20th Century, few homes had electricity or running water. A horse and buggy was the predominant mode of transportation. Radio and television did not exist. It was a different world.

"Now think of the mind-boggling technological advancements we have today. We've learned how to save lives with wonder drugs and to transplant body parts from one person to another. We have wireless phones and the amazing Internet that allows us to communicate instantly with people all over the world.

He leaned back against his desk. "Can you think of other examples that make your life better. I imagine there are a few."

Several students raised their hands.

"Video games!"

"DVR"

"iPods"

"HD TV"

"Yes, to all that and more," Glen said. "As far as science and technology go, humankind has made amazing progress over the past century. Unfortunately, the 20th Century has seen one of the worst, if not the worst, record of human rights violations in history. Not in any one country or continent but all over our planet Earth. There have been mass killings, ethnic cleansings, religious massacres that continue to this day."

Glen saw several students nodding their heads in agreement. Others were quiet, but attentive.

"We could spend a six-week unit on the atrocities committed by people against other people. However, I think it more important that we spend our time on what we can do to avoid repeating the mistakes, the horrors of the past.

"Let's begin with the thinking of Mary Robinson. According to her, the most important thing is how we relate to others. She says,

Two words help me a lot in dealing with this problem: respect—really listening and hearing each side's point of view. And, responsibility—finding the balance between securing my own rights and learning to live by them responsibly so that someone else is not deprived of his or her rights.

Glen printed the two values—*respect* and *responsibility* on the chalkboard. "There is another value we need to include: *caring*. Not just about ourselves and people close to us, but about all people: ones who are like you and ones who are different because of their skin color, their religion, their nationality, the way they think or dress—whatever." He printed *caring* on the chalkboard.

Turning back to the class, he said, "As a starting point, I want you to break into groups of four or five to talk about the meaning of each of these three values—*respect, responsibility* and *caring*—from your perspective. What do these words, these values mean to you? Mary Robinson defined respect and responsibility in terms of behaviors, the way people act toward other people. Do you agree with her? Make a list of specific examples of how these values can be applied to your own lives, your own school day, and most importantly, how you act toward one another."

Toward the end of the period, Glen said, "Your assignment tonight is to share Mary Robinson's words and why she feels they're so important. Tell your family what you and the classmates in your group think and then find out what your family thinks. Do they agree that these values are important and can make a difference in how your family members relate to one another and to other people? Are there other values they want to add? At the start of class tomorrow, I will ask you to share your family's responses."

Glen reached for a book on his desk to hold up to the class. "The literature we'll be reading during this unit will be *The Diary of Anne Frank*. This autobiography is written from the point of view of a young Jewish girl. This book, her diary, has been read by millions of people, and the house where she and her family hid is one of the most visited historic sites in Amsterdam. People throughout the world were deeply touched and shocked by this young girl's story of what happened when bigotry and hate overcame respect, responsibility and caring."

Walking to the chalkboard, he wrote *dis, ir* and *un*. "These are three prefixes that when attached to a word change its meaning to *not* or the *opposite of. Respect* becomes *disrespect. Responsibility* becomes *irresponsibility. Caring* becomes *uncaring.*

"That's the world Anne Frank and her family, Jewish people, experienced in Europe during the 1930s and 40s. Think what your life might be like if positive values that promote harmony and good feelings among people were replaced by negative actions resulting from disrespect, irresponsibility and uncaring."

****

In the past, Glen would remain in his classroom tweaking his lesson plans for the next day based on what was accomplished that day in his classes. That all changed with the birth of his baby.

Moments after the last school bus departed, Glen made a fast walk to his car. He couldn't be late because Katie had adjusted the baby's feeding schedule so that Glen could give him his bottle.

"I just love to hold Glen Junior and watch him suck on that bottle. Do you see the way he's looking at me? Katie, look at how he's looking at me. Yes, you love your daddy, don't you? And your daddy sure loves you!"

Katie laughed. "You were meant to be a dad and . . ." she grimaced.

Glen was startled by the change in her expression. "Are you all right?"

"I'm fine," Katie said, "Just a—I don't know—I seem to be having sharp pains in my back. It's nothing."

Glen was alarmed. "Have you told the doctor about them? You didn't have those pains before, did you?"

"It's nothing," Katie protested. "Probably from holding the baby."

Glen nodded as if he agreed, but he remained concerned. A pallor had replaced the high coloring that had made her so attractive and the shadows under her eyes had darkened. He waited a moment before asking, "When do you start your treatments?"

"Two days from now. I'll be able to have the chemo and radiation here at our hospital so I won't have to go to Dallas."

"That's good. Will your Aunt Molly be able to be with the baby?"

"Yes, she'll be with the baby and my cousin Chrissie will drive me to and from the hospital. Everything will be fine. Aunt Molly will stay with me overnight if I need her."

Glen sighed. "I'm sorry that I'm not your Aunt Molly's favorite person, but I do appreciate her. She's really there for you and the baby."

"I don't know how I would manage without her," Katie said. "That's how she's always been: opinionated and bigoted—she can be so difficult. Yet always there when you need a helping hand. When Mom was going through her problems, Aunt Molly was an angel."

"Hey, little guy, what are you doing with my thumb?" Glen laughed. "Do you see how tightly he's holding my thumb?"

Katie smiled. "He loves his daddy and his daddy loves him. I'm so happy about that. If only . . ." she didn't finish.

Glen shook his head. "There's always something to keep life from being perfect. But we can still have the good life. Katie, we can beat this. You'll get your treatments and everything will be fine. Someday our little Glen will be all grown up and married and he'll have children.

And you and I will be there to love and hold our grandbabies. Now won't that be something special!"

"That would be so wonderful! My dream come true. It would . . ." She hunched over, sobbing.

****

"Jason, it's me, Gentry!"

No response. Just silence. Gentry repeated into his cell phone. "It's me . . . everything's cool."

"We're not supposed to talk to each other. Your father warned me not to have anything to do with you."

"He changed his mind. Mom got to him. I'm sure she did. We can see each other . . . be together. Dad told me to invite you to our home for dinner."

Again there was silence. Then, "I can't believe that. Why would he do a complete turn-around like that? Something must have happened."

Gentry didn't want to talk about his suicide attempt. It was a stupid thing to do. So dumb and he wasn't about to tell Jason about it. "Doesn't matter what happened. The only thing that matters is that Dad asked me to invite you to our home for dinner. You're going to come, aren't you? You've got to come."

"I leave for college next week. It has to be before then."

"Mom suggested Friday. Does that work for you?" Gentry asked quickly.

"Yes, I can be there Friday. You're sure it's okay with your dad?"

"Yes, it's cool with Mom and Dad. By the way, I'm not going to Bob Jones University."

"So what are you going to do? It's kind of late to apply somewhere else, isn't it?"

"I'm gonna take the semester off, and then enroll at U.T. Austin for the spring semester. I was in the top 10% of my graduating class and the person we spoke to in the admissions office feels I won't have a problem being admitted."

"I can't believe this is happening," Jason said. "This is wonderful. We're going to be together!"

"Yes . . . I can't wait to see you . . . to be with you again. When I thought we could never be together again, I was so upset. It was awful."

He started to cry as his voice grew soft and low. "I love you and hope you still love me."

"I do. I love you very much."

"See you Friday about 6 p.m. Okay?"

"Yes. Tell your folks I'll be there."

"I will . . ." Gentry hesitated, not wanting the call to end. "Jason, do you think maybe we can see each other before then? Just the two of us . . . alone?"

"Like tonight? About 8 p.m. at the park." Jason said.

"I'll be there," Gentry took a deep breath. "I can't wait to . . ." his voice became husky, "be alone with you."

****

By September 1, a routine had been set. At the end of each school day, Glen hurried to Katie's home to be with her and, most importantly, bond with his son who was now one month old and seemed to recognize Glen. At least, Glen thought so.

"Do you see how his eyes light up when he sees me? He knows his daddy. That's for sure."

Then, a little later, "Look at that smile! Katie, our son is smiling at me!"

Katie laughed. "It's gas. You just fed him his bottle and he needs to be burped."

About 6 p.m. Glen would return home to be with Keith, and Katie would have her time alone with the baby which she cherished. If she wasn't feeling well, because of a treatment that day, her Aunt Molly would be there to help with the baby and dinner.

On Sundays, the one day Keith did not go to the law office, he would prepare dinner for all of them. Glen would pick up Katie and the baby and bring them to their home.

Keith would be standing at the front door to greet them, and had started to take the baby in his arms. "Little Glen is better looking each time I see him. I really do think he's beginning to look like someone I know."

"Really? You think he looks like me?" Glen asked, obviously pleased.

"No, he looks like Katie," Keith teased. He has her coloring: auburn hair and hazel eyes."

"Oh, he does too look like Glen!" Katie protested. "You're just being mean."

Keith laughed. "Just so you know, I think he's a great looking little guy. Matter of fact, I think he's beginning to look like me."

Katie smiled. "Well, whoever he looks like, he's going to be one lucky boy to have one mommy and two daddies who love him."

Later that evening, when Glen brought Katie and the baby back to their home, he said to her, "When you've gotten the baby settled for the night, we need to have a serious talk."

That morning over breakfast, Keith had said to him, "When are you and Katie going to talk about a financial arrangement to help her with the baby?"

Glen sighed, "I've tried to talk to her about it on several occasions, but she just puts me off. According to her, she made the decision to have the baby. I wasn't a party to her decision and I shouldn't have to be financially responsible."

Keith shook his head. "That's honorable of her, but that's not how it works, especially now that she isn't able to teach because of her medical problems." Then he asked, "Have you ever talked with Katie about her finances? How is she getting by without working?"

"No, that's something we've never talked about," Glen said.

"You need to," Keith replied, "Last Sunday, when Katie was here, I was surprised, actually somewhat shocked, how thin she's become, her pallor and the shadows under her eyes. I don't see her going back to work anytime soon."

****

Before coming to the living room where Glen was sitting on the sofa, Katie had gone to the kitchen to pour a glass of red wine for Glen and herself.

"So, what is this serious topic we need to talk about?" Katie said as she handed a glass to Glen and snuggled up close beside him.

"Money—we need to talk about money," Glen said. "No more putting me off."

"All right, we'll talk about money" Katie said. "So what do you want to say?"

"Who is named as the father on the birth certificate?"

"You."

"Isn't there some responsibility that goes with that? Like child support?"

"I don't think so," Katie said. "Not in this case."

"Why?" Glen asked.

"It was my decision to have this baby. I never intended for anyone else to be financially responsible. Not David and certainly not you."

"Katie, I respect what you're saying. But it takes money to raise a child. I need to be responsible for paying child support."

She raised her hand to stop him. "Paying child support can be a tremendous drain. I saw what it did to David. He has two teenage daughters by his first marriage whom he has to support. He was paying almost $1,500 a month and it wore on him. That's why he was so adamant about not having another child, especially as he would be facing his girls' college expenses in just a few years. He worried about it all the time."

"Katie, I want to pay child support for my son." He reached out to take Katie's hand.

"Glen, I love you for feeling that way, but I don't want you to. After my father died, it was just Mom and me. She supported us on a secretary's salary. A teacher's salary may not be great, but it's more than a secretary earned. I can support my baby without anyone's help."

"Perhaps, when you're working. But you're not working now, and I want to help." He paused to take a sip of wine, before broaching the subject of her finances. "I have no idea what you have or don't have. You've got to give me some idea where you stand so I know what I need to do to help."

"Glen, honey, I inherited this house. It's not much, but it's paid for . . . no mortgage. Mom had an insurance policy that I received, not a whole lot, but enough and I've saved several thousand dollars over the years. I don't have a lot, but I can get by easily for six months, maybe a year without working. Growing up, we didn't have a lot, but we got by. Mom taught me how to keep my want button under control. I know how to do without things I don't need."

"What about medical expenses? Do you have insurance?"

"Yes, that's been a blessing. As I'm still legally married to David, his insurance policy from his teaching position at City College covers me. Once I start teaching, I'll be able to switch over to the school district's group policy."

"Sounds like you have it all under control," Glen said. "As I see it, the only problem you're going to have is what to do with the child support money I'm going to give you each month. He took a check from his shirt pocket and placed it in her hand."

"One thousand dollars? No, that's too much," Katie protested.

"Not for Glen Junior it isn't." He stood up to leave. "Katie, if you need more, just let me know. Keith and I want you and the baby to have whatever you need."

Chapter Fourteen

Mary Phillips had spent the greater part of her morning reading and re-reading in her Bible the verses on the love shared by David and Jonathan in the Book of Samuel.

The soul of Jonathan was knit to the soul of David, and Jonathan loved him as his own soul.—Samuel 18:1

. . . your love for me was extraordinary, surpassing the love of a woman.—Samuel 1:26.

. . . then they kissed—Samuel 20:41

That David and Jonathan loved one another was not in doubt: the Hebrew Bible had detailed a great love shared by the two men. But was it platonic or physical? She searched the Internet for the answer and found that traditional Christian teaching said it was platonic—but others, especially current scholars, believed it was physical, and more than just the kiss revealed in the biblical passage.

In any event, wasn't the real issue biblical approval of a great and intense love shared by two outstanding men?

Mary Phillips was a believer, a devout Christian, searching for comfort in her acceptance of Gentry's love for Jason. What mattered most, she concluded, was the Bible's positive portrayal—its blessing—of the love David and Jonathan felt for one another.

Initially, when he first arrived, Jason said little, he seemed ill at ease as if perhaps he really wasn't wanted in their home. Mary Phillips sensed his discomfort and hugged him. "So good to have you join us for dinner. Just like old times. I made Gentry's favorite dinner, my special turkey and veal meatloaf. Your favorite too if I remember correctly."

Jason smiled. "I'm so happy to be here. Thank you for inviting me." He was still subdued, so different from the upbeat, enthusiastic young man she had known and liked for many years. Jason was a nice looking young man, not handsome, but attractive in an athletic, clean-cut way. His most prominent feature was his large, dark brown eyes that were striking against his fair complexion and sandy-colored hair.

Her husband reached out to shake Jason's hand. "We were pleased you could join us. Come let's sit in the living room and have a glass of iced tea before dinner. We want to hear all about U.T. Austin. Did Gentry tell you he's planning to go there for the spring semester?"

The tense—guarded—look on Jason's face disappeared, and his dark brown eyes regained their sparkle. By the time they were seated at the dinner table, it was like old times with fun-loving and talkative Jason, except for one significant detail.

In the past, Jason and Gentry would have been directing much of their conversation toward each other, teasing and laughing, often reaching over to poke or touch one another in a show of comradely affection. This evening their conversation was directed toward her husband and her. There was no touching of each other.

Mary might have concluded from the lack of interaction between them that their close friendship had cooled . . . except for the flush that had suffused her son's face when Jason first entered their home, and her chance view as she carried their emptied dinner plates from the dining room, not a scrap of meatloaf left on them, that the boys were holding hands under the table.

Later that evening as she and her husband were retiring for the evening, Mary adjusted the lace curtain on her bedroom window to look out at the starlit night. A crescent moon added to the light of the stars, and she became aware that Jason and her son were standing close together beside Jason's silver Honda. She caught her breath as she watched them embrace and kiss . . . . much as David and Jonathan might have kissed in the long ago.

"Mary, what are you looking at?" her husband said from his side of their bed.

"Just the stars and the moon on this beautiful night." She thought it best not to say anything more.

****

As in past years, parental response to Glen's unit was overwhelmingly positive. Several parents had written notes or sent e-mails commending him on the theme for the unit: *Making the World a Better Place through Understanding and Acceptance of Others.* Glen had formed a close bond—a friendship actually—with Mr. Fowler, the school principal, who related that one parent had even called him at home to say how pleased she was that her son had Mr. McLean for a teacher. She was thrilled, she said, that her son was in a classroom where Christian values of respect, responsibility and caring were taught.

Not all the responses were positive, however. Inevitably, there was the occasional parent who detected a devious motive. As a note from one father said,

> *Dear Mr. McLean,*
>
> *My wife and I had serious reservations about permitting my daughter to have you as her teacher. Bowing to her entreaties as well as positive comments about you from others in our Church, we allowed her to be in your class.*
>
> *We are deeply concerned about your classroom focus on teaching respect, responsibility and caring as a possible cover for promoting tolerance, even respect, for homosexuals and their anti-Christian agenda.*
>
> *Please know we will be paying careful attention to what students are taught in your classroom.*
>
> *Sincerely*
>
> *Robert J. Trost*

By his fifth period class, Glen had the day's lesson down pat. As he passed out the activity sheet, he said, "It's one thing to think of ourselves as fair-minded, it's another thing to actually act—to live our lives—that way. I have prepared an activity sheet that you may work on by yourself, if that is what you want, or you may join in a group of up to four other students.

"Let me take you through the steps. The first thing to do is think of someone you dislike—maybe feel you hate. You can choose someone from literature, or someone from history, or perhaps someone living today who is in the news. Write that person's name in the blank space under Step 1 on your activity sheet."

Several students started to call out names:

"Barack Obama"

"Prince Charles"

"Cinderella's stepmother"

"Michael Jackson"

"George Bush"

Glen raised his hand to quiet them. "I was worried that you wouldn't be able to think of anyone you disliked. Apparently, that's not going to be a problem. Next, you need to state specifically why you dislike that person. It can't be a general term such as *he's no good* or *she's mean*. You have to describe the specific behavior—what the person did or does—that makes you judge this person as no good or mean.

"Write your charges against the person under Step 2 in your activity sheet. Have a separate space for each negative behavior."

The class had grown quiet, apparently thinking about why they disliked their chosen person. Glen paused to give them a moment for thought.

"Are you ready now for the hard part? Glen asked. In Step 3 you have to get out of your own head. It's a challenge, I know, to forget about yourself and what you think. You now have to become the person you dislike—get into his or her head. Imagine how they see things and respond as that person would to the charges against them.

"In our legal system, it's called '*due process*'. Mary Robinson would term it *respect*. It means that people are given the opportunity to defend themselves from charges made against them. They are given the opportunity to present their points of view, to explain why they acted in the way they did."

Ty Whiteoak, a serious looking boy with stringy blond hair and bright blue eyes, looked concerned. "Does listening to someone mean you have to agree with him that it was okay to do what he did? Can't you still believe his actions were wrong and dislike him?"

"Good question," Glen said. "And that takes us to Step 4, the final step in this unit. In this step, we apply our values as standards in determining the rightness or wrongness of a behavior.

"The three values we are starting with are *respect, responsibility* and *caring*. These are standards for us to judge the actions of others. Another important consideration would be *truthfulness*. To justify their action or belief, some people may distort the truth, for example, spotlighting the negatives and omitting the positives."

He went to the chalkboard and wrote "*TRUTH versus LIES*". "There are also people who will flat-out lie about someone else—make up a tale to hurt them. I've had the misfortune to know one person like that. What about you? Have you known anyone who would do that?"

Several students nodded. One girl pointed to another, "You told lies about me!"

"All right, the point is made." Glen responded quickly, wanting to avoid a confrontation.

"Few people would knowingly lie," he continued. "but what many people commonly do is repeat hearsay and gossip—or forward to others an item they received in their email or saw on Facebook—without first checking to determine if it's true, and that can be just as hurtful.

"Think of the Nazi soldiers justifying why it was all right to treat Anne Frank and her family the way they did. Or think about a bully justifying his right to torment another student. They can attempt to justify their behavior with their words, but if you put their words to the test of truthfulness, their statements often prove false and show them up as the villains they are.

"Should you ever be in doubt," he concluded, "about the right or wrong of an action, you have the Golden Rule from the Bible to guide you: *Do unto others as you would have others do unto you.* Did you know that every major religion offers the same or similar guidance to its followers?"

****

105

"Hi, Chrissie! Hi girls!" Holding the baby, Katie greeted her cousin and her two daughters. "Come in. The baby just got up for his feeding. His bottle is warming and I . . ."

"Oh, can we hold him?" LeeAnn, the 6-year-old said. "I'll be so careful. I promise, I won't drop him."

Chrissie laughed. "The girls are so excited about their new little cousin. That's all I heard all morning. When are we going to see the baby? Please! Please! Take us there again. He is so adorable!"

Katie said. "I don't blame them one bit because he is a very adorable baby. Yes, he is! And yes, you can hold him, later. But first, he needs to have his bottle and . . ."

"Oh, please let me feed him his bottle!" Betty Jo, who was 8 years old, cried out. "I know I can do it. Please, Katie, please!"

"No, not yet," Katie said. "When he's a little older, maybe next month. For now, only Mama Katie gets to feed him." She saw the disappointed look on the girls' faces and said, "But I will let you hold him."

"Now? Can we hold him now?" Both girls reached for him.

"All right, that's enough," their mother stopped them. "You can watch quietly while Katie feeds him and then after she burps him, if you're good, Katie will let you hold him." She smiled at Katie, "He's the little brother they've always wanted."

Then remembering, she said, "I need to get my camera. It's in the car. Aunt Molly wants photos of the baby. She's just crazy about him. I imagine she'll be showing his picture to all her friends at church. And I want a photo of my girls with the baby. We can pretend it's my girls with their baby brother," Chrissie smiled.

Then in a more somber tone, "Katie, I know those treatments are taking a lot out of you. Is it too soon to know if they're working?"

"Yes, it's still too soon to know. I go for my next chemo treatment on Tuesday," she sighed. "I'm just limp afterwards, but if it works it will be worth it."

Chrissie nodded. "The girls will be back in school so I'll be available to drive you. Aunt Molly told me she'll be with the baby. And I'll make a big chicken pot pie and a salad so you won't have to think about cooking that day or the next."

Katie reached out to take her cousin's hand. "I don't know what I would do if I didn't have you and Aunt Molly to help me."

"Well, you do have us and we're going to be there for you through it all."

Then, after a moment's pause, she said, "What have you told David about—about, you know, the cancer?"

Katie nodded. "I had to tell him everything because I'm on his health insurance policy. He checked and he tells me that it's a good policy. Everything is covered: the surgery, my treatments . . . and that's a relief."

"What about the baby?" Chrissie asked. "Doesn't he want to know about the baby?"

Katie shrugged. "I've told him as little as I need to: the baby's fine . . . healthy. He knows about the fertility clinic and the procedure I used to become pregnant, and that Glen McLean is the biological father of the baby . . . that David is not involved or responsible in any way. That's how he wants it, and that's how we're leaving it."

Chrissie looked perplexed. "Aunt Molly is very upset about you naming a gay man as the father on your baby's birth certificate. She can't put it to rest."

"I know she's upset, and I'm sorry about that. I love her and I need her, very much. But this is my life and my baby. It's my decision to make, not hers."

Chrissie started to say something, stopped herself, then said it after all. "Aunt Molly doesn't believe that gay teacher is the father of the baby. She says your husband David is the father and you're denying it because David told you to have an abortion."

****

Reverend Phillips had promised his wife he would write a sermon calling for tolerance and love for all. Initially, he had planned to draw upon two biblical teachings as the foundation for the sermon:

Judge not and you shall not be judged. Condemn not, and you shall not be condemned. Forgive and you will be forgiven.—Luke 6:37

You shall love your neighbor as yourself.—Mathew 22:36-40

Now seated at his large mahogany desk in his office at the First Baptist Church, he was having second thoughts. Was he really prepared to say that all people were to be loved and not judged for their actions? The Bible condemned homosexual acts. How then could he appear to offer words of support, even love, for people who committed those perversions?

Many of the older and more conservative members of his church would not approve of that message. Nor in truth could he. Where would that line of reasoning lead? Reverend Phillips shook his head. It was the irresponsible approach that liberals took—the slippery slope of moral relativism—that has infected our culture. It would lead to acceptance of other perversions, such as polygamy, pedophilia, incest, even bestiality. Was it not necessary for him to assert God's absolute and unchanging moral law?

He had no choice but to tell Mary that in good conscience he could not give that sermon. She would not be happy with this decision, he knew, but as his wife she was required to accept it. That was God's will.

Reverend Phillips and his wife were seated in their comfortable living room with its traditional English style furniture. Their son was out with Jason, as it was Jason's last evening in Edgemont before departing for the University of Texas in Austin.

"Everett, how is your sermon progressing?" Mary asked.

He cleared his throat. "I've decided not to deliver that sermon. I believe it will be giving a wrong message"

"I don't understand. What could be wrong about not judging others and loving your neighbor? Isn't that the essence of what Jesus taught?"

"Yes, but I fear that some may interpret it to mean that all behavior is acceptable and that is not the message I want to bring to my parishioners."

"What message do you want to bring?" she asked as she leaned forward in her chair.

He heard the edge in her voice and began to speak more slowly, carefully choosing his words. "Am I not as the minister of my church required to condemn unacceptable behaviors such as polygamy, incest, and pedophilia? Does not God expect me to speak out against those who commit acts of perversion, specifically forbidden by biblical teaching?"

"Are you telling me that God requires you to condemn homosexual people for their sin of loving one another?" she asked.

He nodded, "Yes, that is what I'm telling you."

She stood up from her chair and walked to her husband. Standing directly before him, she said in a firm voice, "Then explain to me, Everett, why our God whom we have been taught to love with all our heart, and all our soul and all our mind, would answer our prayers for a child by giving us a wonderful son who is homosexual?"

He shook his head. "I have no explanation."

"Have you so soon forgotten that we almost lost him?" she said. "Things happen for a reason. God's reason. God has a lesson for you to learn so that you as a minister would teach others about acceptance and love of all God's children.

"Listening to you speak, I fear you haven't learned that lesson and that will bring God's wrath down upon us. We could lose our son." She began to cry. "I'm so afraid that you are going against God's will and we will be punished."

Her voice choked with emotion as she clenched her hands. "I have always bowed to your wishes. I believed that was my duty as a Christian woman. But I am also a mother and it is my responsibility to protect my child. I fear that you are placing Gentry in harm's way, and I cannot allow that."

Reverend Phillips lowered his head. "How can I as a minister with responsibility to lead my flock to a righteous life not judge when I hear of homosexuals having sex in bathrooms and public parks. When I read of homosexual men preying on innocent children, hoping to recruit them into their degenerate life style.

"Mary, I love my son with all my heart and the fear that I might cause him harm . . ." He paused, "even more harm than I already have . . . is unnerving me to the core of my being. I understand and respect what you are asking me to do. But how can I in good conscience stand on my pulpit and talk of love and acceptance for people who are violating the morality that I value as a Christian? I'm being torn apart." His voice broke and she saw that his eyes were moist.

Her voice softened. "Everett, I know you're a faithful servant of God and want only to honor his teachings. And this is difficult for you . . . very difficult. We've all heard those terrible stories about homosexual people and judge them by those stories. But I ask you, what if our only exposure to heterosexual people came from the daily news reports of adultery, and killings and violent rapes of innocent women and young girls by heterosexual men? What would we think of heterosexual people?"

She paused, expecting her husband to respond. He didn't. He just shook his head and remained silent.

"Everett, the problem may be that we don't know any gay people. Perhaps knowing gay people—the type of people who don't do wrong and don't appear in news reports—can change the way you feel." She hesitated before saying, "Gentry has spoken so highly of that gay teacher at the high school. Will you allow me to ask Gentry to invite him to our home?"

She placed her hand on her husband's shoulder. "God loves his children—all of them—the straight ones and the gay ones. *He* will show us the way."

Chapter Fifteen

Glen sat on the edge of his desk. "Anne Frank was a teenage girl no different from many of the girls in our school today. The bigotry that was rampant in Germany resulted in behavior against her and her family that was unbelievably cruel; so inhumane, that it's difficult to fathom how civilized people could have acted that way.

"Bigotry is a terrible thing. It brings out the worst in people," he said. "The horrible things that the Nazis did to the Jews, they did to others as well. They tortured and murdered the handicapped, gypsies, Jehovah's Witnesses, and . . . homosexuals. There's a memorial in Paris to all the people they tortured and killed. It shows the colored badges the Nazis forced them to wear." Glen's voice grew husky with emotion, and he stopped.

Several students looked surprised at the inclusion of homosexuals. In past years, no student had ever said anything. This year Linda Hernandez, an attractive Hispanic girl, raised her hand.

"There are people in our country who say bad things about gays, very bad things. Do you think that Americans would ever do anything to harm gay people?"

"I hope not, but I do know that the people in Germany who carried out those cruel deeds, and the people who stood by and allowed the cruelty to happen, were like many people who live in our country today. They thought of themselves as good people—church-going Christians who worshipped then as many of us here worship today."

He paused, allowing his students a moment to think about his comment, before adding, "Do you think it's possible that any of you might have behaved that way if you'd lived in Germany at that time? Do you think you could have been so cruel? Even if you wouldn't have done those terrible things, would you have stood by doing nothing, just watching?"

When the class left at the end of the period, Linda remained. She waited for the last of the students to leave the classroom. Then, speaking in a low voice, "Mr. McLean, do you ever worry that someone might try to harm you because you're gay?"

He appreciated her concern. "I try not to think about that. I know there are some people who wish me, and other people like me, harm . . . but I know also that most people are motivated by good feelings. That's what I think about—not the few who hate, but the many of goodwill—the ones who have love in their hearts."

"I just want you to know," Linda said, "that your students think you're wonderful. You're our favorite teacher. We love you and would stand by you if anyone ever tried to harm you."

****

Glen was lying in bed beside Keith, when suddenly he burst out laughing.

Keith, who was addicted to reading mystery novels, put the book down. "What's so funny?"

"I just visualized you changing the poop in Glen Junior's diaper." Glen laughed again.

"Was it a big poop or a little poop?" Keith asked. "Because if it was a little poop, a real little one, I think I could do it with only a minor gag or two."

"What if it was a big poop, like the one I changed this evening?"

"No problem. I would just call for his daddy. Like, Daddy Glen, hurry, your adorable little guy just had a gigantic poop and needs his loving daddy to clean his not-so-sweet smelling butt."

"Poop aside, you do think he's adorable, don't you?" Glen said.

"For the one hundredth time, let me tell you that I think little Glen Thomas McLean II is the most wonderful, adorable and best looking baby in the world," Keith said. "Especially because he looks more like me every day."

"Like you?" Glen poked him in the belly. "He's my kid and he looks like me."

"You know what I was thinking?" Keith said. "I had this kind of crazy thought."

"So tell me," Glen propped himself up on his elbow.

"I think Glen Junior should have a brother or sister, and it occurred to me that the fertility clinic in New York where you and Katie went would still have her frozen eggs, wouldn't they?'

"I believe they would."

"I've been reading up on in vitro fertilization and was thinking we could use Katie's eggs and my sperm and locate a surrogate mother to carry the embryo. The baby would be a biological half sibling to Glen Junior: the same mother for both, with you as the father of one and me as the father of the other. What do you think?"

"It's a great idea and I love it, except for . . ." Glen paused . . . "you know, her breast cancer. I think it's a genetic issue and that worries me."

"If it were a boy, I don't think it would be a problem," Keith said, "and even if it's a girl, I'm confident in the next 25 or 30 years, there'll be so many advances that it won't be a problem any more. Tell me, are you up for it?"

"Guess?"

Keith grabbed Glen into his arms, embracing him in a tight bear hug. "I knew you'd love the idea! My mother was ecstatic when I bounced it off her. By the way, she can't wait to see Little Glen. Do you think there's a chance Katie will let him spend the night with us?"

"Yes, we've talked about it and when she has her next chemo treatment, the baby will spend the night here. Those treatments take so much out of her she can barely get out of bed afterwards."

Glen hesitated, not willing to express his thought: *What if the treatments weren't halting the cancer's spread?* Katie was now experiencing constant pain in her back, and that couldn't be good.

"So, just give me a date and I'll call Mom," Keith said. "She told me she'll drop everything and drive right up from Austin."

"Okay, as soon as I have the date, I'll let you know. Now, there's something I want you to do for me."

"Can I guess?" Keith smiled. "You want me to put aside my book and take care of your insatiable sexual appetite? Right?"

"Wrong. I want you to get out of bed and walk across the hall to look at the baby's bedroom with me."

"We just looked at it an hour ago. I'm confident nothing has changed. I'm in the middle of the exciting part of this novel and . . ."

"Come! It will only take a minute." Glen jumped from bed, ran to Keith's side of the bed and grabbed his hand. "I know you really want to look at it again!"

"All right, Mr. Daddy, let's go look at Little Glen's bedroom."

"How do you like those cartoon cut-outs I've pasted on his walls?" Glen pointed to the large figures of Snow White and the Seven Dwarfs. "They're really fun, aren't they?"

"I told you they were great an hour ago."

"Really? Tell me again . . . I keep forgetting."

"They're great! And so are the ones on the other side of the room of Donald Duck and Mickey Mouse. I also love the crib with the Humpty Dumpty bumper guards and the bassinet with the Lion King drawings. Have I covered everything?" Keith asked. "I don't want to leave anything out."

"You've forgotten the mobile with the rotating animal figures that plays Rock-a-Bye-Baby."

"That's because it's still in its box. When you set it up on the crib, I'll be sure to include it."

Glen leaned forward to kiss his partner. "I've never been so excited in my entire life! I can't stop thinking about little Glen and all the things we're going to be doing together."

"I'm excited too," Keith said. "Very excited."

"You don't act excited," Glen said.

"That's because I'm a mature adult and know how to contain my excitement."

"Are you suggesting that I'm not a mature adult?" Glen said.

"No, I'm not suggesting that—I'm stating it as a fact. You look like an adult, a very handsome and sexy buck naked one, I might add, but inside you're a child, an adorable, lovable child, and I'm so happy you're mine." He put his arms around Glen and patted him on his bare behind. "I think Glen Junior is so lucky to have you as his daddy."

****

"Hello, Mr. McLean, this is Gentry. My mom asked me to call you."

"Gentry?" Glen was surprised and somewhat uncomfortable with his call. "Your mother asked you to call me? Does she know that your father doesn't want us to be in contact?"

"That's all changed. Dad knows I'm calling."

"And he's okay with that?"

"He is. Actually, I'm calling to invite you to our home. My parents would like to meet you."

For a moment, Glen did not respond. Then, "Why do they want to meet me?"

Gentry cleared his throat. "I guess Dad is trying to accept that my being gay is all right and he's having a hard time with that. They don't know any gay people; at least they don't think they do. Mom thinks it might help Dad if he met an openly gay person that he could like and respect." Gentry stopped, waiting for Glen to respond. When he didn't, Gentry said, "I know he'll like you. Everyone does."

Glen took a deep breath. "Gentry, I would like to help you. But a visit like this would put me on display as some sort of prototype for all gay people. It just doesn't feel like something I'd want to do."

"I was hoping you'd come . . ." The boy's voice broke. "I was really counting on your coming. My dad's trying—I thought meeting you would really help him."

Glen heard the disappointment. "Gentry, you know I want to help you. I think you're a fine young man who's gone through a difficult time. And I . . ."

"Please say you'll come . . . please. Your coming is very important to me. I know it'll help me."

Glen sighed. "All right, I'll come. But just for a short visit, an hour at most."

****

Glen rang the doorbell at the Phillips' home. It was 5 p.m. Friday afternoon, and he would have preferred to still be at Katie's home, holding his son.

The solid mahogany door opened and Gentry was there, his hand outstretched in greeting. "Thank you so much! I can't wait for Mom and Dad to meet you! Come in!"

Gentry was obviously high with anticipation of the meeting. His cheeks were suffused with a reddish glow that highlighted his dark wavy hair and deep blue eyes. For the moment Glen was taken aback by how handsome the boy appeared. *Wow, wouldn't it be something if my son would be so great looking. Maybe he will be. Why not?*

Gentry escorted Glen into the living room where his parents waited. "Mom and Dad, I'd like you to meet Mr. McLean."

Reverend Phillips rose from his chair and reached out to shake Glen's hand. "My son admires you greatly," he said. "My wife and I have looked forward to our meeting."

Glen was surprised by the cordial greeting and even more by the intelligent and sensitive look of this tall, slender man with the wire-rim glasses who had spoken to him on the phone in such a judgmental, almost threatening, manner.

"Please have a seat," Mrs. Phillips motioned him to the sofa where Gentry was now sitting. "May I get you a soft drink, perhaps juice or iced tea?"

"No, thank you. I'm fine." Glen waited, expecting that Reverend Phillips would open the conversation. He was looking at Glen as if he was going to say something, but he didn't and the silence grew uncomfortable.

"You're a fine looking man . . . very handsome," the minister said, as if surprised.

"Thank you." Again there was silence and Glen realized it would be up to him to get the conversation going.

"I understand that Gentry has told you that I'm gay, and that's why you wanted to meet me."

"Yes," Mrs. Phillips said, "We just don't know gay people and feel we should because our son is gay."

Looking uncomfortable, Reverend Phillips remained silent.

Glen smiled at the small, motherly looking woman, just a little bit plump, dressed simply in a floral cotton dress, her brown hair in a bun. She seemed like a sweet lady. "Please feel free to ask any questions you may have. I won't take offense, and I'll answer as honestly as I can."

"Thank you," Reverend Phillips said, "I do have questions, many of them, but I didn't want to say something that might be offensive."

"I promise not to be offended."

The Reverend nodded. "To begin, how did you know you were gay?"

"Let me ask you a question that I believe will help you understand my response," Glen said. "If I were to ask you how you knew you were straight, how would you answer?"

"How would I answer?" Reverend Phillips repeated. "I never thought about it, I guess, because it came so naturally to me. As a teenage boy, I found girls attractive. I responded to them, just like the other boys did."

Glen nodded. "I understand because I was just like you, except it wasn't girls but boys that I found attractive, and I responded to them. That's what came naturally to me and it caused me great anguish. I was raised Catholic and was taught that my thoughts, my attractions, were a mortal sin that could condemn me to hell for eternity."

He shook his head. "A pretty heavy burden to place on a teenage boy who needed the approval that comes from being like everyone else. It was a millstone on my neck and there were moments I felt I would collapse from its weight."

Glen saw Mr. and Mrs. Phillips exchange glances.

"Tell me," the minister asked. "Did you ever try—I mean really try—to change, to become straight."

"Yes, I tried. I prayed night after night. 'Dear God, please, let me awake in the morning and have that attraction gone.' I did everything I knew of to become straight. I dated girls, went steady, acted as if I had the same feelings—desires for girls—that other guys had. I tried to block any romantic thoughts I had for other guys, but it didn't help. I remained gay."

"But what about programs—Christian based programs—such as Exodus International, which have proven so successful in helping gay men and women become straight. Have you heard about them? Maybe those programs didn't exist when you were struggling, but they do today and I . . ."

Glen raised his hand to stop the minister. "Those programs are a fraud. Only the people running the programs and their religious supporters have anything positive to say about their results."

Then, looking perplexed, Glen said, "The failure of the ex-gay programs are so widely documented by objective research, I find it difficult to understand why you didn't know that."

Glen waited for Reverend Phillips to respond. When he remained silent, his brow furrowed, Glen said, "The major psychological and mental health associations of our nation have condemned the practices of the ex-gay groups. You can check their findings on the Internet."

"Does that mean nothing can be done? Are you suggesting that if you're homosexual, that's how you'll remain?" Reverend Phillips' voice registered surprise as he adjusted his bifocals. He appeared to doubt Glen's words.

"What would it take for you to change from being straight to being gay? Can you tell me how that would be done?" Glen said.

"I don't know." Reverend Phillips shook his head.

"And that's my response to you as well." Glen said. "I don't know how I would change from gay to straight."

For the first time, Mrs. Phillips asked a question. "If you had a son or a daughter who was gay what would you do?"

"I would love them," Glen said. "And I would let them know that I loved them just as they are."

Glen smiled at Gentry, who had been sitting quietly. Then, looking back at Reverend Phillips, he said, "I don't know what happened to cause you to change your mind about my being in contact with your son, but I'm glad you did. It gives me the opportunity to tell you that I believe your son has gone through a very difficult time, because his father, whom he loves and respects greatly, has judged and condemned him for being gay—something he couldn't change."

Reverend Phillips shook his head. "I love my son. He is everything any father could want in a son."

"Except . . ." Glen said, "except he's gay."

"Yes," the minister said softly. "The Bible is my teacher, and I find myself torn between its judgment against homosexuality and my love for my son. I am struggling . . ."

"I understand," Glen said, "and if I may, I'd like to ask you a question that has puzzled me for many years. There are so many things in the Bible that Christians don't honor, actually ignore, such as what can and cannot be eaten like pork and shellfish, killing people for working on the Sabbath, condoning slavery, stoning people to death for adultery, not allowing divorce . . . and so much more. How do you as a minister responsible for leading his parishioners determine what in the Bible can be ignored and what must be obeyed?"

"That is a valid question," Reverend Phillips said. "I don't know if I have a satisfactory answer, other than not everything is equal. Some things are more important than others."

"Like not judging people and loving your neighbor as yourself." Mary Phillips looked directly at her husband as she said, "That's what Jesus taught and, therefore, what we must respect and obey above all else."

Then, turning to Glen, she said, "I love my son as he is. My greatest concern is for him to lead a moral and ethical life and to find fulfillment and happiness that can only come from a loving and lasting relationship. I worry he will never find that in the gay lifestyle."

Glen stood up and walked to the chair where she was seated. He took Mrs. Phillips' hand. "You seem like such a sweet and loving woman. I want to assure you that there are many gay and lesbian people in loving and lasting relationships. I have had a wonderful partner for more than four years who has enriched my life. We have friends in Dallas, a retired doctor and a lawyer, who have been together over 50 years."

He smiled, "I know you worry . . . most mothers do. Trust me. Your son Gentry can have a wonderful life."

"Thank you. That's so comforting to hear." Mary Phillips looked up at Glen, approval of him evident in the warmth of her expression. "I would like to meet your partner. Perhaps we could have dinner here."

"Let me talk to him," Glen said. "He's an excellent cook and I think it might be a better idea for you to have dinner at our home, to see first-hand how a gay couple lives."

"What about me?" Gentry said, "I'd like to be included."

Glen laughed, "Of course you're included."

Then Glen turned to Reverend Phillips. "You seem like an intelligent and thoughtful man, and I'm confident you'll be successful in resolving the conflict you're faced with." He shook the minister's hand. "Change is never easy, especially when it involves long-held beliefs."

Walking Glen to the front door, Gentry said, "Dad was impressed. I saw it in his face. I can never thank you enough for being here." Then he whispered, "If you do have us for dinner, can I invite Jason to drive up from Austin to join us? That would be so cool!"

Chapter Sixteen

Glen rang the doorbell to Katie's home. He waited, and when there was no response, he rang it again. When Katie still didn't come, he reached in his pocket for the key to her door and let himself in.

Alarmed, he ran to the bedroom where he saw the baby stirring in his crib and Katie in a deep sleep on her bed.

"Katie, are you all right?" He placed his hand on her arm.

She opened her eyes, and seeing Glen, blinked, obviously startled. "What time is it?" She seemed confused. "Is it four o'clock?"

"Are you okay?" Glen asked.

"Yes, I'm fine. I was just so tired, I closed my eyes. Is it really four o'clock? Oh, it's time for the baby's feeding!" She sat upright.

Later seated on the living room sofa, the baby asleep in his arms, Glen said, "Katie, sweetheart, what's happening? You've got to tell me."

"Nothing's happening." She ran her hand through her thinning hair. "Other than I'm losing my hair. But you can see that, can't you? It's the chemo treatments. I'll have to buy a wig. Do you think you'd like me as a redhead?" She tried to laugh, make light of it, but her voice broke and she started to cry.

"You're in pain. I can see it in your face. What does the doctor say about that?"

She shook her head. "He says we might need to increase the chemo, maybe try something else. I just don't know. Please, let's not talk about it."

Taking the baby from Glen, she smiled. "He's the most wonderful baby in the whole wide world. And he has the most wonderful daddy. In my perfect world there would be the baby, you and me and I'd never want for anything more."

Glen leaned forward to kiss her lightly on the lips. When I think of this little guy—that I have him because of you—it's the greatest gift. Katie, you know I love you. Just be well and we'll have our perfect world."

"I feel better already. Having my two men here beside me makes all the hurt and bad feelings go away."

For a few moments neither one spoke. Glen placed his finger in the baby's hand and smiled, as even in sleep, the little hand closed on his finger. "I just love it when he does that."

"By the way, I was with Reverend Phillips and his family at their home yesterday."

Katie looked surprised. "I can't imagine . . ." she paused. "He obviously doesn't know you're gay."

"But he does. That's why I was invited to their home. He and his wife feel a need to know gay people."

Katie looked doubtful. "Why?"

Glen hesitated, wondering, *Do I have a right to say anything about their son being gay?*

"So, tell me. There had to be a reason." Katie said.

"I'm just not comfortable saying anything," Glen said, already weakening and knowing he would tell her.

"Even if I promise never to repeat what you tell me to anyone?" Katie turned to look directly at him.

"All right, I'll tell you. But first I want to hear you promise. Say, I promise never to repeat what Glen Thomas McLean, father to Glen Thomas McLean II, tells me."

"Okay, I promise," Katie said.

"No, you have to say the whole thing word for word and let me see both your hands so that I know you aren't crossing your fingers."

"Crossing my fingers?" Katie said, "What does that have to do with anything?"

"Don't you know that if you cross your fingers, nothing you promise counts? Don't they teach you Texas girls anything in school?"

"Glen, stop tormenting me! Tell me why Reverend Phillips invited you to his home. Right now!"

"They recently learned that their son is gay," Glen said.

Katie's mouth fell open. "I can't believe it! He's been dating that lovely girl and . . ."

"He's gay." Glen said. "And you are not to tell that to anyone."

"I won't. I promise," Katie said.

"I was impressed with your minister. He seems to be an intelligent and sensitive man who's struggling. He's having a difficult time resolving his past beliefs about gays with the knowledge that his son is gay."

"I've heard him make some very negative statements," Katie said.

"Well, I think that's troubling him now. I wouldn't be surprised if sometime in the future he offers a more positive perspective."

"That could be a problem for him," Katie said. "There are some very conservative and bigoted members in our church—prominent people who would not appreciate hearing tolerance for gays. I've seen them run off one minister who did not say exactly what they wanted said."

"But isn't Reverend Phillips loved and respected? Couldn't he withstand their opposition?"

"Maybe," Katie said. "However, the issues of gay marriage and gays raising children have the conservative members of our church up in arms. You should hear my Aunt Molly on those topics."

****

Reverend Phillips and his family, including Gentry's friend Jason stood on the sidewalk before the grand old home with its rolling front lawn and giant live oak trees.

"Wow, what a house!" Jason said.

"Wait 'til you see the inside," Gentry said. "It's big time."

Reverend Phillips was quiet. He was conflicted about bringing his family to the home of two gay men; he would have preferred to decline the invitation. But Mary had high expectations for the evening, and his son had been so excited that he had called Jason to ask him to drive up from Austin.

Gentry rang the doorbell and in a brief moment Glen opened the door.

"Welcome! So happy you all came." Extending his hand to Gentry's friend, he smiled, "You must be Jason. We're pleased you were able to join us. Then he opened his arms to embrace Mary. "You are such a sweet lady."

"Thank you for including me," Gentry said. "And thank you for allowing me to bring Jason."

Motioning them inside, Glen said, "This house was built by Keith's great-grandfather about 1906, and has been in the Chamberlain family ever since. It's Keith's now and he's allowing me to have squatter's rights."

"It's a beautiful home!" Mary Phillips said. "I can't imagine living in a home this grand."

Glen guided them past the elegant staircase that appeared to be floating on air and into the large formal living room with its 14-foot ceilings and 12-inch crown molding. A crystal chandelier cast a golden glow on the red and yellow striped fabrics on the matching wing chairs facing the yellow, down-cushioned sofa.

Reverend Phillips had been raised in a modest home where they weren't deprived of necessities but didn't have much else. His parents were pious people; they had their love for Jesus, each other and their three children. They often said, "God has blessed us with everything that matters. We have no need for anything more."

Based largely on news reports of arrests in bars, parks and restrooms, Reverend Phillips imagined homosexuals to be drowning in a life of degeneracy and sleaziness. The elegance of the home in which these two gay men lived surprised him.

The door leading to the kitchen opened and an attractive man with dark, short-cropped hair, large brown eyes, and a golden tan entered the living room. His coloring was in sharp contrast to Glen's blond hair, blue eyes and fair skin with its reddish flush. This had to be Keith Chamberlain, Glen's partner, Reverend Phillips realized. Glen was more handsome, but his partner had an athletic build and exuded a masculine presence that gave Reverend Phillips pause, *I would never imagine this man to be a homosexual.*

"Just doing some finishing touches on our dinner," Keith said. "Hope you like down-home cooking, because that's our menu for the evening: tomato-cucumber salad, thick-crust chicken pot pie, followed by a strawberry ice cream dessert. Not fancy, but Glen tells me it's not bad."

"He's being modest," Glen said. "My partner here is one of the world's best cooks. You're going to love his dinner. Now let me take your drink orders. Soft drinks or something with a bit more kick? Tell me what you'd like."

"Iced tea would be fine," Mrs. Phillips said, "for all of us. She smiled at Gentry and Jason." She had been holding a small wrapped package and handing it to Keith said, "I made two loaves of date-nut bread. It's my mother's recipe and I hope you'll like it."

"Thank you," Keith said.

"We'll love it!" Glen said.

Later as they were finishing dinner at the large mahogany dining table, Reverend Phillip leaned forward for the pitcher of iced tea to refill his glass, and observed that his son and Jason, who were seated across from him, were holding hands.

He froze as if in an out-of-body experience. *Did Mary know that the boys were holding hands? And if she did, was she all right with that?*

The conversation never stopped. Everyone was talking, especially about being gay: what it meant to be gay, how it felt to be gay. Then Gentry brought up the topic of gay marriage. "Do you think it will ever become legal in Texas?"

"It's going to happen," Jason said. "Once it became legal in Massachusetts, it's sure to spread."

"Not anytime soon," Keith said. "Not here in Texas. That's going to take a while."

"But if gay marriage becomes legal here, will you and Mr. McLean get married?" Gentry asked.

Keith and Glen looked at one another, and then as if planned, each held up his left hand with the gold commitment band. "In a sense, we are married," Glen said. "Not in a legal sense, perhaps, but in a spiritual one."

Mrs. Phillips smiled. "I think that's very sweet."

"How would you feel, Mom, if Jason and I said we would like to be married one day?"

Before his wife could respond, Reverend Phillips, who had been quiet, allowing others to speak, said, "I don't believe two men or two women should marry. Marriage is a religious rite meant only for a man and a woman. As a Baptist minister, I could not accept being told that I had to perform a marriage ceremony for two members of the same sex."

For a moment, no one spoke. Then Keith said, "I agree with you. No church group should be required to marry two persons of the same sex, if that violates their religious teachings. But there's another dimension to marriage that has to do with hundreds of legal rights including issues as important as inheritance and medical decisions, which have nothing to do with religion. How do you feel about that?"

"I'd feel better if they didn't use the term marriage." Reverend Phillips said.

Mrs. Phillips looked at her son. "To me, the term marriage stands for a full commitment that one person makes to another, to love each other and spend their lives together in support of each other. It has a special meaning that no other word has, and I can understand why gay people would want to have their relationships honored with that term."

Reverend Phillips turned to his wife who was seated beside him. "I believe you are forgetting that the central purpose of marriage is procreation. People marry to have children, and that is something gay people cannot do."

Glen and Keith glanced at each other. Then Glen said, "In all due respect, may I point out that many heterosexual people marry with no intent to have children. Think of older couples, for example. And there are many gay couples today who are having children by adoption or procedures at fertility clinics."

He hesitated, then said, "Two months ago, our son was born, and the little guy has become the center of our lives." He looked at Keith who was seated at the opposite end of the table. "We're a family and I can't think of anything more important—and exciting—than having a child to nurture and love."

****

Later that evening, lying beside each other in bed, Mary Phillips said, "I was impressed by those two appealing men. They seem so supportive of each other—caring and loving. I hope Gentry can have a life like theirs."

Revered Phillips was silent.

"Everett, tell me what's bothering you. You haven't said two words since we came home."

He sighed. "Mary, I saw Gentry and Jason holding hands at the table. Were you aware that they were holding hands?"

"I was," she said simply.

"That disturbs me greatly. They plan to live together when Gentry goes to Austin in January and . . ." He stopped unwilling to say what he was thinking.

"They are two gay men in love. Why wouldn't they hold hands? Why wouldn't they want to be together?"

"It's wrong. I'm trying, but I'm just not comfortable with the thought of my son with another man."

"The Bible tells of David and Jonathan's love for each other. It says they kissed. Don't you imagine David and Jonathan might also have held hands—and more?"

Reverend Phillips remained silent.

"Everett, I know this is difficult for you, but we must love and accept our son as he is, not as you would want him to be. If we—you—can't do that, then I fear one day the distance between Gentry and us will become too great to be bridged. He will not be a part of our lives. I don't want that to happen." Her tone became more firm, "I won't allow that to happen."

"How did you feel about Glen saying he is a father?" Reverend Phillips said. "Do you think it's acceptable for two gay men to raise a child?"

"What if one of those gay men was your son, and their child would be your grandchild? Would you still have a problem?"

Reverend Phillips was silent. Then with a self-deprecating shrug, he admitted, "When it becomes personal, the problem does seem to lessen somewhat, doesn't it?" He smiled, taking his wife's hand in his. "I would love to have a grandchild."

"So would I!" Mary said. "It would bring us so much happiness. I can't imagine anything more fulfilling then to have a grandbaby to love."

Then, reaching out to hug her husband, she said, "Everett, we're going to work this out. You'll come to terms with Gentry's being gay. This is God's doing. It's His plan for us and it will be for the good."

Chapter Seventeen

Katie was upset. Glen could see by her reddened eyes that she'd been crying.

He panicked, not knowing what to think. *Was something wrong with the baby? With Katie? What?*

Glen took her in his arms. "What's wrong? Please tell me."

Katie shook her head, as she led him over to the sofa. "Everything is all right. This is all so silly . . . just nonsense, and I'm sorry that I let it get to me."

"Where's the baby?" he asked, still concerned that there might be a problem.

"He's asleep. He'll be up soon for his feeding. The baby's fine."

"Okay, if everything's all right, tell me why you're crying." He placed his hand on her shoulder.

Katie brushed at her eyes. "It's all so silly! I'm embarrassed that I let Aunt Molly get to me like that. It's my own fault. I never should have told her."

"What did you tell her?" Glen relaxed . . . nothing to be alarmed about, just another Aunt Molly moment.

"We were talking on the phone, and I told her we were planning to have the baby baptized next week when your mother came to visit." Katie shook her head. "I don't know what I was thinking. I should have known better.

"Aunt Molly didn't understand. 'He's an infant? No one baptizes infants. He has to have faith. He has to accept Jesus as his savior before he's baptized.'"

Katie sighed. "I told her, 'That's what Protestants believe, but Catholics believe that infants need to be baptized to ensure salvation, should anything happen.'

"'Since when do you care what Catholics believe?' Aunt Molly said.

"'I really don't,' I told her. 'But Glen is Catholic and his mother feels strongly that the baby must be baptized as a Catholic.'

"There was a long silence on the phone and then Aunt Molly exploded. What an outburst! What was I thinking? My grandmother Collins would turn over in her grave! My father would be shamed for eternity! What would people at the First Baptist Church think? A relative of hers raised a Catholic? She could never show her face at church again!

"She went from screaming about me to yelling about you. 'Not only gay, but a Catholic! Glen McLean ain't even the real father!' It wouldn't stop. She worked herself into a full blown hissy-fit and slammed the phone down."

"Katie, honey, it's not that big a deal to me," Glen said softly. "It's something my mother wants and . . ."

Katie took his hand. "Do you mean that? You wouldn't think it too awful, if we didn't, even after I told you we would? And you asked your mother to fly here for the baptism?"

"Yes, I mean it. I don't want you to be crying over that."

Katie's eyes filled. "You are the sweetest man in the whole world." She took a deep breath, "I was so upset and guilt-ridden, I caved. I called Aunt Molly back and gave in. I promised I wouldn't allow my baby to be baptized in the Catholic faith."

Katie tried to smile, "I didn't know how to tell you, and that's why I was crying."

"It's not a problem for me. As for my mother, that's another matter. I'll call her and explain that Katie has a bigoted aunt who threatened to commit suicide if a member of her family was baptized Catholic. I'm sure my mother will understand."

Glen and Katie looked at each other. Then like two guilty children, they began to plot their plans for next weekend so that Aunt Molly and his mom would not meet.

****

"Mom! Over here! "Glen waved to his mother as she exited through the revolving doorway from the American Airlines arrival gates.

She walked quickly toward him, her face lit with pleasure. "Oh it's been so long! Too long. Can't imagine that I haven't seen you since last Thanksgiving. My goodness, you are so handsome!"

Glen hugged his Mom. Then stepped back to get a better look. "Mom, you look great! No one would ever guess you have two sons in their 30s."

"Oh, you're just saying that," she said, but all the same she flushed with pleasure. Mrs. McLean was an attractive woman, expensively dressed and immaculately groomed. Her hair, a becoming silver-gray, was fashionably cut and neatly combed. Glen noticed that she had put on a few pounds, but knowing his mother, knew better than to mention that.

"Let's get your bags and we'll be on our way." He looked at his watch. It was 2 p.m. and Keith, who as usual had been at the office that Saturday morning, would now be at home waiting for them.

"First, we'll go by the house so that you can meet Keith and spend some time with him. He's really looking forward to meeting you. Then later, we'll go over to Katie's for an hour or two, so that you can meet her and be with the baby."

"I'm going to be here for such a short time, just through tomorrow," his mother said. "I really would like to spend as much time as possible with Katie and the baby. Can't we go to Katie's home first?"

"If that's what you want," Glen said. "I'm sure it will be all right. I'll call Keith and Katie and let them know." He had assumed that his mother would be anxious to meet Keith—his partner for more than four years—and see their home. But, well, turned out he was wrong.

"He's adorable," Mrs. McLean gushed. "What a sweetheart! May I?" She reached out to take the baby from Katie's arms.

"Oh, yes, I'm your Nana," She cooed. "I'm the one who's going to spoil you. Yes, I am." She laughed. "See how he's looking at me?"

Little Glen was staring at her, with uncertainty in his hazel eyes. He looked as if he were about to cry, but surprisingly, he relaxed instead, a contented look on his face.

Mrs. McLean flushed with pleasure. "Oh, he is so darling! And so intelligent! Look at the way he's studying me!"

"Do you remember how Glen looked as a baby?" Katie asked.

"It's hard to remember exactly, but I brought Glen's baby pictures." She turned to Glen, "Please get my rolling bag from the car. There are some things I want to get from it."

When Glen returned, he found his mother seated on the sofa, beside Katie, the baby still in her arms. "Glen, honey, open my rolling bag and take out the manila envelope . . . it's on top. "Yes, that's it. Your baby pictures are in it."

Glen handed the photos to Katie who studied the large one, an 8" x 10", and said, "I do think there's a resemblance. Look at the ears and of course the cleft in his chin. Yes, I see a resemblance."

Mrs. McLean leaned toward Katie. She smiled. "I always thought my Glen was the best looking baby ever . . . but not anymore." She pursed her lips and kissed the baby's cheek. "This little one is the sweetest and best looking baby I've ever seen. So adorable!" She looked at Katie. "He has your hazel eyes."

Katie beamed. "Your mother is so sweet!" Then she said, "Tell me what to call you. Mrs. McLean seems so stiff and formal." She hesitated, "I could call you Mom, if that would be comfortable for you, or grandma. Tell me."

"I would love to have you call me Mom one day. But perhaps for now Nana would be better. That's what my older son's wife and their children call me."

Then she said, wistfully, "I know Glen is so fond of you. He's told me that many times, and being with you, I can see why. You are lovely. I just wish that circumstances were such that the two of you could marry." She sighed, "For the baby's sake."

"I wish we could too," Katie said. "In my perfect world, there would be Glen, our baby and me, but I can't risk changing medical policies at this time. I have to stay married to keep the policy in effect."

"Maybe in the future," Mrs. McLean said. "Once you're married, I would love for you to call me Mom."

Glen started to say there were other significant issues, like his being gay and in a committed relationship. But his mother and Katie seemed to be bonding and so happy with each other, he just let it pass.

Then his mother pointed at the rolling bag. "Glen, honey, please take out the paper bag. I have gifts for the baby and for Katie."

Inside the bag was a gift-wrapped box with a pair of blue pajamas. "Glen had a pair like this when he was a baby with Snow White and the Seven Dwarfs. I just loved those pajamas and when I saw this pair, I couldn't resist buying it."

Then she reached into the bag and removed a small box. "This is for you. It was a gift from my mother. She gave it to me when Glen was born and I want you to have it."

Katie opened the box and saw the gold chain and locket. She clicked open the locket and saw two tiny photos: baby Glen and grown-up Glen.

Katie started to cry. "I can't imagine a more wonderful and thoughtful gift." She turned to hug Glen's mom.

****

As they drove across town to his home, his mother said, "It just breaks my heart to think what that poor girl is going through. She is so lovely and to think she's dealing with such a terrible disease." She shook her head, "I just hope those treatments are working. I'm going to add her to my prayer list and light a candle next week at church."

Glen remained silent. His optimism that all would be fine, that the cancer could be controlled, was lessening. With each passing week, he saw Katie losing vitality and the pain in her back increasing. He had told his mother about the cancer before her arrival, but put a positive spin on the effectiveness of the treatments that he was now beginning to doubt.

"Do you know what I was thinking?" his mother said. "It would be wonderful if Katie and the baby would be with you when you came home at the end of the month for Thanksgiving." She added quickly, "Dad and I would pay for the plane tickets, of course."

Glen remained silent, as he thought, *What about my partner? What about him?* In the four years of their relationship, Keith had never been invited to join them over Thanksgiving or any other time.

"Please ask her. Tell Katie we would love to have her and the baby with us. That would be so wonderful." Then, as if the thought had just come to her, "I could talk to Father Herndon and if Katie was comfortable with it, we could have the baby baptized in our church Friday morning after Thanksgiving Day. Your brother and his wife could stand up as godparents. I know they would love that. Oh, wouldn't that be wonderful! Little Glen Thomas would be baptized in the very same church where you and Geoffrey were baptized!"

Glen looked straight ahead. Instead of responding to her comments, he said, "We're almost home. Keith has been cooking all day to make a special dinner for you. I know he's looking forward to meeting you, and I hope you're looking forward to meeting him." Trying to keep the hurt from showing, he said. "We've been together over four years—four wonderful years that have been the happiest of my life. It's time that you come to know him."

Home for the Thanksgiving holiday four years before, Glen had told his mother he was gay. That was the reason he took a teaching position in Texas, he said, so that he could find himself—be true to who he really was. On some intuitive level, she had already suspected—feared, actually—that he might be gay. Still, even after four years, she remained in a state of hopeful denial: it was just a phase and with time would pass.

During that visit, Glen had told her he intended to tell the family, but she asked him not to. "Let's not ruin our Thanksgiving holiday. I'll tell them later." She did tell her husband, but no one else. She just couldn't bring herself to do that. "What's the point?" she told Glen when later they spoke on the phone. "It's not as if you're living here in Albany and they need to know."

Trying to be upbeat, as he parked his car at the curb of their home, Glen said, "Well, we're about to experience a historic moment—the meeting of my mom and my partner. I'm excited and hope you are too."

Mrs. McLean smiled as if she was looking forward to the meeting, but that was not the case. She was definitely not looking forward to meeting Glen's friend—she still couldn't think of him as a partner, a lover. However, she did intend to be cordial for Glen's sake and because she knew that was the right thing for her to do.

"My goodness," she said as they stepped on the walkway, "I had no idea you were living in such a grand home!"

"Wait 'til you see it inside. It's a work of art. It was built by Keith's great-grandfather in 1906. I know from those two years I worked in Dad's lumber yard, the heart pine used in the hallway would cost a fortune today, if you could even find it. Come, let's go meet your future son-in-law."

Future son-in-law? She assumed Glen was being flippant. Nevertheless, his comment did not sit well.

Keith and Glen hugged in greeting and lightly kissed on the lips. Keith smiled at her and reached out as if to hug her as well. "Welcome! I've been looking forward to meeting you."

Mrs. McLean quickly extended her hand to avoid an embrace. "I have been looking forward to meeting you as well." She had intended her words to sound gracious and warm, but Glen and Keith's embrace upset her. Why were they intentionally pushing their relationship in her face? It was uncalled for and her words came out stiff and formal.

Later at the dinner table, Mrs. McLean took the last bite of the glazed salmon that Keith had prepared. She had had several glasses of chardonnay, far more than she was accustomed to drinking, and a comfortable glow had replaced her earlier angst.

"That was delicious. Glen has high praises for your cooking, and I have to agree. Thank you."

Relaxed by the wine and the soft glow from the rock crystal chandelier highlighting the dining room's elegance, she allowed herself for the moment to admire the intelligent and attractive man Glen had chosen for his partner. If she had a daughter, Mrs. McLean would have been so pleased to have her bring home a man like Keith—a successful attorney from a prominent family. Unfortunately, the relationship was with her son.

Glen was the joy of her life. He was so handsome, and kind and sweet. People had said, "Just wait until your boys become teenagers, then you'll know what upset is all about." And it was true with her older son, Geoff—so many sleepless nights worrying about Geoff, out late with the family car and carrying on with girls. But never a problem with Glen—so intelligent and thoughtful, always there to please. And then to learn he was homosexual. It was a blow that still had her reeling.

Later that evening, Glen and his mom went up the stairs for her to see the baby's room once again. She had been delighted by the cartoon cut-outs on the wall, especially the ones of Snow White and the Seven Dwarfs.

"They're like those on your baby pajamas. I love them!" she said. "And I love you and Katie for having that adorable grandchild for me to love and spoil. Your dad was so sorry he couldn't get away from the business. Do you think there's a chance that Katie and the baby will come with you for Thanksgiving? That would make your dad so happy!"

"Mom, Katie wouldn't be able to make the trip. It would be too much for her. What if I talk Keith into coming with me? Dad has never met him and . . ."

Glen saw the frown on his mother's face and stopped.

****

Glen and his mother had spent Sunday morning at Katie's home with the baby.

"I just love your son! I know you must be so proud of him," his mother said as he drove her to the Dallas airport. "Now make sure you take lots of pictures and send them to me."

"Count on it," Glen said.

"And Katie is a darling! I just pray this terrible ordeal she's going through will be in her past. You hear so many stories of women overcoming breast cancer. The important thing is to catch it early."

"Right," Glen said. He didn't want to tell her that it wasn't caught early and that it was a very aggressive form of cancer. *Why worry her?*

"Have you booked your flight for Thanksgiving? You don't want to wait as the planes get very full around the holiday."

"No, I haven't booked it," Glen said. He had been up most of the night, stewing over his mother's negative response to having Keith come with him.

"But you need to," she said. "You can't wait to the last minute at this time of year."

"I may have a problem coming up for Thanksgiving."

"I don't understand. You always come home for Thanksgiving. The whole family will be with us: your brother, his wife and children. Your uncle and aunt and your cousins. They'd be so disappointed if you weren't there."

"I got the feeling last evening that my partner wouldn't be welcome."

"Wouldn't Keith want to be with his own family for the Thanksgiving holiday?" she asked.

"I am his family, just as he's mine. We're committed to each other and intend to be together on the holidays."

His mother was quiet for a moment as she considered his comment. "Why do you feel it's necessary to force your gay relationship on other people?"

"And how exactly do I do that?" Glen asked, his eyes focused on the highway.

"Hugging and kissing Keith in front of me!" she said. "Do you really think I needed to see that?"

"Do you mean yesterday when we arrived home?" His hands tightened on the steering wheel.

"Yes, that's exactly what I mean and I resented it."

His mother's dismissal of their relationship hurt. Keith was the center of his life: their love the foundation for his feelings of well-being and hopes for the future. Yet his mother dismissed it as an affront, a relationship unworthy of her consideration. Glen was upset and angry and he allowed his feelings to show.

"Seems to me I've watched you and Dad embrace and kiss many times. Were you trying to force your heterosexual relationship on me? Not only that, you're living together, sharing a bed together, having children. Should I have seen that as you forcing your relationship on me?"

Mrs. McLean took a deep breath. "Don't compare your relationship with Keith to the marriage I have with your father. My marriage has the blessing of the Church. Yours . . ." she stopped.

"In any event, there are members of our family who are not comfortable with gay people and their relationships. I cannot allow you to bring Keith into our home and force your being gay on family members."

They drove in silence for several moments.

"So when are you going to book your flight?" his mother asked.

"I'm going to spend Thanksgiving with Keith and his family. If they should see Keith and me hold hands, even embrace, they won't think we're forcing our gay relationship on them. Keith's mother will see it as something two people in love do."

Mrs. McLean sighed. "Glen, I love you with all my heart. I didn't mean to offend you or say something that would hurt you."

"But you did, Mom. I've struggled to rid myself of the guilt and shame I'd internalized about being gay. Those bad feelings came from the church, I know, but I realize now they also came from people like you, who claim to love me, but don't—not as I really am."

His mother started to cry. "I do love you. Don't ever say that I don't!"

"It's been four years since I told you I was gay. I knew it would be a struggle for you to accept, just as it was for me. But I'm winning that struggle. I'm in a loving relationship with an outstanding man. It's a quality relationship—a moral relationship—and at last, I'm feeling good about myself.

"Mom, I love you very much and I love Dad too. But I can't spend time with people who are ashamed of me and the loving relationship that I'm so happy to be in." He reached for his mother's hand to soften the sting. "I won't be coming home for Thanksgiving."

****

It was just a bit past 4 p.m., when Glen pressed the doorbell to Katie's home. He waited and when she didn't open the front door, he took out his key and opened it himself.

"Oh, I'm sorry," Katie said as she entered the living room from the narrow hallway, leading to her bedroom. She was in her bathrobe and Glen suspected she hadn't dressed that day. "I'm just so tired all the time. I guess I fell asleep."

"Is the baby up?" Glen asked.

"I think I heard him stirring. Will you fix his bottle while I change him?"

"Yes, of course," Glen said. He watched Katie as she walked slowly from the room and realized she was in pain. Saturday afternoon and

Sunday morning when his mother had been there, she never let on. But she had to have been in pain, just wouldn't admit it.

"Look at him!" Glen laughed. "Three months is such a wonderful age! Look how excited he gets when he sees me." He took the baby from Katie and hugged him. "Yes, I love you too, and get just as excited when I see you. I just don't flail my arms and legs up and down because I'm a grown up. Otherwise I would."

Katie started to laugh, then winced instead.

"It's getting worse, isn't it?" Glen said.

"Maybe a little."

They sat beside each other on the sofa as Glen held the bottle to the baby's lips. For several moments neither spoke. Then Katie loosened her robe so that Glen could see the locket on its gold chain on her neck. "I love this locket and the little photos of you. I look at them and think how fortunate I am to have you and Little Glen in my life. If only . . ." She looked at Glen as the tears welled in her eyes. "I want to be wearing it when I'm . . ."

"Don't say it! Don't even think it!" Glen stopped her. "You're going to be well . . . you're going to beat this."

Katie shook her head. "Maybe not. I spoke to the oncologist this morning. He had just received the latest test results and . . . they're not good. The cancer is spreading."

"Isn't there something else they can do? A different treatment? Maybe you need to see another doctor. What about surgery?"

Katie placed her hand on his lips. "Let's talk about something else. Like your mother's visit. She is such a lovely woman! That she would give me this locket that her mother gave to her . . . that was so special.

"Your mother just loved being with little Glen! I imagine it brought back memories for her when you were her little baby. And she could hold you and love you, just as I hold and love my own little Glen."

Katie smiled at Glen as she brushed his cheek with her hand. "I was so pleased that your mother liked me. She took me aside Sunday morning and asked if there was any possibility for the baby and me to be with you when you visited them for the Thanksgiving holidays. Wasn't that sweet of her?"

Glen nodded. "She thinks you're wonderful. It would have made her so happy if I had grown up to be straight and found a wonderful girl like you to marry. That would be her perfect world: two sons, each married to a lovely woman . . . each providing her with grandchildren for her to love and spoil and show off to her family and friends and acquaintances at church." His voice broke. "Unfortunately, she wound up with me."

Chapter Eighteen

Keith had changed from his business suit into gym shorts and T-shirt.

"So where's my martini with two olives?" he asked, walking into the living room. "I've been home from the office for almost 10 minutes and I've had nothing to drink. Are you one of those slowpoke bartenders?"

With a twinkle in his eyes, Glen said. "Let me help you overcome your impatience for that martini with two olives. Close your eyes and visualize Mr. Universe standing in front of you buck naked, just lusting to hold you in his muscular arms and perform those titillating deeds you've only read about in porn magazines. Use all your imaginative powers to throw yourself wholeheartedly into that scene: breathe in, breathe out. Exciting . . . so exciting! Greatest sex ever! You're building toward a world-shattering climax . . . you're almost there . . . so close. Stop! I hand you your drink, and you wish I hadn't been so fast."

Keith shook his head. "How in the world did an intelligent attorney like me wind up with a bona fide clown like you?"

"Some things can't be explained. Just accept your good fortune and leave it at that," Glen laughed. "Anyway, I'll fix your drink and a glass of cabernet for me." He poked playfully at Keith's belly as he walked by him to the bar. He started to say something about Katie, but decided not to. Not now. Keith looked forward to this together time as much as he, and Glen didn't want to dampen the good feelings. He would talk it over with Keith later that evening, after dinner.

Glen returned with a martini for Keith and glass of cabernet for himself. Taking Keith's hand, he guided him to the sofa. "How would it be if I went with you to Austin to be with your mom and her family for Thanksgiving?"

Keith took a sip of his drink. "Are you serious?"

"Yes."

"That would be wonderful!" Keith said. "Mom would be thrilled."

"Are you sure it's all right?" Glen said. "You've told me that Thanksgiving dinner is a big production for her. There are relatives and friends. Please call her and check to see if she has any reservations."

"Glen, Mom would love you to be with us. She thinks you hung the moon. I've heard her tell friends that not only are you Hollywood handsome, you're the sweetest, most thoughtful person ever. She couldn't have picked a finer partner for me."

"I like that," Glen said. "You need to tell me that more often." He leaned forward to kiss Keith. "You know, your mom is the real reason I stay with you."

"Is that so? I believe it has more to do with my animal magnetism and the sexual rush you get when I'm near you."

"Well, there's a little truth to that—very little." Glen laughed, and then his cell phone rang.

Glen flipped the phone open. It was his dad.

"Hi, Dad, is everything all right?"

"We're fine. No problem exactly—except you really upset your mother by saying you're not coming up for Thanksgiving."

This was not a conversation Glen wanted to have, especially in Keith's presence. "Hold on a second, Dad." He left the sofa and headed for the front door. He preferred to talk this over in the privacy of the porch.

"Did Mom tell you why I'm not coming?"

"Because you wanted to bring your friend."

Glen sighed. "Dad, I'm so sorry that . . ."

"Son, I don't want you to be sorry. I just want you to come. Your mom and I love you. Thanksgiving just wouldn't be right if you weren't here."

"Dad, the last thing I want to do is upset you or Mom." This was going to be a difficult conversation, but Glen was determined not to give in.

"So don't," his father said. "I've already called American Airlines and reserved a seat for you. They'll hold it for 24 hours. Just tell me you're coming and I'll confirm the reservation and pay for it. How does that sound?"

"It sounds like you're the same wonderful Dad you've always been. Always there to smooth things over, make everything right."

"So you're coming," his father said. "Your mother will be very happy to hear that. You know she loves you very much."

"If I believed that Mom loves and accepts me as I am—a gay man with a partner that I love—I'd be with you for Thanksgiving. But I know my being gay is an embarrassment for her and you. And that's why I'm not coming."

"Glen, don't say that!" his father spoke sharply. "Your mom and I are very proud of you!"

Glen cleared his throat. "Proud of me as I am? As a man who loves another man and has lived with him for four years? Do you think Mom would be proud for the relatives at her Thanksgiving dinner table to learn that her wonderful son is gay and living with another man?"

He heard his father sigh. "Glen, we're trying. It hasn't been easy, but we're getting there. We're just not there yet."

"Dad, if it hasn't been easy for you, what do you think it's been like for me? After all, it's not about Mom and you. It's about me, my life, not yours.

"For so many years I feared that because I was gay, I'd never have the loving relationship that straight people have. That's the message society gave me, but it isn't true. I'm living a moral and ethical life as an openly gay man with a partner whom I respect and love. I take great pride in that accomplishment and in him. Keith has brought great joy to my life that I want to share with the people I love. Do you think that's wrong?"

"No, I don't think it's wrong," his father said. "We just need a little more time—but we'll get there. I promise you. We'll get there." He paused and Glen sensed his father was crying. "I'll tell your mother you won't be joining us this Thanksgiving."

****

After dinner, as Keith and he were finishing their coffee at the small table in the alcove off the kitchen, Glen said, "Katie had a bad report from the oncologist. The treatment isn't working. The cancer is spreading."

"I was afraid of that," Keith said. "She looked so pale and thin when she was here for dinner last Sunday. I was worried then, but I didn't want to say anything that might upset you. Then you told me she was experiencing back pain and I knew—she's in trouble, bad trouble."

"I'm trying to figure out what needs to be done." Glen shook his head.

"We could ask her to move in with us." Keith offered. She and the baby could be in the room next to ours where we would hear them at night if there's a problem. We could also hire a nurse's aide to be with her during the day when we're at work. Would she be open to that?"

"Not really," Glen said. "I don't think she'd be willing to leave her home. She's comfortable there and she does have relatives to be with her, if she needs help. She has an aunt who's like a mother to her and her cousin Chrissie. They'll be there for her and the baby."

"Did the doctor say anything about how long . . ." He stopped. "I'm sorry. It's just we need to start thinking about the baby. Someone will need to be with him during the day when we're at work. I can ask around at the office. Some of the secretaries take their babies to daycare."

Glen was shaking his head. "We would need to ask her Aunt Molly about staying with the baby. She's not my favorite. Actually, I think she's a bigoted old biddy, but Katie tells me she loves the baby and is wonderful with him. Katie would want her aunt to be the one who watches him during the day."

"If there's any problem," Keith said, "I could ask my mom to cover for us until we get things worked out. She'd be here in a heartbeat. We could talk it over with her during Thanksgiving when we're in Austin."

For several moments, they quietly sipped their coffee. They looked at one another, but said nothing—what was there to say? Glen reached for Keith's hand.

Keith ended the silence, "You looked kind of upset when you came in from talking to your dad. Was there a problem?"

"Not a problem really. They were disappointed about my not coming up for Thanksgiving. But Dad understood that this year I would be with my partner and his family. I'd like to think that maybe next year we can plan to be with them."

****

The week following Thanksgiving, Glen's mom called as he had anticipated she might. "Just wanted you to know we're leaving tomorrow for our month in Florida."

His parents had been renting the same condo in Sarasota for a number of years. His mother had already told him the date they would be leaving. He knew that wasn't the reason for her call.

"How is the baby? He's so adorable!" she said.

"The baby's fine. Looks like he's getting ready to crawl. He lifts his chest up and does a rocking movement. I just love watching that little guy."

"And Katie? How is she doing?"

"Not so good. She's having a hard time."

"I'm so sorry. Please tell her I asked about her. She's such a lovely person."

"That locket you gave her. She wears it all the time. She was very touched by your gift."

There was a long pause. "Mom, are you still there?" Glen asked.

"How was your Thanksgiving?" she replied in a casual manner, almost as an afterthought. That was the purpose of her call, he knew.

"Great! Wonderful Thanksgiving! I went with Keith to his mom's home in Austin."

"Oh, it was you and Keith and his mother?"

"No, there were a number of people: relatives and friends. A big gathering."

"Oh, you certainly were missed here." Then as if changing the topic, she said, "Do you remember Mrs. Newbury—oh, probably not—but anyway, one of her daughters is a lawyer in New York City. She came with her mother to the Thanksgiving Service at our church. A lovely girl. She had her partner with her and their two small children."

"Yes?" Glen didn't know where she was going with this.

"Her partner is a woman, a lovely woman," Mrs. McLean said, "People seemed to like her. I heard several positive comments and I saw Father Herndon shake their hands."

Glen smiled. His mother was coming around. He waited for her to continue.

"Does Keith always spend the Thanksgiving holiday with his mother and her family?"

"Either Thanksgiving or Christmas." Glen said and his smile grew even wider.

"Do you think he might be open to be with us next Thanksgiving?"

"I'll ask Keith," Glen said. If his mother had been with him, he would have hugged her.

"Please do. Well, I just wanted you to know we're leaving for Florida tomorrow, and we'll be there for a month.

"I appreciate your letting me know," Glen said. "And by the way, I love you very much."

"I love you too," she said. "Very much."

****

It was unusually cold that mid-December day with light snow flurries falling outside. Katie was in bed, with Glen seated in a chair beside the bed. The hospice nurse had left the room to give them privacy.

"I love you, Katie. You're the special lady in my life and . . ." his voice grew thick with emotion.

Katie reached for his hand. "I know you love me and I love you. We have a spiritual bond that can't be broken." She tried to smile. "Some people don't believe in love at first sight. I do because I've loved you from the first time I saw you.

"It won't be long now and I'll be with Jesus," she said, "and in time you and the baby will join me there. We'll be together for eternity in heaven. That's what my faith teaches and I find that so comforting."

Respecting Katie's need, Glen reassured her. "Yes, we'll be together and then later our baby will join us, and that will be wonderful. It will be the three of us together for eternity."

"Glen, you'll always be there for the baby. I know you will. And you can count on Aunt Molly. She loves him and is wonderful with him. My cousin Chrissie too. They love our baby as if he were their own.

"Did you know that I have a will? A close friend of Aunt Molly's is an attorney. They came here last evening and I drew up a will. I don't have much—this house and a few thousand dollars—but I want it put in trust for the baby so that when he goes to college, the money will be there for him.

"Aunt Molly has agreed to be the executor. I know she'll do right for little Glen." Her voice grew low as if it were difficult for her to speak.

"You look tired and I think you need to get some sleep," Glen said. "It may be a good idea that I take the baby home with me."

Katie shook her head. "I want him to be with me. I need to hold him close as much as I can. Don't worry. The nurse is here and Aunt Molly will be over soon. The baby will be fine."

"All right . . . I'll leave now." He leaned forward to kiss her. "Remember, someone can call me at any time. Okay?" He looked at her drawn and pale face, recognizing that despite the morphine, she was still in pain. It wouldn't be long now and her suffering would be ended.

"Oh, I have something for you. She reached under her pillow and took out a small pink envelope. "There's a note inside. Something I wanted you to know and keep until we're together once again."

Sitting in his car, outside Katie's home, Glen opened the envelope and read the note:

My dearest Glen,

In my perfect world it would be you and me and our baby. That will not happen here on Earth. But perfect can happen in heaven. There will come a day, I know, when the three of us will be together for eternity with Jesus. Until then, I will count on you to love and nurture our little guy. Never forget how much your Katie loves her two men.

Yours always,

Katie

Glen folded the note neatly and placed it carefully back in the pink envelope. He blinked his eyes, then lowered his head and cried.

Chapter Nineteen

Molly Collins stood outside the security area at the Dallas airport, waiting for David Gordon, Katie's estranged husband, to emerge. She had taken a photo from Katie's album to help identify him. They had met only once at Katie's wedding, and with the passage of time, she wasn't sure she would remember him.

A tall, lanky man with dark, wavy hair came through the exit and Molly moved toward him.

"David? You're David Gordon, ain't you?"

"Yes. You must be the Aunt Molly that Katie called each week." He paused. "I'm so sorry. I don't know what to say."

"She's in a better place. Katie's with Jesus now."

David nodded without comment. "It is very thoughtful of you to meet me. I was planning to rent a car and drive to Edgemont. I believe the funeral service is at 2 p.m."

"Yes, 2 p.m. and Reverend Phillips, our minister, is a stickler for starting on time. Come, my car is outside in the parking lot. It's about an hour's drive to Edgemont, and that's good 'cause we have a whole lot to talk about."

"Now I'm going to tell you like it is 'cause I'm no jabbering old woman dancing about the square instead of speaking the truth, plain and simple. You're the baby's daddy. No ifs, ands or buts." She glanced his way to check his reaction as she drove down the four lane highway.

"What?" David Gordon looked stunned. "Katie told me the father was that close friend of hers. I believe his name is Glen. She had a procedure at a fertility clinic using his sperm. That's what she told me."

"That's what she wanted you to think, but it ain't the truth," Molly said. "Katie told me everything—that you didn't want no other child. You said she should have an abortion if she was pregnant by you—that's what Katie told me."

David looked embarrassed. "She said that?"

Molly nodded. "Me and Katie was real close. I was like her mother and there was nothing she didn't tell me."

"That was a cruel thing for me to say. I know it ended our marriage." He shook his head. "I'm sorry about that. But at my age, the last thing I need is to be responsible for another child."

"Well, don't worry none, I'm not going to lay responsibility for this baby on you. My Katie was a real proud woman. She said, he didn't want no responsibility for a baby and I'm not gonna put that on him. So she made up that cock-n-bull story about the fertility clinic to make you believe you ain't the daddy."

"I thought her friend wanted the baby," David sounded concerned. "Katie told me he was thrilled to be the baby's father. Has he changed his mind?"

"We don't need to pay no mind to what he thinks. We only need to do what's right for the baby. A boy being raised by a homosexual man? Think about that. Nobody with a lick of sense would want that to happen!" Molly said. "If Katie had any notion she was going to pass so young, she'd never have made up that story about Glen McLean being the daddy."

"Katie always spoke so highly of him. I thought she wanted him to take care of the baby if anything happened to her. That's what she told me."

"Only because she never wanted you to think otherwise." She lowered her voice as if telling a secret. "Like I told you, me and Katie was real close. She told me things, she'd never tell nobody else. The night before she died, she told me what a mistake she'd made putting Glen McLean on the birth certificate. She was sick and in pain, but she didn't have nothing else on her mind. I promised her I would do something about it and I will." She looked meaningfully at David.

"My other niece, Chrissie Johnson—she was like a sister to Katie—is married to a real fine man who makes a good living. They've got two young girls who love the baby, and they want to adopt him. That's what Katie wanted. She told me so herself."

"Have you talked to Glen about this? Will this be all right with him?" David asked.

"Don't matter what he thinks," Molly said. "Alls we need to think about is what's right for Katie's baby—your baby—and what Katie wanted."

David didn't say anything as Molly continued, "When we get to Edgemont, we'll stop at the office of an old friend of mine. He's a real good lawyer who has some papers for you to sign. He'll have someone there with a kit to take a sample of your DNA to prove you're the daddy."

Molly glanced at David to see how he was reacting. He was looking straight ahead, a perplexed expression on his face. She couldn't tell what he was thinking.

"It's what Katie wanted," she said. Then, even stronger. "Katie made me promise that her baby would be raised by her cousin Chrissie and her husband. It's what Katie wanted," Molly repeated.

Then to cement her point, she added. "They'll pay for raising the baby. I'm the executor of Katie's will, and her house and the few dollars she had will be put in a trust for the baby's college. Everything will be taken care of. You ain't responsible for nothing. The papers you'll sign at the lawyer's office say that real clear and you'll never have to worry that somebody's gonna come after you for money."

"Will there be time to go there before the funeral service?" David asked.

Molly Collins took a deep breath. "Yeah, plenty of time."

****

Glen hadn't realized how beloved and respected Katie had been until the funeral service. The chapel was packed with relatives, friends and former students. Large bouquets of flowers bordered the pulpit.

Reverend Phillips, who had officiated at the service, saw Glen and sought him out through the mass of people milling about after the service.

"Such a shame that a fine woman like Katie Collins would die so young. You know, she leaves behind a baby . . . an infant." He shook his head. "That is so sad. Katie taught math at the high school before her marriage. Is that how you knew her?"

Glen nodded. "That's where we met. We became very close." He considered saying that he was the father of Katie's baby, but didn't. This wasn't the place or time to get into that, especially with people nearby waiting to speak to the minister.

"By the way, before Gentry leaves for college, my wife would like you and your partner to join us at our home for dinner. "I'll have Gentry call you, and I do want to thank you for helping us." He stopped, realizing people could be listening. "Gentry will call."

A cold drizzle was falling at the cemetery as the mourners were leaving. Glen saw David Gordon and started toward him. "David, do you remember me? I'm Glen McLean, Katie's friend. It was so thoughtful of you to come."

David brushed him off. "Can't talk. I have a taxi waiting to take me to the airport."

Glen watched him as he walked away. *That's strange. He'd always been so friendly when I visited. Is he angry about something? The baby?*

Glen looked around for Katie's aunt. A friend of hers was minding the baby at Katie's house, and he thought Molly should be with him when he came for the baby. He didn't see her. Apparently, she had already left.

There were three cars parked in front of Katie's house. He recognized the white Chevy Malibu as Molly's, and assumed another would be the friend's, but who else was here?

The front door was unlocked and Glen let himself in. There was a woman standing beside Molly as well as an older man. No one smiled or said anything in greeting.

Feeling the tension in the room, Glen simply nodded and started toward the bedroom to get the baby. "I'm just going to get the baby and leave."

"Not so fast," the older man said. "I'm Ms. Collins' attorney and I have some papers for you to sign."

"Excuse me? Papers for me to sign? What papers?"

"Christine Johnson and her husband Jerry are planning to adopt Katie's baby. These papers are your acceptance of their adoption. They'll release you of all financial responsibility for the upbringing of the child."

"Is this a joke?" Glen said. "I'm going to get my baby and leave. He walked quickly to the bedroom and found it empty. The crib and bassinet were gone and so was the baby.

"Where's my baby?" He looked directly at Molly.

"He ain't your baby!" She stated flatly. "The baby's daddy is David Gordon and he's signed over his rights to Chrissie and Jerry. They have the baby. The documents are signed and witnessed." She looked at the lawyer. "Tell him that he ain't got no claim to the baby."

"That's right," the lawyer said. "The baby's father has approved the adoption. Now if you'll just sign these papers the matter can be settled without a problem. He pointed to the woman that Glen didn't know, "Sheila and I can serve as witnesses."

"Are you aware that my name is on the birth certificate as the father?" His voice was tight and Glen could hear his heart pounding.

"That's just a formality. The night before she died, Katie told Molly that her husband was the father, not you. The story about the fertility clinic and using your sperm was just that—a made up tale. She never went there.

"We've taken DNA samples from David Gordon and the baby. The test results will prove David Gordon is the baby's father, meaning you have no legal claim to the baby. Waiting for the results will just delay things for a few days, but the outcome will be the same."

The lawyer held out the papers. "You can make it easy for all of us, if you just sign these papers."

Glen's eyes locked on Molly Collins and he saw in her belligerent stance—hands on hips and tight-set lips—the look of bigotry unfettered.

Without a word, Glen turned and left the house.

****

Glen was so agitated, his words tumbling out in a torrent, that Keith listening on his office phone couldn't understand what he was saying.

"Slow down—I'm not following you," Glen was over-wrought. He kept repeating, "They have my baby! They have my baby!"

"Okay, calm down. Just calm down. I'm going to handle this." Keith stood up at his desk. "Now repeat everything, but slowly. I need to take notes. Try to remember exactly what was said, especially by the lawyer."

Keith listened intently, jotting down key points. "Where's the baby now?"

"With Katie's cousin Chrissie," Glen hesitated, realizing he needed to be more exact. "Her name is Christine Johnson and her husband's name . . ." he paused, "I think it's Jerry. I don't know their address but they live here in Edgemont and the baby is with them. They have my baby!"

"Okay, that's all I need. I can get the address. A couple of other questions. You didn't sign anything, did you?"

"No. The lawyer had papers he wanted me to sign, but I wouldn't do it."

"Do you have the baby's birth certificate or a copy of it?"

"Yes, I have a copy at home. It's in a folder in the top drawer of my dresser."

"And it names you as the father?" Keith knew that it did, but he wanted to double check to be certain.

"Yes, it includes my full name: Glen Thomas McLean."

"All right," Keith said. "Try to calm yourself. Go home and wait for me. Don't do anything or talk to anyone. If anyone calls, refer them to me. I'm going to handle this."

Keith took a deep breath and then another. He sat down heavily on his swivel chair and drummed his fingers against his desk top. He needed time to think rationally—to consider the options and the best approach to take.

Chrissie Johnson answered the phone. "Yes?"

"Is this Mrs. Johnson? Christine Johnson?" Keith asked.

"Yes, who is this?"

"Keith Chamberlain . . . I'm Glen McLean's lawyer. I understand you have his baby in your home."

There was a pause and Keith overheard her saying to someone, "It's his lawyer."

Keith said, "I understand from Mr. McLean that you have taken his baby without his authorization."

"It's not his baby!" Chrissie said firmly. "The biological father is David Gordon, Katie's husband, and we have signed papers with his signature authorizing us to adopt his baby."

"The birth certificate names my client Glen McLean as the father. What proof do you have that he isn't?"

There was another pause and once again Keith heard her speaking to someone before responding, "We've taken a DNA sample from Mr. Gordon and the baby that will prove he's the father."

"Do you have the results from that sample?" Keith asked.

"Well, not yet . . . but in a few days," she said.

"In other words, you have no proof, just your speculation. That means, according to Texas law, that you have taken the baby illegally. That's a very serious charge."

There was a long pause. "What are you saying?"

"I'm saying that you have two options. The first option is that when Mr. McLean and I arrive at your home within the hour, you return the baby to him without protest. The second option is that I contact the police department about the kidnapping of Mr. McLean's baby. In that event, I will arrive at your home with a sheriff to arrest you and your husband. I trust you understand that both you and your husband in all likelihood will be taken to jail on the felony charge of kidnapping."

"Just a minute," Chrissie said. Keith held the phone while an apparently intense conversation took place. Then Chrissie returned. "You and Mr. McLean can have the baby—for now."

"We will be there within the hour, "Keith said.

Less than 30 minutes later, Keith and Glen appeared at the Johnson home where the Johnson family and Molly Collins waited for them.

Few words were spoken until Glen took the baby in his arms. Then the two Johnson girls began jumping up and down screaming, "He's taking our baby! Mommy, don't let him take our baby!"

Molly Collins placed her hands on her broad hips, her puckered face red with rage and her voice tight with fury, "You two better not try no funny stuff with that baby! You hear me! You abuse that baby boy and you'll see what happens!"

Then, turning to the sobbing girls, she said in a gentle tone, "Don't you little sweethearts worry none. You'll have your baby brother back real soon. Just a few days and he'll be with his Collins' family where he belongs."

****

Before going home, Keith drove Glen and the baby to the lab at the Edgemont Community Hospital to have their mouth's swabbed for DNA testing. He watched as the lab technician made a copy of Glen's driver's license and took a photo of both Glen and the baby.

Keith explained to Glen, "That establishes a 'Chain of Custody'. It's a legal term concerning proof of whose DNA was actually used in the test."

"How long will it take to get the results?" Glen asked.

"The official word is three to five business days," the technician said. "But it can be a whole lot longer, depending on how backed up the lab might be."

****

As they sat together on the living room sofa, Keith said, "Quite a day."

"If I didn't have you, I don't know what I'd have done." Glen reached for Keith's hand. "The most upsetting day of my life . . . Katie's burial and then their taking my baby." He looked down at the baby who just a moment before had been gurgling and laughing in his arms and was now sleeping soundly."

"December 23, 2008, the day Katie was buried." Glen shook his head, "I still can't believe Katie isn't here. We were so close for so long . . . ." His voice grew husky and he stopped.

Keith placed his hand on Glen's shoulder. "I'm so sorry." In the four years of their relationship, he had never seen Glen so shaken—like a frightened child. It was a side of Glen he had not experienced, and he felt a desire to reach out to him—*I'm here. Don't worry . . . everything will be all right.*

Glen took a deep breath. "Her aunt said Katie lied about going to the fertility clinic. She said it was a story Katie made up because she didn't want her husband to know she was pregnant with his baby." He shook his head, "Her aunt's a hateful person, and I'd never believe that Katie would lie to me, except . . ." He paused.

"Except what?" Keith said.

"It was so important to Katie that we don't check the baby's paternity . . . remember how important that was to her?" Glen took a deep breath. "I don't believe Katie would lie, but . . ."

Keith stopped him. "Katie went to the fertility clinic."

Glen sighed, "I appreciate your saying that. But it doesn't make it true."

"Glen, sweetie, look at me. I'm going to tell you something that I never intended for you to know." Keith hesitated. "First, I want you to promise you'll never throw this up to me. Promise?"

Glen looked confused. "Okay, I'll promise, but I don't know what you're talking about?"

"Do you recall my asking you for the name of that fertility clinic?" Keith said.

"Yes, for a client of yours."

"Actually, it was for me." Keith shrugged. "I got it into my head that you and Katie were having a sexual relationship and I planned to confront you, but I wanted evidence. So I called the fertility clinic and told them I was Glen McLean and wanted to know if they had used up all my sperm in the procedure with Katie Collins. Was some remaining that could be used at another time?"

"Anyway, I found out two things: that Katie Collins' real name was Margaret Katherine Collins, and that she did have a procedure using the sperm of Glen McLean. Oh, actually three things—they no longer have any more of Glen McLean's sperm."

Glen shook his head in disbelief. "I can't believe you did that! But, I'm so relieved! It's something I'd never have thought to do and am so happy you did."

Keith patted Glen's shoulder. "That's the difference between a naïve and trusting high school English teacher and a cynical criminal attorney. And that's why you need me in your life."

Then in a low voice, Glen said, "But I still might not be the biological father. What happens then? Do I lose the baby?"

"I don't know. You're on the birth certificate, and we can argue that means the mother wanted you to be responsible for the baby. But . . . who knows? It will go to trial. Anyway, let's not worry about that now."

Then as an after-thought, Keith said, "That heavy old woman— Katie's aunt—she's trouble with a capital T."

****

Keith was at the office and Glen, still on Christmas break from school, was playing with the baby on the living room floor. Approaching five months of age, Glen Junior was coming into his own: sweet-natured and ready for fun. On the verge of crawling, he enjoyed lying on Glen's belly and rocking back and forth on his hands and knees.

The phone rang and Glen, flat on his back, reached into his pocket to retrieve his cell phone. It was Keith.

"Having fun with the baby?" Keith asked.

Glen laughed. "I don't know who's having more fun, this little guy or me. You should see him laughing."

"What was that, daddy? Are you saying your son is laughing, daddy?" Keith said.

"Yes, he's so happy and I . . ." Glen stopped. "You just said daddy twice—are you telling me something?" He felt his stomach churn.

"I sure am!" Keith's voice was buoyant. "I just received the DNA test result and . . ." he paused to let the tension build.

"Say it!" Glen yelled.

"According to the test results, the DNA of Mr. Glen Thomas McLean and the DNA of baby Glen Thomas McLean II prove that Mr. Glen Thomas McLean is the father of said baby named Glen Thomas McLean II."

"Oh, my God! Oh, my God!" Glen felt the moisture well in his eyes. "I am so relieved! Do you have any idea of how tense and worried I've been?"

"Yes, as a matter of fact, I had noticed that you haven't been able to sleep or finish a meal these past few days, but I had no idea that something might be worrying you." Then he laughed, "Okay, we celebrate tonight! Whatever you want to do."

"You know what I want? Just for the three of us—our family—to be home together. You, me and Glen Junior for the official start of our lifetime together."

He clicked shut his cell phone and hugged the baby to him. "Your daddy is so happy! So very happy!"

It occurred to him to call Katie. She would be so . . . He sighed. For so many years, he had shared all his highs and lows with Katie. She was always there for him and he for her. And now, when he had the most exciting news to tell her, Katie wasn't there.

I hope she knows. She would be so happy. This would be her dream come true. "Katie, sweetheart," he whispered, "wherever you are, thank you. Thank you for always being there for me as I will always be there for our son."

The cell phone rang again. "Yes?" Glen said.

"Hi, Mr. McLean, it's me Gentry. Mom asked me to call. She hopes you and Keith can join us for dinner Friday evening."

Glen hesitated. "I'd love to say yes, but I'd have to make arrangements for someone to be with the baby and I don't know . . ."

"Just a minute. Let me talk to Mom."

In a moment, Gentry was back. "Mom said to bring the baby with you. She'd love to see your baby."

"In that case, the answer is yes. We'll be there."

"6:30 p.m. would be great. And Jason will be here too," Gentry said. Then in a lower voice, "I'll be leaving for college in January. Jason and I will share an apartment. That is so cool!"

ı

Chapter Twenty

"Welcome!" Mrs. Phillips greeted Glen and Keith with a hug, as if they were old friends. "I'm so happy you were able to join us."

Stepping closer for a better look at the baby, she said, "How sweet! It's been so long since I've held a little one. May I?" She started to reach for him, but the baby clutched at Glen and started to cry."

Keith laughed. "He's his daddy's boy. Every now and again, he lets me take him from Glen's arms, and I feel so honored. Otherwise it's all about daddy."

"Especially in the middle of the night or when his diaper needs changing. And that's fine with me," Glen said. "I feel so blessed to have him in my life."

Later, as they sat at the dining table, the baby asleep in his porta crib, Reverend Phillips asked, "I have a question that I hope is not too personal. You'll tell me if it is. My wife and I would love to know how the baby came to you. Did you adopt him?"

"No, it was through the services of a fertility clinic." Glen said. Then observing the blank expressions on their faces, he elaborated, "Four years ago when I was in New York City, I went with Katie to a fertility clinic and had my sperm frozen. Katie then used my sperm in a procedure to become pregnant."

"Katie?" Reverend Phillips was taken aback. "Are you talking about Katie Collins?"

"Yes, Katie wanted a baby and when her husband remained firm about not wanting one, she went to the fertility clinic and had the procedure using my sperm. This baby is my biological child, and Keith and I are so thrilled to have him in our lives. There's nothing we wished for more than to have a child to nurture and love."

Startled by this revelation, Reverend Phillips remained silent. *Gay people not only wanted children, but could actually have them in this manner?* This was a new concept for him. He and his wife exchanged a look.

"Would you want just one child?" Mrs. Phillips asked.

Keith, who typically let Glen do most of the talking in social settings, said, "We're planning on two children. I'll be the biological father on the next one. And . . ." He looked at Glen. "Is it all right if I tell them?"

Glen nodded.

"I've called the fertility clinic that Glen and Katie used. At the time they froze Glen's sperm, they also harvested Katie's eggs. If we can find a suitable surrogate—and the people at the clinic said they could help—I would have the fertilized egg implanted in a surrogate. In that way, my biological child would be a genetic half brother or sister to Glen's son."

Gentry and Jason had been listening intently. "This sounds like something out of a science fiction tale," Jason said.

"I think it's wonderful!" Gentry exclaimed. "I can become a daddy, a biological daddy, and make you grandparents." He looked at his parents. "I hope you wouldn't object."

"God in his wisdom is showing us the way," Mrs. Phillips said. "That would be the greatest gift you could ever give us."

Reverend Phillips saw the tears welling in his wife's eyes. It felt like a surreal, out-of-body moment: four gay men at his dinner table and one of them his son. This didn't seem possible—more like a dream he was living.

He could only shake his head at what he saw before him: two attractive and appealing men, one a highly respected teacher who taught positive values in his classroom, according to parishioners whose children had been in his class, the other an attorney who came from one of the founding families in Edgemont. These were responsible people: gay men in a long term relationship that included caring for a child in a loving manner.

At the other side of the table, sat his son and Jason, a young man that Reverend Phillips had known and liked for many years. These were fine young men, a credit to their families, and their Christian upbringing—and they were gay.

He looked at his son and Jason, and for this moment at least, was able to consider—without upset and pain—the possibility of their having a loving relationship, a gay relationship. They were sitting close beside each other at the table—holding hands he suspected—and that thought didn't unnerve him as it had before.

Perhaps in future years, if they remained together, Gentry and Jason might have children and a quality life, like Glen and Keith. These were new thoughts—revelations—for Reverend Phillips, and he needed time to absorb them.

"Does your family know you're gay?" Mrs. Phillips asked Glen.

"They do," Glen said. "But they didn't know until just a few years ago. My mother suspected, but didn't want it to be true and so she never said anything."

"May I ask if they're comfortable with your being gay?"

Glen smiled, "Let's say, they're becoming more comfortable. Not quite there yet, but getting close."

"And your parents, Keith?" she asked. "Are they aware of your relationship?"

"My dad is dead. He probably would have had a problem with my being gay. As for my mother, I just wish I had told her years earlier than I did. Every gay man should have a mother like mine: totally supportive and loving. In fact, when Glen starts back to school next week, Mom will come up from Austin to stay with us and be with the baby for as long as we need her."

Keith smiled. "My mother is so excited to have our baby in her life. She told me I can't imagine anything more appealing than having a grandbaby to spoil without a daughter-in-law wishing I would pack my bags and head back to Austin."

Jason laughed. "She sounds like my mother. Back in September, my first month at college, I sat up all night composing my coming out letter to Mom and Dad. I sweated over that letter. I wrote it and rewrote it and then was too afraid to mail it. Finally, I did and my stomach was in knots as I waited for the explosion.

"Mom called a few days later to say she had received my letter and was so happy that I was finally able to tell her something that she and Dad had known for years. I was so relieved!"

What about you?" Glen turned to Gentry. "Anything you want to say?"

Gentry looked at his parents. "I was torn apart, knowing that I was gay and fearing others might know it also by something I might say or do. It was this huge secret in my life, and I was eaten up with guilt and this terrible anxiety about being found out.

"My fear of disappointing Dad was so great that I just went crazy." Gentry said. "I should have known my dad would always be there for me—that Dad and Mom would never let me down."

That evening, as they lay in bed in the darkened room, Mrs. Philips said, "Everett, we have a wonderful son and, thank God, he's now at peace with himself. It warms my heart to see him happy after all that he's been through."

Reverend Phillips said, "I was touched by his belief that we'd always be there for him."

"And we will be there for him . . . always." She affirmed.

Reverend Phillips sighed, "I've been wrestling with the terrible knowledge that I've done wrong. I feel the guilt of leading my parishioners in an ungodly direction. I don't know how or when it happened but I lost my way . . . and I am filled with shame."

"What are you saying?" Concerned by the upset she heard in his voice, his wife reached for the lamp switch and turned it on. "Everett, you're judging yourself too harshly."

"Many years ago when I was a divinity student, a beloved teacher said. 'The Bible is an amazing book. People who enter it with purity and love in their hearts will find its pathways to non-judgment, compassion and love for others, as taught by Jesus. But those who enter it with malice and ill-will in their hearts will find pathways to self-righteous judgment and belligerent condemnation against others, all that Jesus stood against."

He reached for his wife's hand. "I've come to see that I had lost my way, and I need to thank you for leading me back on the righteous path that Jesus taught."

"Everett, this is God's doing." She turned on her side to face him. "God is all forgiving and in his wisdom is showing us the way."

They were quiet for several moments. Then Mary said, "If Gentry has a child some day, I would be thrilled to love and spoil my grandbaby."

Leaning forward to kiss her husband, she whispered. "Imagine our excitement the day Gentry gives us a grandchild to love!"

****

Aunt Molly opened the front door of her modest, wood frame home to find an angry Chrissie waving the letter from Keith Chamberlain's office, detailing the DNA report confirming Glen McLean as the father of Katie's baby.

"You lied to me! Glen McLean is the father. Katie never told you he wasn't!"

Aunt Molly motioned Chrissie into her narrow living room furnished with an earth-tone shag carpet and orange sofa that had been the fashion in a long gone era. Then, holding her ground, she said firmly "That's what Katie told me. Anyway, it's what I thought she told me. She was so confused with all that morphine they were putting in her, she probably didn't know what she was saying."

Chrissie took a deep breath as she crossed her arms. "I feel like such a fool for taking his baby to my home. I'm going to contact him and apologize."

"Don't you dare!" Aunt Molly snapped. "Katie didn't want no homosexual raising her baby! That's probably what she was trying to tell me and I got it confused."

Chrissie didn't respond, but she shook her head, indicating her disbelief.

"You just calm down and come with me to the kitchen," Aunt Molly said. "I got some brewed coffee still in the pot and we need to sit and do some talking and planning."

Seated in the stark white kitchen with its avocado green appliances, Chrissie lifted her coffee cup as her aunt said, "Would you want a homosexual raising your baby? Nobody in their right mind would want that! Imagine what men like that would do to a little boy! Makes me sick to my stomach to think about it."

"I don't like it either, but what can we do about it? He's the father and the baby is his." Chrissie said.

Aunt Molly's jaw tightened. "I got some friends at the church, powerful Christian people here in Edgemont. They ain't going to like this either. Not when they hear how on her death-bed Katie begged me to keep her baby boy away from that homosexual man."

Chrissie shook her head, "That's not true. You're making that up."

"Well you just think about this. A baby being raised in a good Christian home with a God-fearing mother and father and two sisters to love him and raise him up right, like your family, blood relatives, I might add. Or a baby boy forced to live in a home with a homosexual who can do whatever his sick mind comes up with."

Chrissie sighed, "Of course the baby should be raised in a proper home with a mother and father to love him. But the DNA results prove that Glen McLean is the father, and there's nothing we can do about it."

Aunt Molly shifted her heavy body forward in her chair. "You give up too easy. This ain't some poor black baby we're seeing on the TV news from Dallas that nobody gives a hoot about. We're talking about a flesh and blood relative—a baby born into our family. You can whine that nothing can be done, but my conscience ain't gonna let me off that easy."

"But what can you do?" Chrissie asked.

"I'll wait for God to tell me," Aunt Molly said, "The Lord knows I'm a true Christian whose only thought is to protect an innocent baby. He's gonna tell me what needs to be done, and I'm gonna do it. No matter what." She gave her niece a meaningful look. "Sometimes, you gotta do what you gotta do.

"Yeah, I'm gonna have a nice, long conversation with God. *He* will show me the way." She pointed her finger at her niece. "In the meantime, you don't go apologizing to nobody, especially that Mr. Glen McLean."

****

Jean Chamberlain stood outside the stately home where 38 years before she had brought Keith, her newborn baby, home from the hospital to join his big sister. Such an exciting day!

She was now a woman in her late 60s, living in Austin with her sister, a widow just like her. Those years in Edgemont living in this grand old home had been wonderful, and she was filled with nostalgia, especially at the memories of her children. The high point of her life had been those early years holding her babies, loving them—the feel of them in her arms. That's what she missed.

Earlier that week, Keith had called. "Mom, Glen returns to work on Monday and we need someone to be with the baby until we set up a permanent arrangement. Any chance you can help out for now?"

What a question! She began packing her bags as soon as she hung up the phone.

"So adorable!" Mrs. Chamberlain cuddled the baby in her arms. "Oh, and he has a cleft in his chin, just like Glen."

"That's my boy!" Glen said. He sat on the sofa beside them as the baby held his finger in a tight grasp.

Keith was in the kitchen preparing dinner, but he heard their conversation and called, "That's my boy, too! He looks more like me every day. Super intelligent too!"

He came to the doorway to tell his mom, "A colleague at the office who specializes in family law, is filing legal paperwork to establish my standing as a guardian of the baby, along with Glen. It's a little tricky because this is Texas and I'm a gay man, but our senior attorney Gordon Mathias Markley assured me he'll establish my parental rights so that it'll stand up in court. If anything were to happen to Glen, the baby will remain with me."

"I'm so happy for both of you," Mrs. Chamberlain turned toward Glen. "Do you recall that dinner several years ago when you said you'd like to have a child, and Katie said she'd love to be the one who gave you a child?"

"I remember that so well," Glen said. "And Katie did just that. There's not a day goes by that I don't think about Katie and what she gave to me—to us."

Glen lowered his voice. "Keith is too macho to show his feelings, but sometimes when he doesn't know I'm listening, I'll hear him cooing to the baby, 'Your Papa Keith loves you and you love your Papa Keith, don't you?"

"I heard that," Keith yelled from the kitchen, "and I deny the part about me cooing. I'm a 38-year-old criminal attorney—successful I might add—and I take offense at your suggesting I coo."

"I'm confident Keith talks to the baby in his most somber courtroom voice." Mrs. Chamberlain laughed. "By the way, if Keith is Papa Keith, what do you want the baby to call you?"

"Daddy Glen hits the spot with me. What about you?"

"Not Granny . . . I'm not old enough for that. Now Grammy Jean has a nice feel. Yes, that would suit me just fine." She smiled. "By the way, Keith tells me you're moving ahead with plans to have a second child."

"We are," Glen said. "We've been in contact with the fertility clinic. They offer all the necessary services: in vitro fertilization, even obtaining a surrogate mother. We're hoping to time this so that Little Glen is about two years of age when he gets a baby brother or sister."

"Grammy Jean can hardly wait! Two grown-up sons, two grandchildren and no daughter-in-law? Who could ask for anything more?"

As Glen left for school early the next morning, he saw a scrap of paper on the porch floor. Thinking it was something the blustery January wind had blown onto their porch, he picked it up to throw away. Then he saw the writing and froze:

If a man lies with another man as with a woman, it is an abomination. They should be put to death.—Leviticus

****

Returning to school after a long holiday always took adjusting. Typically, it required a day or two for students to shake off the vacation mindset. Glen had anticipated a subdued response in his classes—but there was something else on this day.

He couldn't quite put his finger on it, but clearly something was in the air, and it wasn't good. Students who typically milled around his desk, wanting to be with him, kept their distance. He observed students staring at him in a questioning manner.

You're just imagining things, he told himself. But he wasn't. At the end of the day, after the dismissal bell had rung, two girls waited to talk to him.

"At church yesterday, some people were saying very bad things about you." Lynda Mumford, a popular student in his homeroom, spoke first.

"My mother doesn't believe you would do such a thing, but a lot of people at church were saying you did." Shelly Gorman looked upset.

"So what are people at your church saying I did?" Glen smiled, not wanting to appear concerned.

The girls looked at each other, seemingly reluctant to say anything. Then Lynda said, "My mother told me that people at church were saying you do bad things to your baby."

Glen was stunned. "Bad things? What sort of bad things?"

Again the girls looked at one another. "Like touching a baby boy in his privates in a way that you shouldn't." Lynda blushed.

Shelly nodded. "My mom says they're only saying that because you're gay. We go to the First Baptist Church, and some people there don't think a gay man should be allowed to raise a baby."

"But it's more than that." Lynda broke in. "There's a fat, old woman in our church—I don't know her name—but she says her niece gave birth to that baby and before she died, she caught you doing terrible things to the baby."

"That's right," Shelly added, "My mother said this old woman is telling everyone her niece begged her to have the baby taken from you."

Glen shook his head. "I would never do anything to harm or abuse my baby."

"That's what my mom said. I heard her tell people you wouldn't do anything bad like that!" Lynda said.

"So did my mom!" Shelly said. "She thinks the woman spreading those tales is a big liar!"

"Thank you for telling me. Please thank your mothers as well," Glen said. "I have a favor to ask. Please ask your mothers for the name of that old lady who's saying those things and, if possible, the names of people she said that to. Will you do that for me?"

"Yes, we will," the girls said before running to catch their bus.

Glen, stunned by what he had just heard, felt a heavy weight in the pit of his stomach. He visualized Katie's aunt as he had last seen her: bent slightly forward with her hands at her hips in a belligerent stance, her round face scrunched with rage. Keith had said, 'She's trouble with a capital T'—and she was proving him right.

A short time later, as Glen walked to the faculty parking lot mulling over what he had heard, he saw several students standing in front of his new Toyota Camry. As he drew closer, he realized they were staring at his car. Then they saw him.

"Oh, Mr. McLean, we're so sorry. We don't know who would have done this."

"Done what?" Glen asked. Then he saw the slashed tires and the writing on his windshield: *Child Molester.*

****

The baby was now eating solid food, and Jean Chamberlain was laughing at his facial expressions as he experienced his first taste of banana.

"Yes, yes! You like it don't you?" she wiped the banana drool from his chin. "Your Papa Keith liked it also when he was your age."

The doorbell rang, and she was startled and somewhat annoyed at the interruption. It was a few minutes before noon and she wasn't expecting anyone. She knew it wouldn't be Keith, as he had just called from his office to see how she was doing. And this was Glen's first day back at school at the end of the Christmas vacation; he wouldn't be coming home at this hour.

She considered not responding, probably somebody selling something. "Oh, well, let's see who's here." She wiped the banana from Little Glen's mouth and holding him in her arms, went to the front door.

"Mary Ellen, what a surprise." Jean smiled at a former classmate of Keith's who had often attended parties at their home. "How did you know I was in town?"

"I didn't . . . I had no idea. I thought you were living with your sister in Austin. Will you be returning to live in Edgemont? That would be wonderful."

"No, I'm here just until Keith and Glen can make some permanent arrangement for the baby's care while they're at work. But I'm loving being back and I just might shock them by staying," she smiled. "I wouldn't do that to them. But come in and let's visit. You're going to just love their baby. He is adorable!"

When they were seated in the living room, Jean Chamberlain said. "If you didn't know I was back, why were you visiting?"

Mary Ellen appeared uncomfortable. "I'm working for the DFPS and I'm here on an official visit."

"DFPS?" Mrs. Chamberlain said. "You're going to have to help me with those initials. I have no idea what they stand for."

"It's the Department of Family Protective Services. I've worked there for the past three years."

"Sounds very official," Jean said. "What's your responsibility?"

"I'm responsible to make home visits for Child Protective Services to check on the welfare of children whenever our department's been notified of possible abuse."

"That sounds like interesting and very important work," Jean said, "but why are you here?"

Mary Ellen flushed with embarrassment. "I am so sorry. Looking at that happy baby in your arms, I know this is just a . . . Anyway, on Sunday afternoon, we had messages on the hotline from several people concerned about the welfare of the baby in the home of Glen McLean."

Mrs. Chamberlain looked perplexed. "Did they say what they were concerned about?"

"Sexual abuse . . ." Mary Ellen shook her head. "Mrs. Chamberlain, I am so sorry, but it's my job and I will have to check the baby for any evidence of bruising or penetration. I hope you understand."

Later, after the examination, Mary Ellen said, "I knew there wouldn't be anything, but I have no choice, especially in a situation like this when three different people called. It's my responsibility to check and file a report."

"I understand," Jean said. "But I'm very concerned about who would have called and why. Are you at liberty to reveal names?"

"No, their names are confidential, but I can read to you what was said."

Jean nodded, "I want to hear that."

"The first caller said that an infant was in the care of homosexual men and there is reason to suspect the infant is being subjected to sexual abuse."

"The next caller said that the infant's mother, who recently died, observed Mr. Glen McLean manipulating the baby boy's genitals."

"The last caller said she was outraged that in a Christian state like Texas an infant boy would be placed in the custody of homosexual men who could be doing all types of perversions to a helpless baby."

"I'm sorry," Mary Ellen said. "The feeling in our department was this was probably nothing more than homophobia. There are people who just plain don't like homosexual people. Are you aware that the platform of the Republican Party of Texas demands that no child be allowed in the custody of homosexuals? Some people have very strong feelings on that topic.

"Still, the administrator at my office was concerned that we would receive three calls on Sunday. That seemed odd. In any event, we have no choice but to check."

As Jean Chamberlain, holding the baby in her arms, guided Mary Ellen to the front door, she said, "I don't believe it's chance that those three calls all came on Sunday. During my years in Edgemont, I'd noticed that some supposedly good Christian folks use church on Sunday—the holy day—to infect others with the hate in their hearts."

****

That evening, after the baby was settled for the night, Keith and Glen joined Jean Chamberlain in the living room to talk. The mood was somber after the troubling events of the day. Keith, who had filed a police report about Glen's car, was angry. "Secrets don't last long in Edgemont. We'll find out who vandalized the car, and whoever is responsible is going to pay . . . big time."

Earlier Mrs. Chamberlain had told them about the visit from Mary Ellen and the phone calls that had prompted the visit. Then Glen produced the note that he had found on the porch that morning when he left the house. He passed it to Keith, who read the note aloud, "*If a man lies with another man as with a woman, it is an abomination. They should be put to death.*"—*Leviticus* *

Mrs. Chamberlain took a sip from her glass of cabernet. "Leviticus? I knew it was coming from a church! I imagine a minister in one of our churches felt a need to enliven his Sunday morning sermon with a dose of homophobic hate—a sure-fire crowd pleaser!"

"Or in this case, a parishioner made up a story," Glen said. "I had picked up strange vibes from students . . . . a negative feeling," Glen said. "Something was wrong, but I didn't know what. At the end of the day, two students told me that a woman at their church on Sunday was telling people that I had been caught by her niece doing something sexual with the baby." Glen paused to take a sip of wine.

"According to the woman, her niece on her death bed was distraught that her baby would be in my care. She had begged her aunt not to allow that to happen." Glen shook his head, "Apparently, that's what Molly Collins is telling people."

Keith said. "I told you that woman was trouble—big trouble."

"The girls didn't know her name. They just described her as a 'fat, old woman' who claimed she was sick to her stomach at the thought of that innocent baby being abused by a homosexual."

"Well, that would do it," Jean Chamberlain nodded. "Can you imagine how fast something like that would spread?"

For a moment, no one said anything. Then, Keith stated, "I'm going to hit that lying bitch with a lawsuit for slander. But we need to establish some facts. We need to prove it was Molly Collins who originated that lie and that she did it for a malicious purpose."

Glen nodded. "I've asked the girls to find out from their mothers the name of that woman and who she told this story to. Hopefully, they'll be able to tell me tomorrow."

Looking perplexed, Keith reached into his glass for an olive, "We could have a problem. She says Katie was distraught about your behavior with the baby, and you'll say none of that happened—it's a lie." Keith shook his head. "It's one of those 'he says, she says' situations, and Katie's not here to back up your story."

"Let me get something from the study." Glen stood up from the armchair and walked quickly down the hall. He returned in a moment with a pink envelope. "There's a note in here that Katie gave me the evening before she died."

****

The next morning, as soon as the school doors were open, several students rushed to Glen's classroom, among them were Lynda and Sherry.

Mr. McLean, I have the names. Here," Lynda handed a sheet of notebook paper to him. "The woman making up those terrible lies is Molly Collins, and my mother doesn't like her one bit."

"My mom doesn't either," Sherry said. "Mom called some of her friends at church and she got the names of four people that fat old woman told her lies to." She handed Glen another sheet of paper.

"We all know you didn't do those terrible things that people are saying you did," Ty Whiteoak, a student in his fourth period class said.

"Thank you," Glen said. "There is no truth to what Molly Collins has said. Please tell that to anyone who thinks she's telling the truth. Better yet, tell them to come to me so that I can tell them for myself."

"That's what Mom told people at church." Lynda said. "How do you know what Molly Collins said was true? Shouldn't some of you ask Mr. McLean about this before you spread this gossip to everyone you know."

"Mr. McLean," one of the other boys in the group said, "People here know you're gay, and that's okay," he added quickly, "but not with everyone. I talked it over with Dad last night and he believes that's why some people were so quick to believe those bad things about you."

"It's just like in Germany and the lies the Nazis spread about the Jews." Ty added. Then he said, "We're going to find out who slashed your tires and make them pay for the damage they've done."

"That's right," Lynda said, "You're our favorite teacher and everyone's so upset about what happened to your car. Someone will learn who did this—and whoever it might be is going to be punished. You'll see."

At the start of his planning period, Glen received a call to go the principal's office. "Mr. Fowler needs to meet with you and it's urgent," the secretary said.

When Glen entered the principal's office, he was surprised to see that Dr. Ellis, the superintendent, was also present. A tall man with a florid complexion, Dr. Ellis rose from his chair.

"Well, here we go again," he said as he placed his hand on Glen's shoulder. "Hearsay and rumor! Hearsay and rumor! And my wife wonders why I have an ulcer! Are you aware of what's being said?"

"I think so, but maybe not everything," Glen said.

Dr. Ellis looked at the principal. "Before I say anything, I want you to know that Mr. Fowler and I don't believe a word of it. We know it's just malicious gossip from some bigots who can't accept that a gay man could be allowed to teach in our schools. I want you to know that you have our complete and total support."

Glen nodded, "I appreciate your saying that."

"Okay, here goes," the superintendent took a deep breath, "I've received a number of phone calls and several emails claiming that you sexually abused your baby. In each case, I responded that I know Glen McLean and he would never do such a thing.

"Jeanette Haar was one of the callers and I don't have to tell you how opinionated and forceful that woman can be. Mr. Fowler and I belong to the First Baptist Church and we know she has the ear of the most conservative people in our church."

"They're the ones who supported her in her most recent run for the Board of Education," Mr. Fowler added. "Thank the lord she was defeated again."

"Anyway, Jeanette claims to have spoken directly to Molly Collins, Katie's aunt, and knows as a fact that you sexually abused your baby. According to her, just before Katie died, she told her aunt that she had caught you doing sexual things to the baby. Katie begged her to do everything in her power to keep you from having custody of the baby. Jeanette says the poor old lady can't sleep nights thinking about the abuse that baby boy is surely experiencing."

"I told Jeanette that Glen McLean is a fine, ethical man—a credit to our school district—and I don't believe he would do such a thing. That I would speak to him personally to hear what he has to say before I form any judgment."

Dr. Ellis grimaced. "The woman exploded! 'Are you saying you would believe what a known homosexual has to say? What do you expect him to say? Molly Collins is a devout Christian woman who never misses a church service. She has stated that Glen McLean abused his baby! What more could you possibly need to hear?'"

"Well, that's where it stands," Dr. Ellis raised his hands, palm outward, and sighed, "We've got to put this to rest before it goes any further."

"Thank you for standing up for me," Glen said. "Now let me tell you what I believe is going on." He provided the background to Dr. Ellis and Mr. Fowler, ending with "Molly Collins is determined to have my baby taken from me."

"Glen, trust me, we're with you. Our problem is bigotry—how do you counteract bigotry? Let me show you what we're up against." Mr. Fowler stepped to his computer and entered "Republican Party of Texas Platform/Homosexuality." Then he read:

The Party believes that the practice of sodomy tears at the fabric of society, contributes to the breakdown of the family and leads to the spread of communicable diseases. Homosexual behavior is contrary to the fundamental unchanging truths that have been ordained by God, recognized by our country's founders, and shared by the majority of Texans. Homosexuality must not be presented as an acceptable "alternative" lifestyle in our public education and policy, nor should "family" be redefined to include homosexual "couples."

Mr. Fowler looked up. "I'm not going to read it all, except this part further down where it specifically says:

We are opposed to any granting of legal entitlements including . . . custody of children by homosexuals.

Texas is called a 'red state' for good reason," Mr. Fowler said. "Religious fundamentalists like Jeanette Haar are active in Republican Party politics: they've taken control of the party in Texas and are behind the passing of that bigoted platform. That's her mindset and nothing you say or do is going to change it."

Glen nodded. "You may recall that I have a history with Jeanette Haar and her son Mickey. It's not something I'll likely forget. As for Molly Collins," he took a deep breath. "In the next day or two she'll receive a "cease and desist" order and notice of a slander suit."

****

Reverend Phillips was not looking forward to the 4 p.m. meeting scheduled by Jeanette Haar. Mrs. Haar, a formidable member of the church's most conservative faction, had been a major supporter in his hiring six years earlier; and initially, he had seen her as a strong ally in promoting his conservative religious beliefs.

As the years went by, however, and he gradually grew somewhat more flexible in his positions, he found himself walking a tightrope in her presence. He had observed Jeanette Haar becoming increasingly self-righteous and judgmental—even belligerent—and he found himself withholding opinions rather than risking a confrontation.

Promptly at 4 p.m. Mrs. Haar arrived, and Molly Collins was with her. It surprised him that these two women would be together as they seemingly had little in common. Jeanette Haar was college educated with an elitist manner. She had aspirations to be on the Edgemont School Board and had in fact run several times. Always well groomed, her dark hair in a neat bun, Mrs. Haar typically wore a two-piece suit with an expensive silk blouse. She was a tall woman with an intimidating manner.

Molly Collins on the other hand was a "good old girl." She had no sense of style; something was typically amiss in her attire, which she either didn't notice or more likely paid it no mind. She was a short, overweight woman, plain-spoken and devoid of pretense and social aspiration.

The minister couldn't understand what would bring two such different women together, until they began to talk and then he understood: it was their shared bond of bigotry.

Jeanette Haar opened the conversation. "Are you aware that Mr. Glen McLean, a homosexual teacher at Edgemont High School, has custody of an infant, a baby boy?"

"Yes, I am aware of that," he said.

"The mother of that baby is Katie Collins. She's my niece and you spoke at her funeral," Molly said.

"I am so sorry for your loss," Reverend Phillips said.

Molly nodded. "Her dying broke my heart. The good Lord didn't see fit for me to have no babies of my own. Katie was like a natural born daughter to me."

"And that's why we're here," Jeanette Haar broke in. She looked at Molly, "Tell Reverend Phillips what you told me."

"Just days before Katie died, she caught that homosexual man doing ungodly things to the baby. She was so weak with cancer and in so much pain, poor thing, she couldn't do nothing but beg me to see that Glen McLean never got custody of her baby. 'Aunt Molly,' she said, 'Promise me, you'll keep my baby from that man.'"

Molly Collins sighed deeply. "I tried but I failed. That man has custody of Katie's baby. I ain't had one night's sleep, thinking what he might be doing to an innocent boy child."

Jeanette Haar looked at Reverend Phillips. "Heard enough? Just makes my blood boil to think in a Christian state like Texas homosexuals are permitted to have custody of children! That innocent baby must be taken from that man!"

"If you suspect the baby is being sexually abused," Reverend Phillips responded, "Shouldn't this be reported to Family Protective Services? Isn't that the way to handle it?"

"Oh, they're so incompetent! Everyone knows that," Jeanette said. "Several of us called last Sunday when Molly told us what was happening. Supposedly, they sent someone over to check who claimed everything was fine. No problem. Can you believe that?"

These women exude hate and bigotry! Reverend Phillips thought. But even as he was repelled by their belligerent self-righteousness, he felt the prick of conscience: this is what he had nurtured in his sermons.

"You need to do something," Jeanette Haar said. "As minister of the First Baptist Church people will listen to you. Several years ago you gave those powerful sermons on "Homosexuals Versus the Bible" and people listened. The *Edgemont Gazette* printed those sermons. It started people talking about what needed to be done to safeguard our schools and our children. Good came of it."

She gave Reverend Phillips a meaningful look as she pointed her finger at him. "You need to do that again! No one is more highly respected in Edgemont than you. People will listen and once again good will come of it."

Chapter Twenty-One

In past years, Reverend Phillips might have readily joined Jeanette Haar in her efforts to stand firm against homosexuals and the threat they presented to children. In all likelihood, he would have perused the Bible, finding needed justification to properly frame his condemnation.

Now, knowing that his son was gay, his perspective was changed. He called Glen, "I met with two of my parishioners who made some serious charges against you. I think it's important that I meet with you at my home to review their charges and hear what you have to say."

Glen sat in the living room with Reverend Phillips and his family, quietly listening to the minister's recap of the meeting. The minister concluded, "I respect you and know that you didn't do what they said, but their charges cannot be taken lightly. Abuse of a child in the manner they described is very serious. People will be outraged. I asked you here because I didn't know if you were aware of what was being said and to learn if you have an explanation of why they might be saying it."

"I appreciate your respect and the opportunity to explain," Glen said. "Katie's Aunt Molly could not accept that Katie and I had deep feelings for one another, and that I was the biological father of Katie's baby. She couldn't tolerate me because I was gay, and I did my best to have as little to do with her as possible.

"But I did not anticipate the lengths she would go—the lies she would tell—to take my son from me," Glen raised his hands, palms outward. "Katie and I cared for each other deeply to the very end. Let me show you this." He took from his jacket pocket the pink envelope with Katie's handwritten note and handed it to Reverend Phillips. Katie gave this to me the night before she died."

Reverend Phillips reached for his bifocals. He scanned the note and asked, "May I read this aloud so that my wife and son can hear it?"

"Yes, of course," Glen said.

My dearest Glen,

In my perfect world it would be you and me and our baby. That will not happen here on Earth. But perfect can happen in heaven. There will come a day, I know, when the three of us will be together for eternity with Jesus. Until then, I will count on you to love and nurture our little guy. Never forget how much your Katie loves her two men.

Yours always,

Katie

Reverend Phillips sighed deeply. "Katie Collins was a lovely lady." He looked at his wife and saw that her eyes were moist. "Will you allow me to make a copy of this note?" He asked Glen. "I believe I may have a use for it in a sermon I'm preparing to deliver on Sunday. It's a sermon Mary has encouraged me to give for the past several months." He looked at his wife. "I'm ready to do it now."

Turning to Glen, he said, "I appreciate the personal nature of Katie's note to you, but I think it will prove helpful to you if you would permit me to read it from the pulpit."

Glen nodded. "Katie would want that."

Gentry who had been quietly listening spoke up, "Dad, you can also say in your sermon that your son is gay. And that you love him. Will you do that for me?"

"I do love you, and I am very proud of you," Reverend Phillips said softly. "But why would you want me to tell my congregation that you're gay? I don't see that as something people need to know."

"Dad, I'm not doing it for them. I'm doing it for me. I don't want to live with a secret gnawing away inside of me, and a fear that something I would say or do—perhaps the way I held myself or walked—would give me away. I've suspected I was gay ever since I was a little boy. That's a long time to keep a secret."

Looking at his mom and then back to his dad, Gentry said, "Jason and I have talked it over. We're going to be open about who we are when we're together in Austin. No lies or pretense. And that's going to get back to Edgemont, I know. Someone will find out and bring it back here and spread it, as if it were a dirty secret being revealed. We don't want that.

"Dad, tell it from the pulpit and tell it like a proud and loving dad. Can you do that for me?"

****

Chrissie Johnson was vacuuming the beige wall-to-wall carpeting in her living room when she thought she heard someone at her front door. Clicking off the vacuum, she turned to see her Aunt Molly entering from the hallway.

"How many times have I told you to keep your front door locked when you're alone in the house? I could have been a rapist and what would you've done?"

Chrissie laughed. "Fortunately for me, it's my loving Aunt Molly and not a rapist."

"Well, I ain't here to talk about keeping your front door locked. There's something real important that we need to get our heads together on. Put up a pot of coffee and then we'll talk."

"So, what's the real important something we need to cover," Chrissie said as she brought the coffee mugs to the kitchen table.

"I got a certified letter from Keith Chamberlain. He's the one who came here with Glen McLean and acted like a big shot lawyer. I hear tell he's a homosexual, just like Glen McLean. They live together so you get the picture, don't you?"

"What did the letter say?" Chrissie felt a tightness in the pit of her stomach. Ever since church that past Sunday when she had learned her aunt was telling people that Katie had caught Glen abusing the baby, she had been worried. It was a lie, a terrible lie—and no good could come from that.

"They're talking about suing me for slander," Molly snorted. "Let them try. I talked to my lawyer and he told me flat out to win a slander suit they'd have to prove I was lying and that they can't do. It's my word against theirs. I say Katie saw him abusing her baby and Glen McLean says it never happened. Well, who you gonna believe, a homosexual Yankee or a true Christian woman born and raised right here in Edgemont?"

She took a sip of her coffee and made a face. "Too weak! Either you don't know how to measure right or you need to change the brand you buy."

Chrissie ignored the criticism, just Aunt Molly being Aunt Molly. She took a deep breath. "Katie loved him. If Katie knew what you were telling people, she would . . ."

Leaning forward in her chair, Aunt Molly stopped her. "Now you listen to me! Katie wanted the best for her baby. That means being raised in a good Christian home with a husband and a wife. Not with no homosexuals living in sin and doing who knows what to an innocent child."

"Aunt Molly, I know you mean well, but . . ."

"No buts," Molly raised her hand. "We're gonna make sure that baby is raised in your home. Here's what we need to do. I'm telling folks that on her death bed Katie made me promise to make sure her baby wasn't left with that homosexual she caught abusing her baby. Alls you need to do is back up my story."

"Now how am I supposed to do that?" Chrissie asked.

"Just say you heard Katie tell me about Glen McLean abusing the baby . . . that she was real upset that he might ever have her baby. That ain't too much to ask of you, is it?"

Chrissie shook her head. "I'm sorry, Aunt Molly. I'm not comfortable doing that."

"Listen here, Chrissie, everything I'm doing, I'm doing for you and your family. So don't start in with you're not comfortable with the little I'm asking of you. It's no big deal so don't make it into one."

"I'll need to talk this over with my husband," Chrissie said. "I just don't think . . ."

Molly's face reddened. "Chrissie, you don't have no choice at this point."

"Why do you say that?" she asked.

"Because I already told folks you was there and heard everything your cousin Katie said. I told them that you'll back up everything I'm saying." She pointed her finger at her niece. "After all I've done for you and your family, I can't believe you wouldn't be there for me. Chrissie Johnson, I'm telling you plain and simple if you don't back me up, you ain't no kin of mine!"

****

After lying awake for hours, Chrissie finally fell into a restless asleep, only to awaken with a start from a bad dream. She was in turmoil.

Earlier that evening, Chrissie had told her husband about her conversation with Aunt Molly. "I'm not comfortable supporting Aunt Molly in a lie, but she is family and she's doing it for us." Chrissie took a deep breath, "She'd never forgive me if I didn't back her up. She could be sued for slander."

"And what about you?" her husband said. "Couldn't you be sued for slander as well?"

Chrissie sighed, "If Aunt Molly and I both say the same thing, it would be Glen McLean's word against ours. How could anyone prove we weren't telling the truth?"

"And that would be all right with you? It doesn't bother you that God would know an innocent person was harmed because of you?" her husband replied.

Chrissie hadn't anticipated that response, and it upset her greatly. But how could she not stand by her aunt who had always been there for her? Aunt Molly was opinionated and argumentative—an abrasive personality—but when it came to family, she was always there to help you through any difficulty.

Chrissie was deeply ambivalent. One moment, she believed her course of action was clear. If asked, she would tell the truth. As a Christian, she would have to tell the truth. There was no choice. But then, she'd visualize her aunt's response and her certainty would dissolve. How could she face Aunt Molly? Family comes before others. That's what she had been taught. You must always support your family. Through it all, family sticks together.

By the morning, her anxiety had morphed into a throbbing headache. And then her husband, sitting at the kitchen table, reading the *Gazette*, said, "Listen to this! It's on the front page. He read aloud,

Yesterday afternoon at approximately 5 p.m., two young men attempted to burn a cross on the front lawn of the home shared by Glen McLean and Keith Chamberlain.

A neighbor saw them carrying the 6-foot tall wooden cross and called 911. The police arrived just as the young men—Michael Haar, 19, and his brother James, 17—were pouring gasoline on the cross in preparation for setting it on fire. When confronted by the police, Michael Haar responded, "We were only doing this because Glen McLean is a queer who abused his baby."

The two men are now in police custody, pending a formal arraignment. If it can be proved that the attempted burning of the cross was intended as an act of intimidation against the residents of the home, felony charges can be made.

Phone calls by this newspaper to the parents of the young men, Harold and Jeanette Haar, were not returned. Mrs. Haar has unsuccessfully run on two occasions for a seat on the Edgemont School Board. She and her husband are active members of the First Baptist Church.

In an earlier incident, the tires of Mr. McLean's car were slashed and the words "Child Molester" were written on his windshield. According to a statement from the Edgemont Police Department, Michael and James Haar are "persons of interest" in that incident as well.

Jerry Johnson put the newspaper down and said to his wife, "Still think you should support your Aunt Molly?"

Chrissie felt a heavy weight descend upon her, as she thought, *If God knows when even the tiny sparrow falls, God will surely know that I lied . . . and I will be judged.*

"So what are you going to do?" her husband asked.

She began to cry, "I'm going to speak to Reverend Phillips and ask for his guidance."

Because his secretary had stressed how upset, almost distraught, the young woman sounded on the phone, Reverend Phillips rearranged his schedule to meet with Christine Johnson in the early afternoon.

"I believe Molly Collins is your aunt," Reverend Phillips said as he motioned Chrissie to be seated in the upholstered chair beside his desk.

"Yes, she is my aunt and . . ." she hesitated. "I need your guidance about . . ." she stopped.

The minister saw the tears welling in her eyes. "Whatever the problem, trust me. I am here to help. Our meeting will be confidential."

"Thank you," Chrissie took a tissue from her handbag to wipe her eyes. "I'm just so upset . . . I don't know what to do."

Not saying a word, Reverend Phillips reached his hand across his desk to take her hand in his.

Chrissie took a deep breath. "Last Sunday before the church service began, my Aunt Molly told people that Glen McLean had abused my cousin Katie's baby." Chrissie twisted the tissue in her hand. "And that wasn't true. But people believed her and were outraged. By the time the service was over, it seemed as if everyone was talking about it. And then this morning, my husband read in the *Gazette* that there was an attempt to burn a cross on Mr. McLean's front lawn and his car had been vandalized."

"I read that also," Reverend Phillips said. "What those boys tried to do was wrong: it's a stain against our church and our members. Your aunt caused it to happen and needs to pray for forgiveness."

"My Aunt Molly wants me to say that what she said about Glen McLean was true." Chrissie said softly. "And I don't know what to do."

Reverend Phillips said. "*Thou shalt not bear false witness against your neighbor.* That's one of God's Ten Commandments. If you support her in her lie, you will be as guilty as she in God's eyes."

"But what can I do? My aunt received a letter saying she might be sued for slander. She's counting on me to back up what she said."

Reverend Phillips shook his head. "In the eyes of God, a lie is an abomination and one who supports the lie is equal in blame."

"But my aunt is counting on me. She's always been there for me and my family. Whenever we had a problem, I could count on Aunt Molly. Now she is counting on me and I don't know what to do. How can I turn away from her when she needs me? She would never forgive me. It would just tear our family apart. Tell me what I should do, please."

"God has already told you what you must do. *He* has made it abundantly clear that you must not support the liar and harm the innocent man. God will know your choice for he knows all. *But not a single sparrow can fall to the ground without your Father knowing it.*— Mathew 10:29.

"You came to me for guidance and I have told you what God would want you to do. Now it is your choice to decide what you will do."

"But what about Aunt Molly? I don't want her to be hurt. She'd never forgive me."

"It is she who needs to be forgiven, not you. God knows we are all sinners and that is why he brought his only begotten son to Earth so that through his blood on the cross our sins might be forgiven. But the sinner must repent the sin, as all of us must do who wish to enter God's Kingdom."

Once again he took Chrissie's hand in his. "I wish you well in your decision."

****

Jean Chamberlain was watching Glen as he fed the baby from the small jar of apricot baby food. "What a mess!" she laughed. "He has as much apricot on him as inside him."

"You're a funny guy!" Glen said, and leaning forward to kiss him, managed to get apricot on his lips, which he removed with a swipe of his tongue. "Tastes good! I love it too."

Keith, who had been in the kitchen rinsing the dinner dishes and placing them in the dishwasher, joined them.

So how do you like my two men?" Keith asked his mother. "They make me happy. I hope they make you happy as well."

"You have two men to make you happy. By my count, I have three and I am elated. Then in a more serious tone, "I'm glad we weren't home when those boys tried to burn the cross on our front lawn."

"Lucky for them! I would have kicked their butts if I'd caught them," Keith said. "In the meantime, they're in a whole bunch of trouble. I spoke to the arresting officer and he says the older boy, Michael, made some hate-filled comments about scaring queers that can really hurt him if this goes to trial. Plus two students from

Edgemont High have notified the police they heard Michael Haar and his brother bragging about slashing the tires of Glen's car."

Glen shook his head. "Michael Haar—Mickey—was a student of mine my first year of teaching. He was a bigot and bully back then and apparently nothing's changed. He tormented an effeminate boy unrelentingly, making that poor kid's life a living hell. And his mother, Jeanette Haar, was a self-righteous bigot, who hid her mean-spirited nastiness behind a mask of religious righteousness. Those are two miserable creatures that I wish I'd never met . . . and that was before these latest incidents with my car and the cross."

"Jeanette Haar? Isn't she that very conservative Baptist woman who ran for the school board just before I moved to Austin?" Mrs. Chamberlain said.

"That's her," Glen said. "She was so outraged that I wasn't fired from my teaching position that she pulled her two sons out of the public schools. She home-schooled them herself to be certain they were properly educated in traditional Christian values . . . and kept safe from the homosexual agenda."

Glen placed his hands before him, palms outward. "When I was notified that Mickey Haar wouldn't be in my class any longer, I wanted to shout hallelujah from the rooftops."

"Well, I'm sure her minister at the First Baptist Church, can take some responsibility for her sons' actions," Mrs. Chamberlain said. "For a Christian minister proclaiming a ministry of love, Reverend Phillips generated a huge amount of hate. He was frequently quoted in the *Gazette*, and I came to loathe that man as a sanctimonious zealot."

Keith and Glen exchanged glances. "Mom, we've had Reverend Phillips and his family to dinner here." Keith said.

"And we've been to dinner at his home," Glen added.

"Now that's a surprise! Obviously, he didn't know you were gay," she said. "How did you keep that from him?"

"We didn't," Keith said. "He and his wife wanted to know us because we are gay."

"Why?" his mother asked. "I'm missing something."

"You are," Keith said. "Reverend Phillips and his wife recently learned that their son—their only child—is gay."

Mrs. Chamberlain's eyes widened. "Well, that would change things, wouldn't it? How old is their son?"

"He's about 19," Glen said. "He has a partner and they'll be rooming together in college at U.T. Austin. He's a wonderful young man and his parents adore him."

"Now that's poetic justice! Makes you believe there is a God," she smiled. "So how is Reverend Phillips and his wife handling this?"

"It hasn't been easy for Reverend Phillips, but he's trying," Glen said. "From what I've observed, his wife is guiding him through this. He's the minister, but she's the true Christian—a genuinely caring and compassionate person."

"My goodness, but life is full of twists and turns." Mrs. Chamberlain contemplated her glass of wine and said, "I'd love to meet the Reverend's wife! There's so much we could talk about. Let's invite them for dinner while I'm still here."

****

Gentry was at his desk reading when his father knocked at his bedroom door.

"May I come in?"

"Yes, of course, Dad." Gentry walked to the door and opened it. "Is everything all right?"

"It's fine, son. I just want a moment for us to talk about some things. I . . ." he hesitated, not clear about how to begin. "I need you to help me understand about . . . you know . . . being homosexual . . . being gay. That's a better term to use, isn't it? Will you join me in my study?"

Reverend Phillips guided his son to the adjoining room, motioning him to be seated in the straight-back chair beside his large desk. He took a deep breath. "I believe it was Will Rogers who said, 'Everyone is ignorant only on different subjects.'"

He placed his right hand on his Bible. "I am well versed in God's book. Its timeless wisdom and truths have been my education. However, I've come to realize there are other truths . . . other knowledge . . . that I do not know—have not been open to know. And I need you to help me."

Gentry remained silent.

"Son, I'm ignorant on being gay—what it means to be gay—and I thought maybe you could help me with conflicting thoughts that I'm having trouble resolving."

Gentry raised his hands, palms open. "It's kinda new to me too, Dad. But ask me things and I'll tell you what I know."

Reverend Phillips nodded. "I need you to tell me about your experiences—your feelings—so that I can resolve some concerns. I hope that you will be comfortable answering my questions. You'll tell me if you're not."

"That'll be cool . . ." Gentry stopped, "Sorry . . . I know you don't like that word. I meant to say that'll be fine."

"Thanks for remembering . . . I appreciate that." He smiled affectionately, placing his hand on Gentry's shoulder. "Now my first question has to do with when did you first begin to . . ." He paused to find the right word. "experience feelings—attractions—for other boys?"

Gentry ran his hand through his hair. "Dad, I can't say for sure. It was just always there. In first grade, I remember this boy in my class that I really liked. I wanted to be with him all the time. I don't know if that meant anything. Is that what you wanted to know?"

"Maybe . . . I'm not sure if that indicated anything. When did you first experience an attraction that could have made you think . . ." Reverend Phillips hesitated, "You know."

Gentry nodded. "Probably in middle school. I had these feelings— crushes. Dad, it was in middle school when I was about 12 that I began to worry about . . ." He shrugged and stopped.

His father's brow furrowed. "Gentry, this is very important to me. Please, no matter how awkward—embarrassing—it may be for you, I need you to be honest in your answer."

"Yes?" Gentry looked intently at his Dad. "I understand. I'll answer you truthfully."

"Did you ever . . . . I mean, were you ever approached by an older person, a homosexual who did something to you?"

Gentry shook his head. "No, that never happened."

"What about an older boy? Did anything ever happen with an older boy that might have caused you to be gay?"

"Dad, I had those attractions for many years . . . from the time I was 12 at least, but I wouldn't do anything. Those attractions scared me and I tried to block them. It was just this year that my feelings for Jason became too strong for me to deny them any longer."

"What about your attraction for Betty Jean? She's a very pretty girl. You were with her all the time. Didn't you have feelings—romantic feelings—for her?"

Gentry sighed. "I should have. I wanted to because I liked her a whole lot. She's a real nice person, but when we were alone and she wanted to do things, I didn't want to. I told her it would be wrong for us to do anything . . . sexual," he flushed. "I told her anything like that would have to wait 'til we were married."

He shifted in his chair. "Dad, when I told her about me—that I was gay—I was afraid she'd be angry, but she wasn't. She said she'd suspected something wasn't right because I never . . . you know. Other boys always had. They'd come on to her . . . try things. And she couldn't understand why I didn't. She worried I didn't find her appealing in that way. I think she was relieved when I told her the truth."

"Just a few more questions," Reverend Phillips said. "Will that be all right?"

Gentry nodded. "It's okay, Dad."

"Your feelings for Jason . . . how are they different from your feelings for Betty Jean."

Gentry hesitated, trying to find the words to describe his feelings. "I'm attracted to Jason in every way you can be attracted to another person. I think about him all the time, even in my dreams," he reddened. "I want to touch him, be with him. It wasn't that way with Betty Jean."

Reverend Phillips sighed. "I have just one more question that's been troubling me greatly. All those years you were hearing my sermons condemning homosexuals . . . how did you feel? What were you thinking?"

"I felt . . ." Gentry shook his head. "I felt shame. That I was a terrible person. That if you knew what I was feeling inside, you wouldn't love me. That I had to hide the real me . . . never letting you or anyone else ever suspect what I was feeling inside."

Gentry had avoided looking at his Dad as he spoke. When he looked up to face him, he saw his father was crying. "Dad, I'm so sorry. I didn't mean to upset you."

Reverend Phillips brushed the tears from his eyes. "When you were born, I fell on my knees to thank God for giving you to us. If I close my eyes, I can see you in your mother's arms and the love in her eyes as she held her baby. I felt that love as well and promised myself that I would be the best father in the whole world. That I would love you and nurture you all the days of my earthly life."

Hearing the pain in his father's voice, Gentry reached for his hand. "Dad I love you and I know you love me. You never meant to hurt me. Please don't blame yourself. Please don't."

"But I have hurt you. Tell me . . . please, what can I do to make up for the hurt I've caused you?" his father asked.

"Just tell people that your son is gay and that you love him and are proud of him. That would mean so much to me. It would mean that I'm okay just as I am . . . that I don't have to hide the real me ever again.

"Dad, I've always wanted to please you . . . to have you be proud of me. Nothing is more important to me than that." He tried to smile, instead he began to cry. "Dad, just tell people that your son is gay and that you love him and are proud of him. Okay?"

Chapter Twenty-Two

Reverend Phillips watched as the late-comers rushed to fill the few remaining seats in the rear of the large sanctuary of the First Baptist Church. His wife and son were seated in the first row, center aisle and as he looked their way, prior to beginning his sermon, he saw his wife mouth, "I love you."

He smiled, knowing that she had to be as nervous as he. They had been up most of the night, reviewing what he would say and how he would say it. He typically felt a touch of nervousness prior to beginning, but this sermon would be different and he was feeling intense anxiety. He removed his wire-rimmed bifocals to clean them with his handkerchief.

Then rising from his chair, he stepped to the pulpit.

Without his usual introductory remarks, he began, "This has been a bad week for honoring our commitment to the teachings of God and our Savior Jesus Christ. One of our members has violated the 9th Commandment by bearing false witness that brought harm to another person. Many more of our members, while not initiating the false charges, spread it by gossip and in so doing became equally guilty in God's eyes.

"A number of you have left messages of your revulsion at what that homosexual teacher supposedly did to the baby of Katie Collins, a recently deceased member of our church. Those messages stated as fact that Katie caught this young teacher abusing her baby and was horrified that he might gain custody of her baby after she died. Many of you requested that I act on her behalf, and I did. I contacted this man, a wonderful teacher who happens to be gay, and asked him to respond to the charge. He gave me this note from Katie, dated the evening before she died.

Dearest Glen,

In my perfect world, it would be you and me and our baby. That will not happen here on Earth. But perfect can happen in heaven. There will come a day, I know, when the three of us will be together for eternity with Jesus.

Until then, I will count on you to love and nurture our little guy."

Yours Always,

Katie

He paused to look at the now silent congregation. "Earlier this week, two young men whose mother and father are active members of our congregation attempted to burn a cross on the front lawn of this teacher's home, bringing shame on our church and its teachings."

With these last words, all noises—shuffling, coughing, page-turning, whispering—ceased. Many eyes turned to the pew where Jeanette Haar and her husband always sat. They weren't there. But Molly Collins was in the sanctuary and the color had drained from her face.

"I am not here to speak out against others," Reverend Phillips said. "That would surely be hypocrisy. *Why do you look at the speck of sawdust in your brother's eye and pay not attention to the plank in your own eye.—* Mathew 7:1-5. Rather I am here to condemn myself and ask your forgiveness and more importantly the forgiveness of God."

Once again, Reverend Phillips removed his glasses to wipe them clean. "As your minister, it is my responsibility to lead you in the path of righteousness, through the gospel of Jesus. And that is not what I have done. Many Baptists believe in the inerrancy of the Bible. Many do not. Without saying who is right and who is wrong, it can be argued that there are many passages in the Bible that we may not know are there, or we ignore them, or we violate them knowingly without a qualm.

"We eat pork and shellfish, we do not kill people who work on the Sabbath or children who disrespect their parents, and we gossip. Religious Baptists get divorced and remarry, making them, according to the Bible, adulterers. We do not stone young women who are found not to be virgins on their wedding night. Nor do we condone slavery and expect the slave to honor his master. So why do we condemn men who love other men? Leviticus says that a man who lies with another man as with a woman is committing an abomination and should be condemned. And I ask now, why do we honor that prohibition with self-righteous fervor, while dismissing so many others?

"As Christians, is it not the New Testament teachings of Jesus that we adhere to as the true teachings in the Bible? Are they not the teachings most important for us to follow? Yet Jesus does not say one word condemning the love of a man for another man. Or the love of a woman for another woman.

"Why then do we self-righteously condemn the homosexual without first knowing him: judging him to be evil, a predator, someone who tears at the fabric of society? Why? Because that's what we've been taught by people in authority. People who are supposed to guide us to an understanding of what is right and what is wrong in the eyes of Jesus Christ, our savior—people like me.

"As I think back about the many sermons I've delivered from this very pulpit condemning homosexuals, I am filled with shame. And when I think of the potential harm done to an honorable teacher—who happens to be homosexual—by members of our church, I feel the heavy weight of blame.

"'Teacher, which commandment is the greatest?' He said to him, 'You shall love the Lord your God with all your heart, and with all your soul, and with all your mind. This is the greatest and first commandment. And the second is like it. You shall love your neighbor as yourself. On these two commandments hang all the law and all the prophets.'—Mathew 22:36-40.*"

Reverend Phillips paused. "Not a sparrow falls that God does not know. Surely, God heard my condemnations of homosexual people. It was my responsibility as your minister to guide you in *HIS* path of righteousness. Instead I guided you to judgment and condemnation in violation of biblical teachings. *'Do not judge and you will not be judged. Do not condemn, and you will not be condemned.'*—Luke 6:37.

"There was a lesson I needed to learn and God was my teacher." Reverend Phillips looked at his wife and son. "The Lord God brought to me my amazing wife Mary, who guided me to understand and accept God's lesson, which I will now reveal to you.

"After many years of trying, God blessed Mary and me with a baby who *He* knew would be the center of our lives. Our son grew into an outstanding young man: intelligent, kind, generous of spirit, a true Christian who accepts Jesus in his heart. And knowing that I loved my son with all my heart and all my soul, God made my son gay."

Reverend Phillips saw the shocked faces of the congregants. More importantly, he saw pride and love in the expressions of his wife and son, and he continued:

"Let it be known that nothing happens by chance. It happens as God in his infinite wisdom plans it to happen. I needed to cast away judgment and open my heart and mind to love all people, for they are all God's children. That is the lesson I needed to learn, and I thank our Heavenly Father for his teaching and I thank him for my son—my wonderful son—who God made gay.

"Let all bitterness and wrath and anger and clamor and slander be put away from you, along with all malice. Be kind to one another, tenderhearted, forgiving one another, as God in Christ forgave you.—Ephesians 4:31-32.

"Allow me to end this sermon with our revered verse: *For God so loved the world, that he gave his only begotten Son, that whosoever believeth in him should not perish, but have everlasting life.*—John 3:16."

Reverend Phillips bowed his head. "In Christ's name we pray. Amen."

****

As soon as the school doors opened, several students, including Lynda and Sherry, rushed into Glen's classroom.

"Reverend Phillips read Katie Collins' note to you yesterday in church!" Lynda said.

"It was so beautiful!" Sherry exclaimed. "My mother cried when she heard it."

"Ms. Collins really loved you, didn't she?" another girl exclaimed. "Did you love her also?"

"I did," Glen said. "I loved her very much in a spiritual way."

"Would you have married her, if you weren't . . ." Lynda hesitated, "you know . . . gay?"

"Yes, I would have," Glen said.

"My mother sent a note to Reverend Phillips," Sherry said, "thanking him for his wonderful sermon. Everyone just loved that sermon! Well, maybe not Molly Collins. We were all looking at her and she wouldn't look at anyone. You could tell she was upset, but I don't feel sorry for her one bit. Not after the lies she told."

"Mr. McLean, did you know Gentry Phillips is gay?" Lynda said. "We were so surprised to learn that! Gentry is so handsome and popular. Everyone likes Gentry and . . ."

Sherry interrupted, "He's gay because God made him gay to teach Reverend Phillips to love all people and not say bad things about gays in his sermons."

"Wow, sounds like Reverend Phillips made a powerful sermon," Glen said.

"Oh, he did!" Lynda said. "Dad said it was wonderful to have our minister talk about God's desire for us to love one another. He said Reverend Phillips' sermon made him feel proud to be a Christian."

Then Lynda and Sherry looked at one another and almost simultaneously said, "Will you let us babysit for you!"

"I can't stay out later than 9 p.m. on a school night," Lynda said. "But if it's the weekend I can babysit until 11."

"We'd love to do it," Sherry said, "and we'd be very good with the baby."

"I'll remember that," Glen smiled, "and if I should need a babysitter, I'll call on you."

"That would be wonderful!" Sherry said.

As the girls rushed from his classroom to get to their homeroom in time, Glen heard Sherry and Lynda exclaiming to other students in the corridor, "Mr. McLean is going to let us babysit for him!"

The principal's secretary called Glen to ask him to stop by Mr. Fowler's office at the end of the school day.

Hand outstretched, the principal stood up from his desk to greet him. "Last week a pariah. This week a hero! The roller coaster of life right here in Edgemont!"

Glen laughed. "Music to my ears!"

"To my ears too," Mr. Fowler said. "When the minister of the First Baptist Church states from the pulpit that one of our teachers is wonderful, that resounds big time in Edgemont. "I've had calls and notes from parents saying how proud and happy they are to have a teacher of your caliber at Edgemont High. 'A true Christian,' as one mother put it."

"Must have been a wonderful sermon," Glen said.

"It was," Mr. Fowler said. "Spoken from the heart. This was a new Reverend Phillips, and his words resonated with the people. We have a number of churches in Edgemont, but First Baptist is the big one. What Reverend Phillips says in his Sunday sermon will be repeated in homes throughout this community. It will have an impact."

The principal shook his head. "After all those years, hearing his negative words about homosexuals, I was delighted yesterday to hear Reverend Phillips talk about love for all people."

The principal smiled. "Nothing like having a gay child to remind a conservative Southern Baptist minister that the gospel of Jesus was about compassion and love, not judgment and condemnation."

****

Molly Collins sat across the desk from Reverend Phillips, her eyes averted. "I only done what I thought was right . . . what God wanted me to do."

Reverend Phillips remained silent. This was a very uncomfortable meeting. The woman had told lies—mean spirited and vicious lies— that were unconscionable. But his hands weren't clean, as he well knew: he had helped shape her bigotry. That was undeniable and it weighed heavily upon him.

"It ain't right for a homosexual to be raising a baby, especially a helpless boy child. You can't be thinking that's right, can you?" Molly leaned forward in her chair. "You yourself told us that homosexuals preyed on children," she said accusingly, "Ain't that what you told us?"

Reverend Phillips sighed. "I did."

"Don't you believe that no more? Just 'cause you learned your boy was homosexual . . . that doesn't change anything, does it? Truth is still truth, ain't it?"

"Reverend Phillips nodded. "Truth is still truth . . . and a lie is still a lie. God doesn't want you to lie, especially when it will hurt an innocent person. God made it one of his Ten Commandments."

"But God don't want no homosexual to be raising a baby boy. I only done what I did to protect Katie's baby. I was only trying to do the right thing. God has to know that, don't he?"

Sensing her upset beneath the veneer of self-righteous defiance, Reverend Phillips reached across his desk to touch Molly's hand. "I'm sure God knows what was in your heart, and *He* is all-forgiving. But you must acknowledge your sin and ask to be forgiven."

Molly Collins straightened in her chair. "I didn't sin! I only done what I had to do as a Christian. I don't see I had a choice."

He saw her lower lip quiver. Reverend Phillips had heard that church members were shunning her, and a few had even confronted her about the shame she had brought upon the church.

"It can be difficult to determine right from wrong, especially when the Bible guides us in paths that seem to be in conflict. It does condemn homosexual behavior as an abomination. That is clear. But it also admonishes us not to judge others and to love our neighbors. And that is strongly stated, especially by our savior Jesus."

Molly Collins swiped her roughened hand across her eyes to stop herself from crying. "I only done what I thought was right to protect Katie's baby." She repeated. "Why is that a sin?"

Reverend Phillips sighed. "You went against God's teaching about speaking truth. You provided false witness against an innocent person and could have brought great harm to him."

The heavy woman hunched forward, her shoulders sagging. "What should I do?"

"Pray to God for forgiveness. God is compassionate and *He* will forgive you." Reverend Phillips paused. "You might also consider apologizing to Mr. McLean and asking for his forgiveness. Will you do that?"

Molly shook her head. "He won't want nothing to do with me. Why would he? He'll probably never let me see Katie's baby and . . ." she began to cry, no longer attempting to hide her upset.

"I've come to know Mr. McLean and I believe he's a kind man," Reverend Phillips said. I could tell him how sorry you are and ask him to forgive you. Would you like me to do that?"

She nodded. "I love that baby . . . and . . . yes, tell Mr. Mclean how sorry I am." She bowed her head and in a low voice murmured, "I'm so ashamed."

Reverend Phillips clasped her hand. "I'll do what I can."

****

The late January wind whistled through the twisting branches of the live oak trees on the rolling front lawn of the Chamberlain home. It was a cold night, with the expectation that a light snow might be falling in the later evening hours.

In honor of the gathering and the unusually chilly Texas evening, Keith had several large logs burning in the brick fireplace at the far end of the formal living room. Reverend Phillips and his wife were seated beside each other on the yellow damask Chippendale sofa. Jean Chamberlain, Keith and Glen were seated on striped red and yellow antique arm chairs facing them. Gentry and Jason, who had driven up from Austin, squatted on the floor beside the roaring fire.

"This is such a lovely home," Mary Phillips said. "I understand you raised your family here and lived in this house until a few years ago."

"That's what makes it so special for me," Jean Chamberlain said. "I have so many memories of Keith and his sister growing up in this house, and now to have the pleasure of being with this baby—my grandson—in this same house is just so heartwarming for me." She held the sleeping infant in her arms. "Did you know that Keith and Glen plan to have another baby?"

"God has surely blessed you," Mary Phillips said. Then looking at her son, she smiled, "You don't even have to ask. My answer is yes, I would be very happy if one day I would have a sweet grandbaby like this one. Actually, make that two or three grandbabies. There's a whole lot of love stored inside Dad and me."

Gentry laughed. "I'll do it. I promise. But give me a little time. I'm just 19." Then, looking at Glen and Keith, he said, "I'm so sorry you weren't at church to hear Dad's sermon. It was wonderful, especially when Dad said how much he loved his gay son. I started to cry and Mom was crying too. Every time I think about my dad and what he said to hundreds of people that day in church, I cry again. Like right now." He brushed at his eyes.

Jason reached for Gentry's hand. "I can't believe we're all here this evening. I never thought that this could happen. Reverend Phillips, your support has made a world of difference to Gentry. I've never known him to be so at peace with himself."

Reverend Phillips turned to face his wife. "Mary deserves the credit. Without her guidance, I don't know if this evening would have happened." He took her hand in his. "There are so many moments in a lifetime and so many wrong paths to stumble onto. Looking back, I can't say exactly where or why I started down the path of judgment and condemnation." He shook his head. "It's not where I wanted to go."

He paused. "Thank goodness, I had Mary to take my hand and . . ." his voice broke.

"God led you back. I was just his messenger," Mary said.

Then, regaining his composure, Reverend Phillips said, "Jesus teaches forgiveness and there is a member of my congregation who is in pain." He looked at Glen. "I was hoping you could find it in your heart to forgive her. I'm talking about Molly Collins."

Glen looked at Keith, before saying, "If things had gone her way, our son would have been taken from us."

"I know and I would understand if you could not forgive her for what she did. But I do want you to know, the woman has met with me in my office and is overwhelmed with guilt and shame. Her action will be a stain on her ledger when she faces God on Judgment Day. She knows that and it troubles her greatly."

"I imagine what's really worrying Molly Collins is our threat to sue her for slander," Keith said. "If it were left to me, that's exactly what would be done. However, Glen feels her public humiliation is punishment enough. Above all, he believes Katie would not want us to do that."

"Thank you. It did worry her," Reverend Phillips said. "But I would also like to tell her that you forgive her."

"Tell her that I'm working on forgiving her, and maybe one day it will happen." Then looking upward, he said, "Katie, I'll need your help on this one."

Reverend Phillips nodded. "I know you'll try. Now one more thing. Shortly after the false charge against you began to spread, Chrissie Johnson, Katie's cousin, spoke to me in confidence. 'My aunt is not telling the truth,' Chrissie said. 'Glen McLean did not abuse the baby.'"

"I'm glad you told me," Glen said. "That makes a difference."

Then Keith stood, "I'm all for a toast to good people and good feelings. Tell me what you'd like to drink and Glen will fill your order." He smiled at Glen, "I could never do it as well as you."

"Chardonnay," said Jean Chamberlain.

"The usual," Keith said, "a martini with two olives."

"Iced tea," said Reverend and Mary Phillips.

"And you?" Keith turned to Gentry and Jason.

Gentry looked at his Dad. "Would it be all right if I had one glass of red wine? Just one?"

Reverend Phillips sighed, then smiling said, "I believe biblical teaching would permit you to drink one glass of red wine."

"That's what I'll have also," Jason said quickly.

As the wood logs crackled in the fireplace and the freezing January wind careened through the twisting branches of the giant live oak trees outside, they all raised their glasses in fellowship, "To good people and good feelings."

Following the toast, Reverend Phillips raised his glass of iced tea once again, "Thank you, Lord, for opening my heart and mind to an appreciation of all that you have created, and especially for the wonderful son you have chosen to bless my wife and me."

****

Lillian McLean called Glen, just moments after he had placed the baby in his crib for the night.

"Good timing, Mom. Just put Glen Junior to bed. Did you know he's sleeping through the night?"

She laughed. "Makes a difference, doesn't it? Anyway, I just received the photos of him you sent and he is so good looking. I do believe he's looking more like you."

"I agree," Glen said. "Except for his coloring and his features, he's the spitting image of me."

"Well, he does have the cleft in his chin."

"That's true and he is super intelligent and so adorable. He surely is my son."

There was a pause and then his mom said, "Do you remember my telling you about that woman who brought her daughter and the daughter's partner with their two little girls to church for the Thanksgiving service?"

"I do," he said. "You said they were lesbians."

"Yes, that's right. I had lunch with the woman today and do you know what she told me?"

"What did she tell you?" he asked, as he thought, *this is the purpose of her call.*

"She said her daughter and her friend are planning to drive to Boston to get married."

"And how does her mother feel about that?" Glen asked.

"Oh, she is very approving! She feels it's the right thing for them to do since they have two little girls. How do you feel about that?" his mom said.

"I don't have a problem with that. It's their life," he smiled, realizing now where she was heading. "So, tell me how do you feel about it?"

"I think it's the right thing for them to do . . . for their children's sake." She paused, "Is that something you and Keith would consider?"

"We've talked about it, but in reality getting married in Massachusetts wouldn't change anything for us here in Texas."

"Don't you think it might strengthen your bond to one another by making your relationship official."

"So you think Keith and I should get married?" Glen asked.

"For the baby's sake, it might be a good idea. But that's up to you and Keith. It's not my place to tell you what to do."

"Mom, I love you," Glen said, "and I know you would never tell me how to lead my life."

"Are you making fun of me?" Mrs. McLean said. "I'm only thinking of what's best for you and your family."

My family? A broad smile lit Glen's face. *Wow, she's coming around . . . big time!* "So what else did that woman tell you?"

"Her daughter and her family will be here again next Thanksgiving. They always get together on Thanksgiving. I told her that you and your family will be here also. Perhaps we could all get together at the Thanksgiving church service," she said.

"Now you are all coming, aren't you? You've covered it with Keith, haven't you?"

"Yes, it's firm." Glen heard the concern in his mother's voice. "Mom, we'll be there."

"I've discussed this with your father, and we want to pay for your plane tickets. In fact, we think you should book your flight now."

"Mom, Thanksgiving is months away. We can wait. And Keith and I are grown-up men. We can pay for our own plane tickets." If they had been together, he would have hugged her. "Mom, please don't worry about our coming. Keith, the baby and I will be with you in Albany next Thanksgiving. It's a promise."

"I was so upset that you weren't with us this past Thanksgiving. Everyone asked about you . . ." her voice broke and he knew she was crying. "Next Thanksgiving I'm going to invite all the family so that they can meet Keith and the baby."

Glen felt the moisture welling in his eyes. "Mom, I know you love me and I hope you know how much I love you and Dad. I couldn't ask for better parents than the two of you."

"Really?" Mrs. McLean said. "I hope you mean that. I've always tried my best. Maybe sometimes I get a little confused . . . but anyway, I love you very much and am so happy you and your family will be with us Thanksgiving."

"We will," Glen said. "It's firm. We'll be with you and even go to church with you, if that's what you'd like."

"That would be so nice. And wouldn't it be wonderful if we could have little Glen Thomas baptized while you're here!"

****

Chrissie Johnson had obtained the phone listing for Glen McLean and Keith Chamberlain in the Edgemont Town Directory, but was hesitant to call. What if Glen refused to talk to her? Or said something nasty to her?

She was horribly embarrassed and ashamed, especially knowing how outraged Katie would have been if she knew that they'd attempted to take her baby from him. But it wasn't her fault, Chrissie rationalized. Hadn't Aunt Molly assured her that David Gordon was the biological father, not Glen McLean? And hadn't David signed the legal papers permitting the adoption of his baby by Chrissie and her husband?

Chrissie picked up her phone several times to call, only to put it back down again. *I don't know. I just don't know.* Then screwing up her nerve, she dialed Glen's number.

"Yes?"

"Is this Glen McLean?" she asked.

"It is."

"Hi, this is Chrissie Johnson, Katie's cousin." She took a deep breath. "I'm calling to apologize for . . ." She hesitated again, not certain how to phrase it, "for all that happened."

"From what I've gathered, it wasn't your fault," Glen said.

"I appreciate your saying that," Chrissie said. "I still feel terrible that I was involved in any way."

"If it helps, I don't have any bad feelings toward you or your husband," Glen said. "Katie often spoke of you. She said you were like a sister to her and that goes a long way with me."

"Thank you so much for saying that!" Chrissie said. "It makes it so much easier for me to ask that you allow my daughters to know their baby cousin. Is that possible? It would mean so much to them . . . and to me."

"Chrissie, I believe my little guy would love to know his cousins and grow up loving them, just as Katie grew up loving you."

"Oh, I am so relieved!" Chrissie exclaimed. "I can't tell you how nervous I was to make this call. You are the sweetest man!" She paused. "I wonder how far I can press my luck?" she asked.

"Yes?" Glen waited for her request.

"What about Aunt Molly? She is so upset. She's been meeting with our minister to work through her guilt and shame. It would mean so much to her, if I could tell her that you'd allow her to see the baby."

"I'm not ready for that," Glen said. "Let's start the healing with you and your daughters. Somewhere down the road, perhaps, we can include your aunt. Not now."

"I understand," Chrissie said. "Would it be all right if next Saturday we set aside an hour to be together, the girls and me. Perhaps in the morning?"

"That will be fine." Glen said, "Family was very important to Katie and to me as well. I'm glad you called."

****

"Now, remember, anytime you need me, I'm just one call away." It was an unusually warm, Sunday afternoon in early February. The baby was in his crib napping as Jean Chamberlain backed her Lexus down the driveway and with a goodbye wave was on her way back to Austin.

"What a sweetheart!" Glen said. "She took care of everything, including the arrangements with the daycare provider for caring for Glen Junior while we're at work. Your mom's been here for almost a month, and truthfully, I wouldn't mind if she stayed longer."

"She is the best," Keith said. "Always has been . . . but you know what?"

"What?" Glen said.

"I love that it will be just us in our house. You and me and our son."

"Come, let's go inside," Glen said, "There's something I've been thinking about and want to talk over with you."

"All right, I'm ready to listen," Keith said. He seated himself close beside Glen on the down-cushioned sofa.

"Now just be patient and let me build up to it. Okay?" Glen said. "I have this unit that I start off each school year in which my students name a villain, someone they really don't like. They list the charges against their villain. Then they have to get inside their villain's head to see it from his or her point of view. It's called having respect for another person.

Glen reached for Keith's hand. "It's a great exercise for building understanding and tolerance, and sometimes even appreciation for someone you thought you disliked."

"So what's your point?" Keith said.

"I've been thinking about Katie's Aunt Molly."

"No! Absolutely not!" Keith said. "I know where you're heading with this and my answer is no. That woman is a mean-spirited bitch and . . ."

Glen raised his hand to stop him. "I know you feel that way. I did too, and that's why I want you to go through this. Respect means listening to the other person's point of view. Putting yourself in their position. Please just bear with me.

"Think about this from Molly's viewpoint. Granted, she's a bigot, but in fairness to her, she had some influential people guiding her in that direction. Reverend Phillips for one and he'd be the first to admit it. Given what she'd been taught about gay people, how do you expect she'd feel about Katie's baby being raised by a homosexual man?"

Keith sighed deeply. "All right, so she's now Saint Molly saving an innocent baby from homosexual predators."

"There's more," Glen said. "She was devoted to Katie. She was over there at all hours caring for Katie and the baby. Katie couldn't have managed without her."

"Okay, I can see where your bleeding liberal heart is leading you. You've forgiven her. Now what?"

"I keep thinking about Katie," Glen said. "She'd be so upset to know we wouldn't allow her Aunt Molly to be with the baby."

May I remind you if Molly Collins had her way, you wouldn't have been allowed to be with your baby," Keith said. "I doubt very much if that would have troubled her."

"That's true, I know. And that would have been wrong, not fair. Just as it would be unfair of me, because of my grievance toward her, to keep her from knowing Katie's baby. Katie told me her Aunt Molly loved the baby . . ."

Keith stopped him. "So it's not enough that Katie's cousin and her daughters will be involved in our baby's life? You're wanting to add bitchy Aunt Molly as well?"

Glen squeezed Keith's hand. "They're his family, his great aunt and cousins. I don't want our son growing up in this community without any contact with blood relatives."

Keith shook his head. "It's not how I would go about it. You're a whole lot more caring and forgiving than me." He shrugged, "Maybe that's why I love you."

Glen leaned forward to kiss him. "You're a lot more caring than you'll admit. It just takes you a bit longer to get on the forgiving trail."

"Since you're in such a forgiving mood," Keith said, "tell me your feelings about Jeanette Haar and her son Mickey."

"You want to know how I feel about them?" Glen's voice tightened. "Mickey Haar is a vicious bully who made that poor Danny Anderson's life a nightmare. And his mother, Jeanette Haar, raised him to be that way. She brought a group of fellow bigots from the First Baptist Church to a Board of Education meeting to have me fired because I was gay."

Glen stood up and started walking about the room as if in search of something.

"What are you doing?" Keith asked.

"I'm looking for the forgiving trail," Glen said. "Must have gotten lost somewhere because I can't find it for the life of me."

Keith laughed. "What about her point of view? Aren't we supposed to provide her the opportunity to explain her position so that we can learn to appreciate her?"

"I'm sure that's going to happen sometime in the future. Like 20 years from now. In the meantime, she's going to be very busy making certain her two sons pay for damages to my tires and fulfill their 200 hours of community service for attempting to burn that cross on our front lawn."

Glen returned to the sofa and settled down close beside Keith. "Let's not spend time on the mean-spirited people, the ones who wear a religious mask to hide the hate in their hearts, when there are far more good people with love and caring for others in their hearts."

He took Keith's hand in his. "I used to worry that I'd spend my life looking through the window at others—straight people—leading the life I desperately wanted and I'd never have because I was gay."

"And what was that life?" Keith asked.

"In my perfect world," Glen said, "I'd want an intelligent, loving partner, an adorable baby son and a beautiful home. And do you know what? That's exactly what I have."

Keith said, "Guess what? I want—and have—the same perfect world as you. Lucky you, lucky me!"

Keith's face became animated with a thought. "If you scurry to the bar to make your outstanding martini for me and pour a glass of cabernet for you, we can clink our glasses to our special toast. Now hurry!"

In just a few moments, Glen returned with the two glasses. He handed Keith his martini with two olives, and they raised their glasses, saying in unison, "'To the Rest of Our Lives Together."

The End

35068631R00133

Made in the USA
Lexington, KY
28 August 2014